THE INCUBUS IMPASSE

A CHARLIE RHODES COZY MYSTERY BOOK SIX

AMANDA M. LEE

WINCHESTERSHAW PUBLICATIONS

❀ Created with Vellum

PROLOGUE

SEVEN YEARS AGO

I was late.

That rarely happened to me.

Charlotte "Charlie" Rhodes was almost never late.

Sure, my parents had claimed I was scatterbrained and would forget my head if it wasn't attached to my body, but I was a stickler for punctuality. I had no idea why. I didn't get it from my mother. I was adopted, though, so that wasn't all that surprising. My father loathed lateness to the point he complained bitterly about anyone who caused him to wait. Apparently it was learned behavior I'd picked up from him.

I didn't make a conscious choice to ignore my curfew. I'd simply lost track of time. I was in the library and found a book about people who claimed to have telekinetic powers — like Carrie in that old Stephen King book — and I was curious about if there were any documented cases. The author was enthusiastic and held every story up as fact, but I was skeptical. Still, there were a few stories that rang true, and I'd managed to read the entire book before looking at the clock and realizing how late it was.

It was spring in Minnesota. The days were getting longer, but the sun still set long before eight. My curfew was ten on a school day —

which this was — and I was already fifteen minutes late. My parents were undoubtedly worried, and I hated that.

My pace was brisk as I moved away from the shadow of the library and toward home. I had seven blocks to traverse and I was determined to erase the distance in as little time as possible. The sooner I got home, the better.

It wasn't exactly cold — especially compared to the long winter we'd just escaped — but the wind was strong and I shivered as I tugged my coat tighter. Perhaps I'd given up my heavy parka too soon. Once fifty-degree days hit in the Midwest, residents couldn't wait to embrace spring. I had switched to my spring coat right away.

That was probably a mistake.

I bent my head low and tried to ignore the biting wind. My cheeks were so frigid they felt as if they might actually chip away from my face if I accidentally brushed them too hard. All I could think about was the pot of tea my mother likely had brewing and the fuzzy pajama pants that I knew were waiting for me in my dresser.

I had to stop at an intersection and wait for the traffic to clear. It was the lone obstacle between me and home. Once on the other side, I tuned out the traffic — which was sparse this evening — and focused on the sidewalk ahead of me.

Five more blocks.

I was already imagining what my parents would say. Would they ground me? I'd been grounded before, but not in a long time. I tried to be a relatively diligent kid. After all, I was adopted. I didn't want to give them a reason to return me to whatever adoption agency had put me in their care.

On the surface, I recognized that was a ridiculous thing to worry about. My parents had never hidden the fact that I was adopted. That probably had something to do with the fact that I was older when they took me into their home. At four, I should've been able to form some memory of the life I'd had before them.

But I didn't. No matter how hard I tried to focus on that period of my life, I came up empty. My parents reassured me that the memories were probably still there. I'd simply tucked them away until I felt comfortable enough to access them. They'd been telling me that since I was old enough to voice my concern about the blank spot in my memory. I'd been eight at the time. I was a teenager now and nothing had changed. If there was anything to access, it remained cut off from me.

There's a lot of fear associated with being adopted. Perhaps there shouldn't be, but reality is different from what should be. My parents swore up and down that they loved me as if I'd come from them. My father insisted that they'd chosen me, which made our familial bond all the more strong. I believed that. Er, well, mostly. I still had nagging doubts in the back of my mind.

If one family thought I was too much trouble, not worth the effort, and abandoned me in the middle of the night, what would stop a second family from doing it? I hated myself for doubting the Rhodes. They'd given me their name and everything else I could've ever possibly needed, and yet I couldn't stop myself from wondering.

My mother said that was normal. *It's human nature to wonder about where you came from, Charlie. You don't have to hide it when you're feeling vulnerable.* She'd said that over and over and I believed her. That didn't change the fact that I felt guilty about wondering. Why would I possibly care about people who abandoned me when the ones who took me in were so perfect?

It was something I struggled with.

Four more blocks.

The rain started. It was more than a gentle mist or light spatter. It was a deluge, almost as if the sky decided to open up and douse me simply because I'd been wondering about my past ... again. I grimaced as I steeled myself against the rain. Not much farther now. I would be warm and potentially in trouble within a few minutes. I welcomed the coming reprimand because at least I would be out of the rain. Besides, I was one of those kids who would punish myself under a blanket of guilt if my parents didn't do it for me. That's simply how I was wired.

Three more blocks.

I couldn't see the house. Not yet. The lights on the main streets were ample. Those on the side streets were few and far between. I'd never really thought about it before because I wasn't the sort of girl who struggled with fear ... at least not physical fear. I always rationalized that someone would have to be a complete and total idiot to approach me. I was stronger than the average teenager. My gifts were greater.

I thought about the book on telekinesis. That was me. I could've been included in the book. I could move things with my mind, drop signs from overhead on enemies and even break off tree branches to use as weapons if I needed to. I was careful to keep my abilities secret. They'd manifested at a young age. At the time, my parents had been confused, although they swore they weren't afraid of me. I was afraid of myself, so I had trouble believing them. Ultimately it didn't matter.

Through the years, my powers grew. I could see inside people's heads, read their surface thoughts without even trying, and dig deep if there was something worth unearthing beneath mountains of guilt. My parents always warned me about invading the privacy of others, and I took those admonishments to heart. Still, I grew stronger.

When it became apparent that I could really move things with my mind, my father insisted on trying to train me in the backyard. He waited until it was dark, when no one could see, and forced me to practice over and over. It was their true fear that I would lose my temper and inadvertently attack another student. I would regret it immediately, but if the damage was already done ... .

Two more blocks.

Over the years, my father had turned me into a lean, mean fighting machine. Those were his words and he laughed like a loon whenever he said them. Apparently they were from a movie or something.

I could protect myself, both mentally and physically. I could run two miles without breaking a sweat, and I was sharp in the face of untenable circumstances. He'd made me practice fighting him off, pretend he was a stranger trying to grab me. He'd drilled me should a stranger approach and say he or she was a member of my biological family. He made sure that I didn't immediately try to cut them off as much as call him or my mother for backup.

I understood everything I was supposed to do in case I was

attacked or approached by an unknown individual. I didn't often feel fear. And yet, something had me slowing my pace now.

One more block.

I could see the house, every window illuminated. I knew my parents were waiting for me, anxiety probably coursing through them. Something inside wouldn't allow me to run the final distance. I sensed trouble ... and it was close.

Slowly, I turned my eyes to the bushes crowding the sidewalk ahead. I was only about five feet from them. They were the square hedges that so many people use to hide their yards from the prying eyes of neighbors, which meant they were tall enough for someone to hide behind.

And that's exactly what was happening now.

I had no idea how I knew it, but I did. I was no longer alone. Whoever hid behind the bushes waiting for me to pass so he or she — no, it was definitely a he — could jump out and attack.

Why? What was the motive here? Robbery? I had three bucks on me so that would be a fruitless effort. Rape? The notion sent a shiver down my spine, but I didn't allow fear to crowd my heart. Something else? Ultimately, it didn't matter. I wasn't about to make myself a victim.

"You might as well come out," I offered in a clear voice, my eyes never leaving the bushes. "I'm not walking past that spot."

The declaration was met with silence for a beat, and then there was a distinctive rustling. I couldn't immediately see who I was dealing with, but my heart skipped a beat when a hulking figure detached from the hedges and stepped onto the sidewalk in front of me.

"Hello, girlie." The voice was a low growl. I probed his mind quickly. It didn't take long because his surface thoughts were so shallow. What he wanted was filthy, disgusting, and so not going to happen. "Why don't you come a little closer so I can get a good look at you? I won't hurt you. I promise. I just want to look."

My father didn't raise me to fall for a line that weak. "I'm good here." My hands clenched into fists at my sides as I risked a glance at the surrounding homes. The lights were on in most of the windows, but there were no silhouettes to signify that anyone was watching. That was good. I didn't need help. I simply needed to make sure that no one saw what I was about to do.

I forced a tight smile. "You should probably go." I decided to give him an escape hatch even though he clearly didn't deserve it. "This isn't going to go down like you think."

"Is that so?" When he smiled, he displayed two rows of jagged and yellow teeth. He didn't look homeless, but he obviously wasn't keen on personal hygiene. "What makes you say that?"

"I already know how this is going to go."

"Oh, yeah? How?"

I didn't wait for him to move toward me. That would've put me in a vulnerable position despite my power because he was absolutely huge. If I had to guess, most of his girth was flab, but that didn't mean he wouldn't be able to take me to the ground if he got his hands on me. I weighed a hundred and twenty-five pounds soaking wet. Physically, I was the exact opposite of imposing. Mentally, I could run laps around him.

The magic was already bubbling when I tapped into it. I didn't think before unleashing it, instead going with my initial instinct ... which was to physically hurt him. The magical wave — which he obviously couldn't see — hit him hard ... right in the face.

He reared back, his eyes going wide as he looked in every direction, panic evident. I hadn't as much as twitched during the attack. I remained rooted to my spot. It must've felt as if an invisible being had slapped him across the face. It was only the opening volley, a warning of sorts. He could still run.

I wasn't surprised when he didn't. "What was that?" His voice dripped with menace.

"I have no idea," I lied blandly. "Perhaps you should go that way and find out." I pointed in the direction of the busy highway I had crossed earlier. "You're better off leaving."

"I'm not leaving." Determination etched across his stubbled face as he took another step toward me.

This time I reacted with enough force to level him. The magic I unleashed was a fiery pulse. It escaped from my fingertips and slammed directly into his chest. His eyes went wide at the impact, and for a second it looked as if he was going to turn in the other direction and run, but he continued moving forward.

The magic I enlisted was a trap of sorts and it wrapped around him like fiery razor wire. He made a guttural sound as the net tightened, wrapping around his neck and causing him to gasp as he struggled against the sudden change.

"What is this?" His hands moved to his neck as he tried to remove the barrier constricting his breathing, something he couldn't even see. "I ... what are you doing?"

"I told you to leave me alone." I was matter-of-fact as I stepped around him, giving him a wide berth as he dropped to his knees. The sounds he made were disturbing, but not nearly as bothersome as the images I'd gleaned from his mind. "You should've listened."

"Help me." He moved his hands from his neck to his chest and clutched at it, as if having a heart attack. "Stop. You can't just leave me here."

My mind was already back on what I would tell my parents about missing curfew. I was unlikely to mention this incident because it would only make them worry. Instead, I would simply accept my lumps, take whatever grounding they handed out, and call it a day.

"You'd be surprised at what I can do," I shot back. "Don't worry. You're not going to die. You will be trapped there until the cops show up. I'll make sure that happens before dawn."

"Come back," he growled, flopping like a fish on the sidewalk as he tried to regain his footing. "I'm going to kill you."

"And you wonder why I don't want to help you."

"I'll make you pay."

"That's unlikely. But if you manage to come around again, just remember that I can make things even worse for you." As if to prove my point, I tightened the net on his nether regions and cringed as he screamed. There would be no explaining that noise if the neighbors decided to look out their windows. It was time for me to go. "Stay away," I warned. "You'll regret it if you don't."

"I will find you. Kill you." His voice was ragged. "Gut you."

"I look forward to the attempt. You have a nice night now."

I didn't laugh as I turned up my sidewalk. This was hardly a funny situation, but victory was, of course, sweet. I would have to keep that to myself. Some things were better left secret, and this was one of them.

ONE

PRESENT DAY

"What am I thinking?"

Jack Hanson, my boyfriend and co-worker, was the persistent sort. That's why, two weeks after the horrifying truth about my magical abilities came out he was still trying to get a handle on what I could do.

I was starting to tire of the game but appreciated his enthusiasm.

"You're thinking that we should go out and get something to eat," I replied after a beat. No, I didn't actually take the time to read his mind. His stomach was growling in time with mine and we'd accidentally skipped lunch.

"I *was* thinking that." Jack's expression was hard to read. "How did you know?"

I wanted to shake him. With that shoulder-length black hair and those mesmerizing eyes it wasn't really an option. He was too handsome to scream at.

Besides, he'd been nothing but great since he found out about my secret. Ever since we returned from New Orleans — after an initial few days of reticence and awkwardness, of course — he'd bent over backward to give me what I needed without pressuring me. It was only in the last two days he'd found the courage to start pushing me on what I could do. I was so relieved things were going back to normal that I didn't want to risk ruining our progress, so shaking him until he stopped speaking was out of the question.

"Jack, we were both thinking it," I offered pragmatically. "We haven't eaten since this morning."

He narrowed his eyes, speculative. "So ... basically you're saying you deduced what I was thinking rather than read me. That's not how this is supposed to work, Charlie."

I held back a sigh ... but just barely. He was trying so hard to ingratiate himself into my world that I couldn't slap him back. Part of me wished he would continue giving me space and not push so hard, give me some time to come to grips with the knowledge that he was in on the big secret. I was psychic, telekinetic and any number of other things. He was a non-believer at heart, so I was terrified he would run when he learned the truth. On the contrary, though, he held fast. He was obviously stunned, needed some time to absorb what had happened, but even from the first moments in the immediate aftermath there was no dissuading him.

He was determined to stick ... and I'd never been more grateful for anything in my life. Er, well, other than the people who adopted me when I was a child and did their best to give me an idyllic childhood, that is. The Rhodes saved me from what I was convinced was a fate worse than death. I owed them everything.

Jack saved me a second time.

Instead of being irritated, Jack flashed me an amusing smile before scooping me around the waist and dragging me to my couch. It was secondhand — like almost everything I owned — but East Coast garage sales were high class enough that I got a nice piece of furniture for a song.

"Fine." Jack heaved out a sigh as he grabbed the stack of takeout menus from the coffee table. We'd been ordering in a lot and had developed something of a pattern. Our days were taken up with work at the office — we hadn't been called out to an assignment since the rising dead in New Orleans triggered the last one — and each other. As much as I loved spending private time with him —

and I genuinely did — I was starting to get antsy. I joined the Legacy Foundation because I thought I would be learning about other paranormal creatures. The past few weeks had been spent learning about Jack's morning beauty ritual and nightly snoring pattern.

In truth, we needed the time together to get through what happened. Jack's faith in everything he believed was shaken by the fact that I happened to be the exact sort of entity the Legacy Foundation sought. He was pragmatic, preferred believing we were chasing our tails rather than embrace the possibility of the fantastical. The revelation of what I could do shook him to his core. But it didn't shake him loose.

"What do you want for dinner?" Jack rested his chin on my shoulder. His breath was warm against my ear and caused the hair on the back of my neck to stand on end as an involuntary shudder passed through me. His presence was always intoxicating.

"Pizza is the easiest," I offered. It was also cheap and allowed me to pitch in for the meal.

"We've had pizza three times this week," he countered, grabbing the menu from the corner restaurant. It was much ritzier than the pizza places and cost three times as much. "How about some seafood pasta? This place has the best shrimp Alfredo on the planet."

"Whatever you want." I forced a smile for his benefit and started doing the math in my head. "I'm not all that hungry. I'll just get a cup of soup and the dinner salad."

Suspicion flitted through his eyes as he shifted his gaze to me. It was obvious I'd taken it a step too far. "You just said you were hungry."

"I know. I … ."

He waited. There was a challenge to the tilt of his head. After the revelation of my abilities I'd promised there would be no more secrets. He obviously was trying to decide if I planned to hold true to that promise. I didn't really consider my financial issues — not all of us at the Legacy Foundation were paid as handsomely as Jack — to be a secret. It was an embarrassing subject to talk about.

"I only have fifty bucks for the rest of the month – and that's five days," I volunteered finally, averting my gaze. "It's fine, though."

Jack stilled. "Charlie ... ."

"I said it's fine." I adopted a brisk tone and forced a smile. "I like salad."

"Nobody likes salad." Jack made a face. "We don't have to get the pasta. We can get pizza."

"But you want pasta."

"No, I want you." His words were earnest enough to warm me. "I didn't think about the money. I would offer to buy dinner, but you only allow that once a week. The rest of the time you come up with excuses for why you have to contribute."

My cheeks colored as I stared at my unpolished fingernails. "I didn't realize you were aware of that."

"I'm head of security," he noted, tapping the end of my nose. "It's my job to be observant ... and you're often an open book." He pressed his lips to my cheek. We'd grown incredibly close the past few months but we were still a new couple and needed to feel our way around one another. "I'm sorry. I'll do better remembering about the money stuff."

I expected him to say something else. "You're not going to fight me on this?" I angled my head to better study his strong profile. "Why?"

"I want you to feel comfortable." His answer was simple. "I won't say we've had an easy time of it lately, but I think we've navigated it pretty well. We've had a bumpy couple of weeks and you deserve to be comfortable. If pizza is what you want, pizza is what you're going to get."

I'm embarrassed to admit that I went warm and fuzzy all over. He had the power to make me go weak at the knees, something I never thought possible. I fancied myself immune to that. It turned out, because of Jack, I wasn't. "Thanks."

He slid me a sidelong look. "You don't have to thank me. I'm ordering wings, breadsticks and that giant cookie thing. Oh, and I'm also paying."

I balked. "What's the point of that? I'm supposed to contribute."

"Because you're a financially independent woman?"

I nodded. "Yes. Don't even think of making fun of my beliefs."

"I'm not making fun of your beliefs. You're too important to me for that. However, I want all those things and I'm going to get them. I also want you to eat them ... so we're going to have to compromise."

"How is that a compromise?"

He poked my side. "Because I said so and I'm the boss."

"I don't remember agreeing to you being the boss," I argued. "I think I should be the boss. I have the better temperament. I ... ." I yelped when he rolled me to a flat position on the couch and started tickling me. That was his go-to move when he wanted to shut me up.

"That's not fair," I protested, gasping as I fought the urge to laugh. "You know my secret tickle spots. You have me at your mercy."

"I do indeed." He ceased tickling me and planted a lavish kiss on the corner of my mouth. "I'll place the order and then we'll get back to you reading my mind."

My mouth dropped open at his words and I was already thinking of a reason to fight him on the subject when I rolled to a sitting position and watched him place the order.

"I'll take an extra-large with garlic parmesan crust," he started. "I want ham, tomatoes, mushrooms and onions." He paused a beat and fixed his gaze on me. "Actually, scratch the onions and go with green peppers."

My heart gave a little jolt at his flirty expression.

"I also need twenty wings with ranch, an order of breadsticks with extra dipping sauce and that huge cookie thing you guys have that comes warm from the oven," he added. He was silent for a few minutes and then nodded. "Yeah. That's the address. We'll see you in thirty minutes."

He disconnected and turned his attention back to me. "We've called so many times the past few weeks that they know the address."

"I guess we're creatures of habit." Absently, I ran my fingers through his silky hair. "I bet it's that blond delivery girl again, the one barely out of high school. She goes all googly-eyed for you."

His smile turned mischievous. "I can't help it that I have power over female hormones." His lips curved as he slanted them over mine. "You can rest assured, though, that I care only about your hormones."

We spent the next five minutes making out like horny teenagers who had limited time before our parents returned. I thought he'd given up on the notion of me reading his mind, but he disabused me of that idea fast.

"Okay. Let's do this." He grabbed my hands and dragged me toward the floor. "Come on. I'm dying to see what you can do."

"I thought I was going to show you what I can do on the couch," I grumbled, my skin still flushed from the kissing. "I was looking forward to that."

The grin he shot me was impish. "I promise we'll get back to that after dinner. We don't have enough time to thoroughly enjoy ourselves anyway. It's better we table that activity until after I can wash my hands and give you the hours of dedicated attention you deserve."

If I wasn't hot already, that would've done it. "Oh, well ... ."

His grin only widened. "I love it when you get all flushed and worked up." He nipped at my bottom lip. "I still want you to read my mind, though."

Frustration I thought I'd tamped down returned with a vengeance as I settled on the floor next to him. Jack loosely folded his legs and then drew me to his lap, causing me to frown.

"This is an invasion, Jack," I argued. "You don't want me in your head."

"Charlie, you're already in my head," he insisted, causing me to blush. "I'm trying to understand what you can do. You agreed to let me in. You can't go back on that now."

I didn't want to shut him out. Quite the contrary, actually. But what he was asking felt unnatural. "Jack, everyone has things they want to keep to themselves," I started, licking my lips. "Those will be the things you naturally try to cover up ... so they'll be the first I see."

"It's fine." He took me by surprise when he grabbed me around the waist and held me tight in his lap. We were positioned in such a way that I was on top of him, my face inches from his, his arms wrapped around my back.

"This doesn't seem like an educational position," I offered after a beat, my breath ragged.

He laughed at my reaction. "I want us to be close so I can reassure you. I know you're nervous. This is a big deal. The sooner I understand what you can do, the easier this is going to be.

"Millie and I know the truth, but I think it's better — at least for the time being — that nobody else knows," he continued, solemn. "I'm not saying it has to be that way forever, but for now … ."

"For now it makes sense," I finished. "I happen to agree with you, Jack. I never intended to tell Millie. It just sort of happened. And, as for you … ." It was hard for me to explain how things went down with him. "I didn't expect to find you when I came here. I thought maybe they would have answers, and I've always been curious about the paranormal. But you … ."

He was patient as he slipped a strand of hair behind my ear. "We're fine, Charlie," he promised. "I understand why you were afraid to tell me."

"I was going to tell you," I promised. That was the truth. I'd made up my mind that he needed to know because our relationship would never truly be real until he knew everything. "I wanted to wait until we got back from New Orleans."

"Well, we're back and I know. That's the most important thing." He kissed the tip of my nose. "I need to do this with you because it's important for me to understand. I'm not trying to push you or anything — I swear — but I want to see you in action.

"It's my job to keep you safe," he continued. "That involves a level of secrecy that we're both going to have to come to grips with. Your abilities make you important to this team on a level I didn't realize. I just want to understand."

He was so earnest I couldn't deny him. "Okay. But if you have any embarrassing secrets in there I'm going to see, you've been warned."

"I'm perfectly fine." His smile was indulgent. "I honestly don't have any secrets."

I didn't believe that. Everybody had secrets. He was insistent, though, and I wanted him to feel involved. "Don't say I didn't warn you." I blew out a sigh and leaned forward, resting my forehead against his. Jack's strong hands automatically went to my back and began to rub, lulling me until I was completely comfortable.

"You secretly like watching old reruns of *The Golden Girls*," I offered after a beat.

He chuckled. "My grandmother loved that show. She made me watch it, but I actually liked it."

"It's a good show." I kept my eyes squeezed shut. "You're trying to figure out a way to convince me to allow you to pay for all our meals. Just for the record, that's not going to happen."

"I get paid more than you," he protested. "I mean ... by a long shot. You're basically a glorified intern and this is an expensive city. I think it's only fair that you allow me to pay for the meals."

"No." I was firm on that and sighed, digging deeper into his head. The next secret I stumbled over was a doozy, and it set my teeth on edge. "You're covering the difference on my rent."

He went still under me, his hands freezing in place. "I ... you ... ."

"Don't bother denying it," I warned, my temper flaring as I leaned back to stare into his eyes. "I wondered how I could get this apartment for the same price as the other when it was so much better. It turns out I wasn't getting it for the same price."

Jack was resolute in the face of my burgeoning anger. "You can be as angry as you want, but I'm not sorry. You weren't safe with that ground-floor apartment. I won't apologize for getting you out of there."

My mouth felt unusually dry. "You could've told me."

"No, I really couldn't have told you," he countered. "You wouldn't have allowed me to help."

I wanted to argue the point, but he wasn't wrong. "Jack ... ." I glanced around the apartment I'd come to adore and frowned. "I guess I should start looking for a cheaper place."

"No." Jack's frustration came out to play. "This is a nice apartment. It's right around the corner from my apartment, which makes it convenient. Don't be a stubborn idiot. You're safer here, away from the ground floor. And I don't want you to move."

"I can't afford this apartment."

"Oh, shut up, Charlie," Jack growled, shifting so I had no choice but to climb off his lap. "I agreed to pay two hundred bucks a month on this apartment for you. It was the best thing for you – which means it was also the best thing for me – and I'm not sorry. Maybe I should've told you, but you're funny about money.

"I get that, by the way," he continued. "You want to take care of yourself. There's no shame in allowing someone to help, though. I get paid five times what you do and we basically do the same job."

That was a wild stretch. "You're head of security," I reminded him. "There are dangers inherent in that job. I'm a glorified intern. You've reminded me of that repeatedly."

"No, I said you got paid like an intern," he corrected. "You're much more than that and we both know it. Stop being a pain. I'm not withdrawing the money and you're not moving."

"I didn't realize you were the boss of where I live."

"I'm not falling for that." Jack dragged a hand through his hair and fixed me with a pointed look. "I want you safe. I get that you want to be independent and everything, but there are no reasonable apartments in this city at your price range and I've decided your safety is more important than your financial independence."

I understood his worry but still felt leery. "I at least have to look." I was adamant. "Maybe there's something out there that will surprise both of us."

"There isn't. Trust me. I've been looking for myself. Everything good is expensive ... and geared toward two people. In fact ... ." He trailed off and stared at me for a long beat, making me feel uncomfortable.

"In fact what?" I asked finally.

"Nothing. We're not ready to talk about that quite yet." He was thoughtful. "Soon, though." His head jerked toward the door at the sound of a knock. "That's our dinner. We're going to table this discussion until ... well, until you're willing to give me my way. I don't want you moving to an unsafe apartment and I'll have a meltdown if you try."

"That sounds like a threat," I muttered as I followed him to the door.

"It's a promise."

I was quiet as I watched Jack pay for the food and carry it into the kitchen. We got comfortable at the table — well, as comfortable as we could get with the threat of a fight hanging over us — and immediately dug in. We were both starving.

"I don't want to be a jerk and point out that you were keeping a secret from me," I said finally, licking the ranch dressing from the wings off my fingers. "We agreed there would be no more secrets."

He was calm as he used his napkin to wipe at the corner of my mouth. "I wanted to tell you, but I was afraid you would freak out. You were keeping a secret from me, so I guess we're even."

"That's the only secret, right?"

He nodded. "Well, I also have a fetish for skinny-dipping, but that's something we can talk about later."

My cheeks colored, something I was certain he'd intended. "You just like throwing me off my game."

"I do," he agreed, leaning in and giving me a kiss before holding my gaze. "I'm sorry I didn't tell you, but I need you to be safe. I know we're spending every night together now, but when this went down we weren't and I spent my nights worrying someone was going to break into your apartment and try to hurt you.

"Now, I get that you can take care of yourself in ways I never envisioned, but I still feel better with you on the second floor," he continued. "Can't you just give me this?"

The imploring expression he lobbed at me was enough to weaken my resolve. "For two months," I said finally. "I'll give you this for two months. Then we're going to argue about it again."

"Two months is more than enough time."

He looked like he was plotting something else, but I decided to let it go. "While we're having serious discussions, I think I should be done reading your mind. That's as dangerous as living on the main floor."

"I'm not sure I agree with that, but we can be done for tonight," Jack countered. "I have different plans for you once we've devoured all this food."

"And what do those entail?"

"I think I can paint you a picture." He leaned in again to give me a kiss, a smug smile on his face, and swore viciously when his phone dinged with an incoming message. He finished the kiss and then reluctantly pulled back to read his screen.

"Well, crap," he said after a beat. "Apparently we have a job."

I was caught off guard. It had been weeks since we'd had an assignment. I was starting to think we would never get one again. "Where are we going?"

"Charleston."

I was intrigued. I'd never been to South Carolina and Charleston was supposed to be one of the most haunted places in the world. "That sounds cool. What are we looking for?"

"Chris didn't say," he replied, referring to our boss. "Knowing him, though, it'll be a doozy."

I was totally looking forward to it. "We should finish our dinner and get packed. I don't want to miss the plane."

His easy smile was back. "You're so cute. You're like a teacher's pet who insists on being prompt. You have time to digest your food. We're not leaving until tomorrow."

I couldn't hide my disappointment. "We're not?"

"It's late," he reminded me, inclining his head toward the clock on the wall. "By the time we got there, all we could do was go to bed anyway. This is better, but we have to be up early."

"I guess that means you're spending the night at your apartment," I said ruefully. "So much for your dirty plans."

"On the contrary," he countered. "Your apartment is closer to the airport. I'm going to run home, pack a bag, and then come back to spend the night here. I believe we'll have plenty of time to embrace my plans ... if you agree to hold off on eating that giant cookie until I get back."

I loved it when he negotiated. "Okay, but I'll want something in exchange."

"What's that?"

I leaned close and whispered a flirty suggestion. For a change, he was the one blushing.

"I think that can be arranged," he said in a strangled voice. "Give me thirty minutes to pack and get back. Then I'm going to change your world for the better."

"You've already done that," I said. "I think you managed to achieve that within a few days of meeting me."

He sobered and held my gaze. "Right back at you. As for the rest of it ... think of it as a work in progress. We'll figure it out."

I had no doubt he was right. There was strength in our union, and it would carry us through. "Go get your stuff. I want to eat the cookie and it's going to be pure torture to wait."

"You'd better wait. You have to share."

"There's no one I would rather share with than you."

He leaned over and smacked a loud kiss against my lips. "Good to know."

TWO

The plane was scheduled to leave early the next morning. Jack woke in a surprisingly good mood, which expanded when we stopped at McDonald's for his favorite breakfast sandwich — the steak and cheese bagel — before hitting the airport.

The Legacy Foundation had its own private jet and our co-workers were already seated when we boarded. Our boss, Chris Biggs, merely gave us a nod of greeting from his spot next to his girlfriend Hannah Silver. She was a scientist, one of the smartest women I'd ever come in contact with, and she looked like a swimsuit model. Sometimes life simply wasn't fair.

"You're late," a rancid voice called from the middle of the plane. Laura Chapman sat with an apple in her hand and a hateful glare on her face. She'd perpetually looked as if she'd smelled something foul the last few weeks, and that expression was often aimed at me. She had attitude where I was concerned, and only part of it was on a professional level. The other part — the bigger part — was because she had feelings for Jack that weren't reciprocated. Our relationship had pushed her over the edge and she was constantly digging at us these days.

"We're five minutes early," Jack countered, dropping our bags at the front of the plane so the flight attendant could stow them. He took the bags of food I carried the minute we sat down and waited until I'd buckled my belt before doling out the items. "Mind your own business, Laura."

"Yes, mind your own business, Laura," drawled Millie Watson, glee practically flowing off her in waves as she reclined in her seat. She was located in the section of the plane between Laura and us — her boyfriend Bernard Hill seated beside her — and she looked as if she was spoiling for a fight.

That wasn't unusual for Millie, of course. In addition to being Chris's aunt, she was the ex-wife of the foundation's chief executive officer. The divorce, which she described as amicable —though I had my doubts — had left her in a unique position. She was basically untouchable and she knew it. Laura, a genuinely unlikeable person, was the only member of our team who didn't essentially have a partner, and Millie enjoyed messing with her. It was becoming an everyday occurrence.

"Oh, stuff it," Laura shot back, making a face. "Nobody was talking to you."

Jack nudged my hand with my breakfast sandwich. He'd gotten four hash browns for us to munch on, too. He was clearly determined that I start the day with a full stomach. "Eat," he prodded in a low voice. "Ignore her. She only wants to get under your skin."

She was good at doing just that. I knew as well as Millie and Jack, though, that it irritated her more when I didn't respond, so I acquiesced.

"Everyone eat breakfast," Chris ordered. "I'll wait until we're in the air to tell you about our case." His eyes sparkled. He was clearly excited about the investigation. He was the enthusiastic sort, determined to find proof of paranormal shenanigans. He'd done just that on multiple occasions. He simply didn't realize it.

I was used to flying at this point. It was almost a weekly occurrence before the last assignment. Since then, we'd been hanging close to the office. It was a timely break — and Jack and I needed that time to re-forge our bonds and get over what had happened in New

Orleans — but I was happy to be back to work. Given the way Jack smiled when I bit into my Egg McMuffin, he obviously felt the same way.

Twenty minutes later, we were at cruising altitude and everyone had finished eating. Jack collected our refuse and tossed it in the garbage before settling next to me. He held his coffee and sipped as he waited for Chris to start explaining. Our gregarious boss needed little prodding.

"We're after an incubus," he announced, grinning.

"What the heck is an incubus?" Laura asked, her voice shriller than usual. She was obviously still agitated by Jack's lackluster greeting. The more he ignored her, the more desperate she became to garner a reaction from him. It was getting rather pathetic.

"An incubus is the male form of a sexual demon," I volunteered without thinking. "The female form is a succubus. According to legend, he invades the bedroom of sleeping women and basically ... um ... loves them to death."

Jack arched an amused eyebrow at my discomfort. "Loves them?"

"You know." I shot him a dark look. "I'm not saying more than that."

Jack chortled as Chris took over the educational portion of the conversation.

"Charlie is essentially right," he volunteered. "An incubus is a demon who uses his sexual prowess to invade a woman's dreams, lull her into a fall sense of security, and then extracts her life force through sexual acts."

Jack looked horrified at the prospect. "Excuse me? Are you saying he literally kills a woman with sex?"

Chris nodded without hesitation. "That's exactly what I'm saying." He looked far too happy at the prospect, but I didn't take it personally. It wasn't that the notion of innocent women being essentially raped to death excited him. He just liked the demon part. He wanted to see one more than anything.

Jack's gaze was speculative as he shifted his eyes to me. "Are demons real?"

The question likely wasn't directed toward me, but it felt that way. "How should I know?" I shrugged, uncomfortable. "I know what you know."

He realized his mistake too late to take it back. "I wasn't directing the question at you."

"He was directing it at me," Chris volunteered. "Although I'm not sure I have the answers. I believe in demons. And there are more than incubi and succubi out there. As we all know, though, Jack is harder to convince when it comes to creatures with a paranormal bent."

That certainly used to be true. Given recent events, though, I couldn't help but wonder if he would change his tack moving forward.

"I don't always jump to the conclusion that it's not possible," Jack hedged, although he didn't look as if he believed the statement. "It's just ... demons are so fantastical."

He'd met one in New Orleans. Harlequin Desdemona Stryker — or Harley for the great unwashed — was a crossroads demon who inserted herself into our lives when the zombies called forth by an evil bruja threatened to overwhelm us. She tipped us off to what was happening and tried to help. After that, she disappeared into the night. I had no idea if I would ever see her again. I used my magic to eradicate the rest of the zombies once she figuratively (and kind of literally) lit a fuse for me, something Jack witnessed from a prime seat. He'd obviously been more focused on that, which was understandable. Apparently we needed to have a discussion about Harley and her origins when we got a moment alone.

"And yet they have ties to biblical times," Chris noted, oblivious to Jack's inner turmoil. He wasn't a bad guy by any stretch of the imagination, but he often missed social cues. Jack wasn't always easy to read anyway. Chris naturally assumed he was reticent about the existence of demons for the same reasons he always was. He couldn't possibly know about what had happened in New Orleans to change Jack's outlook.

For that, I was grateful.

"So ... are you saying angels are real, too?" Jack queried.

Chris nodded without hesitation. "Most certainly. But we're not dealing with an angel. What's happening in Charleston is decidedly ... evil."

"And what's happening in Charleston?" Millie asked, directing the conversation to safer waters. She knew Jack was still struggling to wrap his mind around the expanded world he found himself living in. She wanted to give him a moment to regroup, which he desperately needed.

"Well, in a nutshell, women are dying," Chris replied, his expression darkening. "It's really more convoluted than that." He pulled a file from the briefcase he carried only when traveling. "We have eight dead women so far."

"Eight?" I was flabbergasted.

Jack, who tried not to display our relationship when we were on the job, automatically reached for my hand. Either he no longer cared about keeping up a professional front or he simply lost track of his emotions before he could think better of it.

"That's a lot of bodies," he noted after a beat. "What sort of timeframe are we dealing with?"

"Three weeks."

"Three weeks?" Jack's eyebrows practically flew off his forehead. "Are you kidding me? That's ... I mean ... ." His mind was clearly busy as he leaned back in his seat and rubbed his cheek. "Serial killers usually have a cooling down period between kills. This speaks to escalation, the exact opposite."

"We're not dealing with a serial killer," Chris pointed out.

I stirred. "Aren't we?" I felt the need to take Jack's side, even if it was in a roundabout way. "You're saying eight women have been killed in the past three weeks, and there's obviously enough evidence to suggest that a single culprit is responsible for all the attacks. If that's not a serial killer, I don't know what is."

"Point taken," Chris conceded. "This is obviously a ritual killer, albeit a supernatural one."

Jack cleared his throat and his expression told me he was

returning to reality ... with a big, loud thud. "What evidence do we have that we're dealing with a supernatural killer?"

Chris beamed at him. "I'm glad you asked." He removed a small stack of documents from his folder and handed them to Jack. "Here are the police reports from several of the scenes. Not every death is being investigated by the Charleston Police Department. Three of them belong to a neighboring community, Summerville, which is about twenty minutes away."

"Far enough for neighboring departments to have a pissing contest, but close enough to detect a pattern," Jack mused as he perused the documents.

I looked over his shoulder, not caring in the least that I was crowding him, and frowned when I read the portion about how the bodies were discovered. "This says there were no marks on the bodies," I noted. "How do we know the women didn't die of natural causes? I mean ... it would seem unlikely for younger women, but it's not out of the realm of possibility, especially if we want to include potential environmental factors that might've impacted them."

Jack shot me an appraising look. "Nice. You're thinking like a cop."

The way he phrased it didn't sound like a compliment. "Oh, I still think it's an incubus," I warned him. "I just like having all the information at my fingertips."

"My earlier statement stands." He shot me a wink — something that wasn't lost on Laura because she made a disgusted sound deep in her throat — and then turned back to the files. "It says here that full autopsies were performed on all the women and no cause of death could be ascertained."

"That's correct." Chris bobbed his head. "All the women were in their early to mid-twenties. None of them were over the age of twenty-seven. None were younger than twenty-three. All were brunettes with blue eyes. No deviations. We're talking fit women, all considered attractive by generic standards, and they all had long hair, which they wore straight, past their shoulders."

"It sounds like Charlie," Millie noted out of the blue, causing me to cringe.

Jack, his eyes thoughtful, pinned me with a worried look. "It does sound like Charlie," he agreed.

I sensed the discussion turning in an uncomfortable direction. "Let's not get ahead of ourselves."

"Nobody is jumping to conclusions," Jack reassured me. "You're not sleeping alone in Charleston, though. I mean ... just to be on the safe side."

Laura snorted. "I guess that means you're bunking with Millie, huh, Charlie? What a bummer for you."

"She'll be bunking with me," Jack corrected, his tone confrontational. He appeared to be channeling Millie this morning and was apparently ready to throw down if need be.

"Fraternization is against the rules," Laura shot back.

"Not for our group," Chris reminded her. "Thanks to the fit you threw in St. Pete Beach — and the recent sensitivity seminar we were forced to attend because of you — the rules of our group have been expressly laid out. If group members want to share a room, no matter the configuration, it's encouraged because it will save on costs. I initially booked Charlie and Jack separate rooms, but that will be easily rectified when we reach the hotel."

Jack shot Laura a smug look, which only seemed to darken her mood ... if that was even possible.

"Well, how great for you guys," she drawled, hatred practically dripping from her tongue when she focused on me. "Everything seems to be turning up roses for you, huh?"

I managed to keep my temper in check, but just barely. "I'm actually a fan of hydrangeas. Roses are nice, don't get me wrong, but hydrangeas are fancier."

"I'll mark that down for the first time I need to bring you flowers to dig myself out of a hole," Jack offered. "And that will happen, by the way. You might want to buy some vases now."

I laughed. He was happier, freer even, than he was on previous assignments. I couldn't help but wonder if the truth coming out about my abilities had allowed him to lighten up.

"Oh, I just can't take the cuteness overload," Laura complained, bitterly. "Can we talk about something else? Anything else, really. How about we go back to the dead women? That's preferable to this conversation."

"I hate to agree with Laura — honestly, you have no idea — but we probably should focus on the bigger picture rather than how adorable Charlie and Jack are together," Millie offered, causing Jack to scowl. "That's a lot of women for such a short amount of time. What are the specifics of the attacks?"

"There aren't any specifics," Chris replied. "All of the women were tucked safely in their beds. They were thought to have died in their sleep because their expressions were peaceful. Some of the bedrooms were on the first floor, others on the second floor. All the bedroom windows were open. There wasn't a mark on any of the bodies."

"Were the women single?" I asked, searching for another pattern that might help us narrow down potential victims. "I mean ... was the incubus relatively certain that he wouldn't be interrupted during the act?"

"Actually, I don't know the answer to that question," Chris mused, scanning the paperwork in front of him. "It doesn't really say. The only information on the individuals who discovered the bodies comes in the form of 'male' and 'female.' There's no way of knowing if we're dealing with a parent, sibling, friend or significant other. I will be sure to ask, though. That's a very good point, Charlie."

"Yes, well done, Charlie," Laura whined. "You're perfect and the rest of us bow at your feet."

Jack shot her a quelling look. "Why must you always make things difficult?"

She was incensed. "Me? I'm not the one fawning all over a co-worker and creating a toxic work environment. That would be you. I mean ... do you really think anyone wants to see you making a fool of yourself by kissing her ass? It's gross."

"I love watching him kiss her ass," Millie countered. "It's a highlight for me ... and only partially because it drives you crazy. That's just an added bonus."

"You know what?" Laura looked as if she was going to stand and I couldn't help but wonder if she would actually travel the five feet to the back of the plane and physically attack Millie. Jack would step in at that point and Laura would likely lose her job. While I didn't want anyone to go through a financial hardship — even Laura — I couldn't deny the notion appealed to me.

"Sit down, Laura," Chris ordered, his eyes flashing with impatience.

One look at him told Laura all she needed to know. He meant business.

"We don't have time for this," Chris insisted. "There are innocent women out there, probably being stalked, and it's likely they've already been marked for death. We need to hit the ground running on this one. We don't have time for tedious games."

I shot a sheepish look toward Jack, embarrassed, but he was busy glaring at Laura. Apparently he didn't care if his hatred was deemed tedious.

"The only thing we know for certain right now is that every woman in question appeared to have had sexual contact before her death, but there were no fluids left behind. There were no fingerprints of note. The front doors were locked and only the windows were open. That's what we have to go on right now."

"Then we'll go from there," Jack said, dragging his eyes from Laura. "We'll figure it out, Chris. We always do. You can count on us."

"I certainly hope so. I told my uncle that the personal relationships in this group weren't a problem. I would appreciate it if you didn't make a liar out of me."

"We won't," Jack promised. "You have my word."

THREE

The hotel fronted Folly Beach, an absolutely beautiful spate of land that offered one of the best views I'd ever seen. The sun was high in the sky, the water crystal clear, and the grand pier I could see about a half-mile down the beach beckoned.

"Look at that."

Jack moved to my side, his lips curving. "It's cool. We'll check it out when we have a few minutes of free time."

"I've never seen anything like that," I admitted. "The pier we saw in St. Petersburg was cool, but that is … wow."

"It's very cool."

When he didn't expound, I slid my gaze to him. "Have you been here before?"

He nodded. "Quite a few times, actually. My grandmother was a fan of the area and she used to bring my cousins and me to Charleston at least once a year for a two-week vacation to give our parents a break. We stayed at the hotel down the way."

"That's amazing."

"I take it you didn't get to go on many vacations."

"Not really. My parents were amazing, but they didn't always have a lot of extra money. We weren't poor, but our vacations usually consisted of trips to the Upper Peninsula of Michigan to camp."

"Ah." His hand automatically moved to my back so he could lightly rub. "Well, you're not in Minnesota any longer. With this gig, you'll see a lot of the country."

I could hardly wait.

The Legacy Foundation had rented the beach villa on the hotel property other than the individual rooms Chris had mentioned, something that was arranged while we were in the air. It boasted five rooms, three of which looked out at the beach, and Jack ensured we snagged one of those rooms. He carried our bags up the stairs and put them on the settee on the far side of the suite — we had our own private bathroom, which was a bonus — while I checked out the balcony.

"What do you think?" he asked from behind me.

"It smells great here," I admitted, my enthusiasm getting the better of me. "I love the smell of the ocean."

"I take it you want to end up someplace with beach access."

I'd never really given much thought to where I might end up. For a long time, survival was the name of the game and I couldn't see past my next meal. It seemed strange to suddenly be plunged into a world where I had options. "I like the beach. Who knows? I might find a spot I like even better."

"You might," he agreed, although he didn't look convinced. "Folly Beach is a seafood town. I know you're a big fan of shellfish. The main road is only a half mile that way. I figured we could break from the others and head in that direction once we're finished with work for the day."

There was nothing I liked more than an adventure, so I readily agreed. "That sounds good." I turned to face him. "I can't believe you requested a room together. Aren't you worried that Chris might come to regret it?"

His smile was smug. "Why? Are you planning to be particularly loud?"

It took me a moment to grasp what he was insinuating. "Don't be a pervert." I lightly slapped his arm. "Now you're not going to get any action because I won't be able to think of anything but the others knowing what we're doing."

"I have news for you, Charlie; they're well aware that we have sex."

My cheeks burned and I could just picture the flush stealing over my face.

"You're cute," he teased, giving me a quick kiss. "As for the other stuff, we'll worry about it later. Chris expects us to meet in the living room so he can dole out tasks."

"Okay." I closed the sliding glass door behind me as I returned to the room, arching an eyebrow when Jack immediately double-checked to make sure I'd locked it. "You're really worked up about the possibility of an incubus, huh?"

The question obviously caught him off guard. He shrugged. "I don't know. Until today I never really gave demons much thought. I always assumed they were myths, remnants of fairytales long since passed. I thought that about a lot of things."

His eyes were contemplative when they snagged with mine. "You've changed things for me," he continued. "You've widened the scope of my life. I'm pretty sure that's a good thing. It's a daunting thing, too. I don't know how to handle myself in this brave new world."

His honesty was raw, on the surface, and it made my heart roll. "I'm sorry if I ruined things for you."

He immediately started shaking his head. "Don't say that." His tone was sharp, probably more so than he intended. "You've made my life better just by being." As if to prove it, he pulled me in for a demanding hug. "You make me happy, Charlie." His voice was barely a whisper. "Don't think otherwise. We're going to have things to overcome — all couples do — but what you are isn't one of them. Please don't think that."

Tears pricked the back of my eyes. "Thank you for saying that." My voice cracked and I felt like a ninny. "You've made my life better, too."

He chuckled as he rubbed his hands over my back. "We're still getting used to our new reality. It's going to be okay." He repeated those words regularly. They were becoming his mantra. "We're going to be stronger going forward. I'm lagging right now because I didn't want to see the truth about paranormal beings before you. Now I have no choice but to see. I will catch up."

"You're not lagging." I pressed a kiss to his cheek. "You're perfect the way you are."

"Yeah. You're perfect, too." He held on for a moment longer and then released me, offering up a lopsided grin that increased my heartbeat. "We're kind of the schmaltz twins now, huh?"

"We definitely are." I squeezed his hand and exhaled heavily. "We should probably get downstairs." I started for the door and then pulled up short. "Just one thing. I know the demon thing is throwing you for a loop, but the woman on the roof, the one who warned us the zombies were coming before sending the fire — she was a demon."

Whatever he was expecting, that wasn't it. He was utterly flabbergasted as he stared. "What?"

I nodded. "She wasn't the same kind of demon. Not all demons are bad. She was a crossroads demon, which I can explain in more detail later. I just didn't want to give you the impression that it was still possible demons aren't real. That's not true. Whether this demon is real is another story. I don't have an answer for you."

"And that's why I want that door shut after dark every night." He pointed toward the sliding glass door for emphasis. He didn't appear angry as much as worried. "The victims look like you. I don't want to frighten you — not ever — but if this creature picks up that we're on his tail he's probably going to be attracted to you. It's important we don't give him an opening to get to you."

"Trust me. I have no interest in hooking up with a sex demon. I can barely handle you."

He mustered a smile. "Let's keep it that way, huh?"

"Absolutely."

EVERYONE WAS GATHERED IN THE living room when we arrived. Laura sat in the middle of the couch, a move that felt purposeful because Jack and I had no choice but to separate on either side of her.

"Thank you for coming," she drawled sarcastically.

Jack ignored her and focused on Chris. "So, what's the plan?"

"A little background to start," Chris replied, clapping his hands and then rubbing them briskly. "Charleston is one of the oldest cities in the United States. It's been a hub of activity practically from the start. That means it has a rich mythology and history, two things that we can't overlook.

"First, Charleston is known as the holy city because of all the churches," he continued. "The bulk of the population is religious, so we need to be careful talking about demons. It could set certain people off."

"I don't think you have to worry about that," Jack said dryly. "I don't plan on using that word in front of anyone outside of this group. I doubt anyone else does either."

"Oh, not me," Laura countered. "I'm going to tell anyone who listens about the demon prowling the streets. I figure if I act like enough of a basket case that will garner some attention from you. I mean ... it worked for Charlie."

He scorched her with a death glare. "Have you ever considered taking a vow of silence? I know you're not a nun — half the East Coast can vouch for that — but it might be an interesting change."

Millie chortled as Chris shook his head.

"The sniping needs to stop," Chris ordered. "I get that tempers are running high given some of the things that have happened of late — and ninety percent of that is Laura's fault because she keeps pushing the envelope — but we have to find a way to work together."

Laura balked. "Ninety percent?"

"More like a hundred percent," Jack muttered.

Sensing trouble, I attempted to re-direct the conversation. "The churches could actually appeal to the demon," I offered. "From everything I've read, demons enjoy messing with symbols of faith and hope. Churches would definitely fall into that category."

Chris beamed at me. "See. Charlie's done her research. I've also been wondering if that's a possibility."

"Yes, Charlie is perfect," Laura muttered under her breath.

"She is," Jack agreed, blasé. "What else do you want us to know?"

"The South Carolina Ports Authority is one of the top ten container ports in the United States," Chris replied, happy to unleash his mountain of trivia. "The authority is responsible for almost two hundred thousand jobs, which means people are coming and going in the city via the Atlantic Ocean every day."

"You're suggesting that our demon works on the ships," Jack surmised, rubbing the back of his neck. "It's not a bad idea, but how do you plan on proving it?"

"I'm not suggesting anything of the sort," Chris countered. "I'm merely considering it as a possibility. There's a heavy transient population here. That means individuals — men in particular — come and go from Charleston regularly ... and they have money. I don't know how we would go about checking those individuals, but I haven't ruled out giving it a shot."

"So ... what do you want to do?" Jack queried. "Do you suggest we head down to the port and start questioning random people?"

"No. But we're going to need to split up."

Laura's hand shot into the air. "I think you should split up Charlie and Jack because they don't seem to focus on work when they're together. I'll go with him and someone else can go with Charlie, just to make sure they do their jobs."

Jack's glare was pronounced, but Chris didn't seem to notice.

"I've already divvied up the work assignments," he said briskly. "Millie and Bernard are going to head to the port to look around. I don't expect them to find anything, but I would like to know the lay of the land. Bernard, you have access to one of our good cameras. Please take some photos."

Bernard nodded without hesitation. "Absolutely. We can do that."

Chris smiled before turning to Hannah. "I've made arrangements for you to get in and see the most recent body. The Charleston County Coroner is expecting you. You probably won't be able to do your own autopsy, but any insight you can give us into the cause of death will be of use."

Hannah offered up a pretty smile meant only for him. She excelled in a scientific setting. "No problem."

"I'm sending Laura with you," he added.

Hannah's smile slipped. "That's really not necessary. I can handle the body on my own."

"Nobody can run around on his or her own," Chris countered. "Especially because we're most likely dealing with an incubus, who will be attracted to the women. No one of the female persuasion is allowed to go anywhere alone."

My mouth dropped open. "Wait a second … ."

Jack shot me a quelling look. "I think that's a fine idea," he said pointedly. "We should definitely make that a rule while we're in town."

Of course he would think that. I wanted to argue the point, but it seemed a waste of breath. It was better to pick my battles, and this one was a losing proposition. "I have no problem sticking with a chaperone," I said sweetly. "It sounds like a great time."

"That's good," Chris noted. "You'll be coming with Jack and me. The most recent victim, the one Hannah is going to see in the morgue, had an apartment about three miles from here. We'll be heading there. I've secured permission to search the premises."

I wanted to ask how, but it really didn't matter. "That sounds like a good place to start," I said. "Are we heading there now?"

Chris nodded. "Shortly. Does anyone have any questions about what they're supposed to be doing?" he asked the group.

"I do," Laura replied, her voice like grinding gears on a dying machine. "Why does Charlie get to go to the scene and I have to go to the morgue? I think our roles should be reversed. I've been with the group longer, after all. My instincts are sharper."

Chris didn't appear to agree. "Charlie's instincts are infallible. She's stumbled across more clues in her short tenure with us than you have over the course of the past few years. I want her with me."

Jack's smile was smug as he risked a glance at Laura. She looked as if she was about to melt down, but managed to hold it together.

"Okay then." Chris clapped his hands. "Let's get to work."

SAVANNAH BILLINGS — SHE WAS CLEARLY named after the southern city — had been a neat freak. That was the first thing I noticed upon entering her apartment.

She didn't have many decorations, only a few framed photographs on the tables scattered about the living room. There were no tchotchkes on the shelves or artwork on the walls. Everything was decorated in sterile colors. White, gray, beige. There wasn't a splash of color to be found in the apartment, even in the closet.

"This is a nice place except for the way it makes me want to slit my wrists," I commented as I sifted through the bills on the counter. There was nothing of interest, only the standard gas and electric bills that would never be paid. "Apparently she didn't like color."

Jack smirked as he glanced in my direction. He was going through Savannah's iPad, which she'd failed to lock. "It's a little drab," he agreed. "I notice you like a lot of color, whether everything matches or not."

"I do love color," I agreed. "As for everything matching ... sometimes I don't really have a choice in the matter. I bought the couch because it was comfortable and in my price range. If I had unlimited funds and could go to a store and buy everything new, I guarantee my life would be color coordinated ... just not like this."

He stared at me a moment, his expression unreadable, and then went back to his snooping. "I like your apartment. It's comfortable, homey. This place doesn't feel homey."

"No, it doesn't," Chris agreed as he strolled out of the bedroom. "According to the police report, the bedroom sliding glass door was open. That means whoever entered somehow managed to fly to do it."

Jack lifted his chin and frowned. "Fly? Can demons fly?"

The question was directed at me. "I have no idea," I answered. "I'm guessing yes, but I'm not an expert."

"They can totally fly," Chris offered. "Trust me. I've researched this front and back. Demons can fly and they don't need capes to do it."

"Good to know," Jack said dryly, shaking his head as he turned off the iPad and left it on the counter. "There's nothing in her electronics. She was a real estate agent and had a variety of appointments lined up for later in the week. I can check those to see if any of the names hit on a search, but I don't expect they will. She didn't have a datebook in there, so I have no idea what she did in her free time."

"I do," I supplied, smirking when he shot me a sidelong look. "I do," I repeated. "I know exactly what she did with her time."

"Would you like to share with the class?" he prodded.

"Absolutely." I bobbed my head and held up the Bible I'd found on the end table. "Charleston Church of the Divine. According to the inside jacket, she was a part of the fellowship ministry and went to at least three sermons a week."

Jack frowned. "She went to church three times a week? I'm not religious, but that seems like a lot. Is it a lot?"

That was another question I couldn't answer. I was always afraid of churches in my youth because I was convinced I might turn to ash if I tried to cross the threshold. I watched a lot of movies that only fueled my imagination. I wasn't keen to test my theory now, but I didn't want to be cut out of the action, so I would have to suck it up.

"If anyone can tell us about our dead woman, I'm guessing it's the people at the church," I said. "I think that should be our next stop."

"Agreed," Chris said, exhaling heavily as he took another look around the living room. "There's nothing here. We need help if we're going to figure this out."

"Church it is," Jack said, pushing himself to a standing position. "I don't see where it can possibly hurt."

"Then let's go," Chris prodded. "I'm anxious to find a direction to start looking in."

That made two of us.

FOUR

Jack drove the rental car as Chris pored over maps of the area. He was the sort of guy who absolutely loved anything visual. He kept rattling off observations from the passenger seat as I watched the scenery fly by the window. I was looking forward to having a chance to explore later with Jack. For now, I had a job to focus on.

"It kind of makes sense for the incubus to be transient," I offered, my mind busy. "I mean ... the murders only started a few weeks ago. Our guy had to be somewhere else before then."

"I don't know," Jack replied, his eyes bouncing from the GPS unit in the dashboard to the road. "I have a hard time believing a demon needs to work on a ship."

"Why not?" I was curious why he believed otherwise. "Even a demon has to find a way to fund his lifestyle."

"Can't he just — I don't know — snap his fingers and make people bow to his will? Can't he steal from his victims?"

"Even paranormal creatures have rules to follow," Chris countered. I wasn't even sure he was listening to us until he spoke. "I think if it was easy to steal money, every demon in the free world would do it."

"How do you know they're not?"

Chris shrugged. "I guess I don't. But according to the police reports, nothing of value appeared to be missing from any of the homes. That seems to indicate that the murderer was there for a different reason."

"Like sex and essence stealing," I muttered darkly.

Jack lifted his eyes until they locked with mine in the rearview mirror. "You make sure you stick close to me," he ordered. "I'm serious."

"Yes, Dad," I said dryly.

"I agree with Jack," Chris said. "You resemble all the victims, Charlie. We don't want to take a chance with one of the most valuable members of our team."

I preened under the compliment even as I fought my disgust at being guarded like a prissy princess who couldn't take care of herself. "I very much doubt an incubus would go after me," I said after a beat. "He probably has his victims scoped out days or even weeks in advance. I'll be fine."

"You *will* be fine," Jack agreed as he pulled onto a one-way street. "I'm going to make sure of it."

I remained quiet until he parked in the lot of one of the fanciest churches I'd ever seen. It was huge, the spire jutting high into the sky. The lot was so big I found myself counting spaces as I exited the vehicle and stretched my legs. I wasn't tall, but the backseat was hardly comfortable.

"This congregation must be humongous," I noted as Jack moved to stand by me. His eyes were alert as he scanned the parking lot. "Chill out," I suggested. "The incubus isn't going to come for me in a church parking lot in the middle of the day. He attacks at night."

"You're the only one convinced it's a demon," Jack argued. "If it's a bargain-basement serial killer — one who somehow managed to kill without being overt — he very well could attack in the middle of the day. He could also simply be scoping out the church for new victims, and if he sees you he might be intrigued."

"I think it's a demon," Chris volunteered, winking at me as Jack scowled. "Charlie isn't the only one."

"Sometimes I want to gag you two so you can't feed off each other," Jack complained, inclining his head toward the large wooden doors at the front of the church. They were beautifully ornate, to the point they took my breath away. The inlaid stained glass was a work of art. "Let's see if we can find someone knowledgeable inside."

Even though he acted annoyed, Jack made sure to fall to the back of our formation, sandwiching me between him and Chris. I could've called him out on his overprotective nature, but he was simply trying to protect me.

Chris pushed on the heavy doors, which opened with an echoing creak that reminded me of an old *Scooby-Doo* cartoon. Jack arched an eyebrow, amusement evident when I spared a glance for him, and then prodded me forward.

The church was immaculate. It was obviously old, probably built in the 1800s if I had to guess, but it had been painstakingly restored. The arched ceiling and pews were carved from polished mahogany. The floor was marble, the grout pristine, and the air was fresh and clear as the overhead ceiling fans did their job.

"Wow," I intoned, my voice echoing.

"It's pretty fancy," Jack agreed, his eyes moving to the front of the church, to where a casually dressed man stood. He seemed surprised to find interlopers in his building. "I'm guessing he works here."

"That would be my guess, too," Chris agreed. He plastered a friendly smile on his face — he was ridiculously good with people, strangers and friends alike — and extended his hand as he approached the man. "Hello. I'm sorry to bother you in the middle of the day. I'm sure you have work to do.

"My name is Chris Briggs and I'm here as part of an investigative group that's been put together by the city to look into the deaths that have been occurring," he continued, not pausing even for a breath. "The most recent victim, Savannah Billings, was a member of your congregation. We have some questions."

The man, who looked to be in his early thirties, arched an eyebrow. "That was a mouthful," he said after a moment's contemplation. "I'm not sure I absorbed everything you said. Give me a moment."

"Certainly." Chris rocked back on his heels and waited.

After a few more seconds, the man nodded. "Okay, I think I've got it. You've been brought in to work on the law enforcement task force that's investigating the serial killer the police believe is hunting in our fair city. Do I have that right?"

Technically we weren't involved with the task force — at least not officially — and I was curious if Chris would correct the man. He didn't.

"That's it in a nutshell," Chris agreed. "We're with the Legacy Foundation out of Boston. We just arrived today and we're digging into Savannah's background because she's the latest victim. Her ties to this church seem deep, and I was hoping you might have time to answer some questions."

That man didn't look thrilled at the prospect. "I cannot divulge secrets about our parishioners."

"Not secrets," Chris said hurriedly. "It's more that we're looking for insight. It's possible that whoever did this inserted himself into Savannah's life within the last few weeks. We were hoping you might know if there was any such individual."

Instead of immediately responding, the man licked his lips and dragged a hand through his sandy hair. He looked conflicted, as if he was having trouble making up his mind. Finally, he nodded and gestured toward a door at the back of the church. "Come to my office. I'm Samuel Rodriguez, but everyone here calls me Reverend Sam."

"You look young to be a reverend," I noted.

"I'm thirty-one." He flashed me a friendly smile. "I grew up in this parish and discovered my calling at a young age. I returned to the church after my schooling, and I don't foresee ever leaving."

"Are you in charge here?" Jack asked.

Sam shook his head. "I'm second in command, I guess you could say. The head reverend has been here for a number of years."

"And who is that?"

"I'll introduce you."

Since Jack and Chris seemed to be taking the lead, I fell into step with them and studied the church. The adornments on the walls were ornate, so overblown as to be almost garish. I'd never been one for church decorations. Religious icons — it didn't matter the religion because they were all the same — gave me the willies.

The office Sam led us into was simpler than the public areas of the church, which allowed me to breathe a little easier. The furniture he directed us to sit in was comfortable. He held up a finger indicating we should wait before disappearing through yet another door.

"What do you think?" Jack asked in a low voice as we arranged ourselves in the chairs.

"Churches are freaky," I automatically answered, frowning at the crucifix on the wall. It looked to be homemade, a regular piece of art, and someone had gone overboard with the blood. "Seriously freaky."

He chuckled and patted my knee in a reassuring manner before turning his attention to the opening door. Sam entered, followed by a much older man who wore formal black robes and had snowy white hair. He looked to be in his eighties, and the juxtaposition between the two men was on full display.

"This is Reverend Alexander Johnson," Sam offered. "This is his church."

"This is the Lord's church," Alexander corrected, his sparkplug eyebrows furrowing as he glanced between faces. He didn't look all that impressed by what he saw, but because he had that "Hey, you kids, get off my lawn" vibe going for him, I didn't hold it against him. "Reverend Rodriguez says you're here about Savannah. We heard about her death, of course, and the entire congregation is stunned. We want to help ... within reason."

His knees creaked as he took the big chair at the edge of the room. It gave him a position of dominance over the rest of us. That was clearly by design. "You understand that we can't share personal information about one of our parishioners. That would be breaking faith and that's something we just won't do."

"We don't want you to break faith," Chris assured him. He took a moment to make introductions, something that was uncomfortable for me because Reverend Alexander gave me a long once-over that caused butterflies to flit through my stomach. He had an overbearing presence that made me nervous.

"We're here because we're trying to help," Jack explained. He was seated next to me but made sure we weren't touching. I had a feeling he was just as uncomfortable with the religious icons littering the room — which all seemed to be staring at us — as I was. "What's happening in Charleston right now is a travesty. We want to catch the individual responsible and make sure he's put behind bars."

"It's not a man," Alexander shot back. "It's a devil."

I leaned forward, my interest piqued. "What have you heard?"

"Just what the news is reporting. A man didn't do this. You know that, right?"

"You think it was a demon, too." The statement escaped before I could think better of what I was saying — which was normal for me — and I didn't miss Jack's groan as the older reverend shot me a curious look.

"Men have personal demons they sometimes can't overcome," he said finally. "If that's what you're talking about, I agree."

It wasn't what I was talking about, but he gave me an easy way out, so I took it. "Personal demons are the worst."

Jack shot me a quelling look and shook his head as Chris took over the conversation.

"We understand that Savannah was a regular here," he started. "I don't suppose you saw anyone new in her life, perhaps someone on the perimeter who was always looking in? We're not necessarily saying the culprit could be a member of your congregation, but it's likely he would've watched her given the time she spent here."

"The time she spent here?" The new voice that took over the room was female and I jolted when I realized a third individual had joined us from the back room. The petite brunette, her dark hair sprayed to the point it didn't as much as flutter despite the strong fan blasting overhead.

"Gretchen," Alexander said, shaking his head. There was an

admonishment in his tone. "I thought I told you we would handle this."

"You did." Contrition flitted across her face. "I heard the discussion from the office, though, and I finished recording the tithes from last night's service. I couldn't stop myself from adding my two cents. I knew Savannah better than you and Reverend Sam combined." Her tone was pious and she batted her eyelashes when appealing to the older man. "I meant no disrespect."

Her demure attitude when talking to Alexander made me uneasy. I glanced at Jack to see if he felt the same way, but his expression was unreadable. If he thought there was anything weird about the interaction, he didn't show it. I, on the other hand, couldn't stop myself from squirming. Gretchen was almost being treated like a misbehaving child rather than an autonomous woman, and it was ... well ... weird.

"This is Gretchen Dunlop," Sam offered, a tight smile clamping down on his features. "She volunteers her time to work in a secretarial position three days a week."

"And I'm here the other four days a week," Gretchen added. "I know the inner workings of this church better than anyone."

Alexander shot her a questioning look.

"Well, almost anyone," she conceded. "As for Savannah, while she was in regular attendance here, she was hardly what I call pious."

Oh, well, now we were getting somewhere. I was a fairly good judge of character and it was obvious that Gretchen didn't like Savannah.

"I don't know what that means," Jack said. "Everything we found in her apartment seemed to indicate this church was her life."

"And it was," Sam reassured us. "She was a regular face under this roof. She attended Sunday and Wednesday services, was a member of the adult fellowship group that met every other Thursday, and was a regular participant in the Saturday singles group."

The way Gretchen's lips twisted told me the singles group was the avenue to drive down. "What's the Saturday singles group?" I asked.

"It's an excuse for heathenism," Gretchen replied before either man could answer.

Alexander shot her a look that would've shriveled the nerves of most ordinary individuals. Gretchen obviously noticed and took a pronounced step back.

"The singles group is for parishioners who have not yet married," Sam explained. "Most of our members hope to find love within our group because it's simply easier. Savannah was one of our most popular members."

"Popular?" Gretchen snorted and rolled her eyes. "We all know why that is."

Alexander looked to be at the end of his rope as he cleared his throat. "Gretchen, we're all aware that Savannah was not your favorite person. There's no reason to speak ill of the dead, though. She was a young woman, in her prime, and there's a chance she was stolen early by a violent individual. Show some respect."

Gretchen had the grace to be abashed. "I'm sorry, Reverend. I didn't mean to sound disrespectful. I just ... I ... I'm sorry." She clasped her hands, lowered her eyes, and stared at the floor. "I apologize for speaking out of turn."

Okay, that was definitely weird. This time when I glanced at Jack I found his forehead wrinkled. He was obviously picking up on the same strange vibe.

"You'll have to forgive Gretchen," Sam said hurriedly. "She's a good woman who can occasionally come across as harsh. Her heart is pure. She is dedicated to the Lord.

"As for Savannah, her path was a bit ... rockier," he continued, holding Alexander's gaze long enough to get a nod from the older man. It was obviously a silent acknowledgment that he should continue. "She was a true believer. That was never in doubt. She didn't always live the life, though."

"I'm not sure what that means," Chris hedged.

"She was a partier," Gretchen sputtered before either reverend could respond. "She went out to clubs all the time. That strip of down-and-dirty clubs near the port in the downtown area? She was there at least twice a week, and we know the sort of filth that occurs there."

I pressed my lips together and fought to maintain an even expression. I wanted to laugh, but I knew that wouldn't go over well. Instead, I folded my hands on my lap and let Jack and Chris run the conversation. Anything I said was bound to come out as accusatory ... and maybe a little angry. That wouldn't help our cause.

"I don't suppose you have the name of those bars?" Jack asked.

Gretchen nodded as Sam let loose a world-weary sigh.

"We can get you the names of the bars," Sam answered. "That's hardly a secret; nor was Savannah's regular attendance at the establishments. However, there's not much else we can help you with."

It was a dismissal, cold and to the point.

"That's fine," Chris said, his smile never wavering. "You've been a great deal of help. We really appreciate it."

I wasn't sure how much help they were, but I was eager to get out of the church. "Yes, thank you for your time," I said when I finally found my voice. "Hopefully Savannah's charlatan ways didn't hasten her demise." It was meant as a sarcastic response, but Gretchen took it as truth.

"Oh, it was her charlatan ways," the secretary intoned. "God paid her back. You can be assured of that."

FIVE

There were five bars on the list Gretchen supplied. Three had stars by their names because they were regular haunts. Two were establishments she didn't like because she was certain those who frequented them were getting freaky with one another. I kept my opinion on her to myself — which was a mighty struggle — until we were back in the rental.

"She's nuts," I announced as I fastened my seatbelt.

Jack lifted an eyebrow and eyed me over the seat. "Is that your clinical opinion?"

"That's easily discernible from watching her for thirty seconds. She's crazy ... and she's got a really weird thing going with Alexander."

Jack narrowed his eyes, as if he wanted to ask me a question. I had a feeling I knew what the question was — he was obsessed with me being able to read people's minds — but he wisely avoided that particular topic. The question was obviously still to come when we were alone, though. "What do you think is going on with Alexander?" he asked finally.

"I think he's got control over her, and it's freaky. She's a grown woman. He treated her like a child ... and she let him."

"Maybe she has impulse control problems and he had no choice but to rein her in."

The look I shot him was withering. "That was more than reining in. It was ... embarrassing. If someone tried to do that to me I would melt down. I wouldn't care if he was my boss. There's a line and he crossed it."

"I thought he was a little weird," Chris volunteered, his eyes back on the map. "She obviously puts up with it. If she had a problem, I think she would say something. She doesn't seem to be the quiet type. I mean ... she had no problem telling us about Savannah's issues."

I'd been thinking about that, too. "I don't think Savannah had issues."

"Gretchen certainly thought so," Jack noted as he navigated onto the highway.

"She's a judgmental freak. I'm guessing that Savannah was looking for a man and it bothered Gretchen because they're hunting in the same forest. Gretchen saw them as being in competition and was jealous."

"Because Savannah was prettier?" Chris asked absently. He appeared to have only one ear on the conversation, which was fine because I was about to start ranting.

"It's not just about being prettier. I mean ... looks aren't everything. I like to think personality plays into it, too."

Jack met my gaze in the rearview mirror. "Personality is the most important thing for a lot of people," he offered, his eyes piercing to the point I felt uncomfortable. "Physical attraction is based on chemistry, though, and looks are often a part of that. It's not necessarily a bad thing."

"Jack is right," Chris offered. "I knew that Hannah was the prettiest woman I'd ever seen the second I saw her. It wasn't until I'd spent some time with her that I realized we were compatible. I'm sure it was the same for you two."

A burning sensation crept up my neck at the offhand comment. "I very much doubt Jack thought I was beautiful when he saw me," I said finally. That wasn't a word people used when describing me. Cute.

Feisty. Mouthy. Sarcastic. Those were words people used. Beautiful? Not so much.

"That's not true," Jack countered as he checked the GPS. I didn't remember discussing our next stop, so he must've made up his mind without input. "I knew the second I saw you that you were going to be trouble for me."

I was confused. "Why?"

"Because I couldn't stop staring at you and you made me want to hide in bed to get away from you."

That didn't exactly sound flattering. "That's not attraction on a physical level."

"Oh, I was attracted to you." His expression momentarily darkened. "I was attracted right away. I didn't know what to do with the feelings because that had never happened to me before. I was confused, so I decided to keep you at a distance because I figured the feelings would just go away."

"And?" I prodded.

"And they didn't, and here we are." He flashed a warm smile. "I knew from the start that I was attracted to you. That part of a relationship is chemical. You have to get past that part to know if you're compatible."

That was an interesting observation, and I filed it away to think about later. "Well, I'm guessing that Savannah had the looks and personality sewn up ... at least more than Gretchen, who looks as if she spends her days eating lemons."

Jack barked out a laugh. "She does have a way about her, and she clearly didn't like Savannah. I don't know if that hate was warranted or if she's simply crazy."

"Oh, she's crazy." I was certain of that. "She hated Savannah and isn't sad in the least that she's gone."

"She's the one who told us about the bars where Savannah hung out," Jack reminded me. "The two reverends were going to sweep that under the rug until she opened her mouth. In this particular case, I think the hate is good."

Honestly, I agreed with him. "Yeah, well ... which bar are we going to first?"

"Apparently this beach bar was the one Savannah went to most often. Two of the others are on the same strip. The other two are farther out, so I think we should start with this one, especially since the beach grill is close to port."

"You think someone coming in from sea might've seen her at the bar," I mused. "You're considering the beach bar as a hunting ground."

"It's way too early for that," Jack countered. "We don't even know if the other women were regulars at the bar."

"According to this map, the area we're heading to is known for the nightlife," Chris volunteered. "There's a lot to do other than visit bars, although there are plenty of those to choose from."

"What else is in the area?" Jack asked. "It's going to take us about ten minutes to get there. I would like a picture of the area before we land."

"Sure." Chris nodded. "Let's see. There's a popular hotel, a waterfront park and some famous restaurant everyone raves about called Fleet Landing."

"That sounds interesting." Jack winked at me in the mirror. "If they're famous, they must have good food. I know someone who loves good food."

"Yes, good food is great," Chris replied absently, completely missing the fact that Jack was flirting with me directly in front of him. That was one of the great things about Chris. When he was focused on a case, very little else entered his brain. Jack liked to take advantage of that, which always made me laugh.

"This is the historic section of Charleston," Chris noted, turning serious. "The old slave market was located in this area – somewhere – and there are a lot of museums and nods to the past."

My stomach tightened. "I didn't really think about that," I said, rubbing my forehead. "Charleston would've been a hotbed for slavery back then."

"It was," Chris agreed. "I was reading a book on our flight here — just general tidbits about Charleston — and it said that forty percent of all Africans forcibly brought to the U.S. set foot on this soil before being dispersed to their owners."

The notion made me distinctly uncomfortable. "That's … interesting."

Chris carried on, oblivious. "City Hall was built by slaves. Gadsden's Wharf is where slave ships docked, and they believe more than one-hundred-thousand slaves landed in the city there. There's something called the Sugar House, which sounds horrifying. It was located directly next door to the jail. I guess it was a slave torture chamber."

The more he talked, the more uncomfortable I got. "Is it still standing?"

"No," Chris replied. "It's gone. It was a factory — or I guess they called it a workhouse — and a lot of slaves died there because of the tortures they endured."

I shifted on my seat and forced my gaze out the window. "I'm guessing the entire city has a harsh history."

"Any good city does," Chris agreed.

Jack cleared his throat to get us to stop talking. "I don't think the city's history of slavery has anything to do with what's happening today. We should focus on that and leave the other stuff for another time."

"You're right," Chris agreed, unruffled. "Let's check out that beach bar. What's the name of it?"

"Blessed," Jack replied.

I wrinkled my nose. "That's a weird name for a bar."

"It's a saying in the south," Jack explained. "Bless your heart. It's used as an insult toward people who are idiots."

"Seriously? How do you know that?"

"I watch *Southern Charm*," he teased, grinning. "It's common knowledge. The bar is reportedly popular."

"After that, we'll call it a day and regroup," Chris suggested. "I want to touch base with Hannah and find out if she discovered anything in regard to the body. I'm not sure where we should be looking at this point."

"Sounds like a plan," Jack agreed. "The bar shouldn't be packed, so we'll know right away if there's anybody worth questioning."

BLESSED BUSTLED WITH SO MUCH ACTIVITY I was immediately swallowed by a bevy of tanned and muscular men, all of them offering me drinks.

"Well, you're new," one of the men noted, grinning. He was young, twenty-five at the most, and he had a charming smile he wasn't afraid to beam at anyone who caught his attention. "Did you just move to the area?"

I glanced around for a sign of Chris or Jack and came up empty. Because it was the middle of the afternoon, the sun still high in the sky, I didn't feel vulnerable. Jack would find me eventually. Until then, I might as well take advantage of my freedom because he was going to smother me eventually.

"I'm just visiting," I offered, flashing a smile as I glanced around. There seemed to be a rousing game of volleyball on the beach and what looked to be a modified tiki bar serving as a drink station in the shade of an older building. "This place is ... neat."

"It's great," the man enthused, gesturing toward an open seat. "Sit down and I'll order you a drink."

"Oh, well ... ."

He pretended he didn't hear me mustering the words to shoot down the alcoholic option and instead signaled for a waitress. "We'll have two Painkillers," he ordered with a smile. "Put them on my tab."

The waitress returned the smile. "You've got it."

I worked my jaw when he took the seat next to me. The smile on his face was amiable enough, but I was on alert given the reason we were here. "What's a Painkiller?" I asked for lack of anything better to talk about. I wasn't the smoothest conversationalist.

"Oh, it's the absolute best drink," he enthused, rubbing his hands over his knees. His skin was so bronzed he looked like a tanning lotion model and his eyes were bright against his chiseled features. Before Jack, I would've considered him handsome. No one compared to Jack, though. "It's rum, pineapple juice, cream of coconut, orange juice and nutmeg."

I wrinkled my nose. "That sounds ... weird."

"You'll love it." He patted my arm. "I didn't get your name."

I was uncomfortable with him touching me so I turned my body so it would be more difficult for him to comfortably invade my personal space. "Charlie Rhodes," I replied. "What's your name?"

"Liam Walsh."

"Are you a local, Liam Walsh?"

He nodded, grinning. "I grew up on Drum Island, but I live in the downtown area now. It's closer to work and more convenient, but I do miss the island life occasionally."

"Are your parents still there?"

"Unfortunately, no. They passed away and I couldn't afford the upkeep on the house so I had to let it go."

My heart went out to him. "My parents died, too."

"See, we already have something in common," he teased, grinning. "I knew I was going to like you from the second I saw you."

I took a moment to glance around the bar, dubious. "That might have something to do with the fact that the men outnumber the women right now," I pointed out. "I think it looks like three-to-one." I frowned when I finally caught sight of Jack. He was near the bar and a blonde in a low-cut top was boxing him in. She appeared to like what she saw and was putting the full-court press on him, the hussy. For his part, Jack didn't look particularly engaged in the conversation. He was obviously going to pull whatever information he could from her. That's why we were here, after all.

"Do you come here a lot?" I asked, focusing my attention back on Liam.

He nodded without hesitation. "At least three times a week. I'm a regular. This is my favorite bar."

"And it's open all year?"

"Yeah. I mean ... I'm not sure what you're asking."

"I grew up in the Midwest," I explained. "Bars like this wouldn't survive all that long up there because people could only enjoy them a few months out of the year. The climate is much different up there."

"Oh, right." He bobbed his head in understanding. "Yeah, this place is definitely open all year. There are a few weeks in the dead of winter where it might not be comfortable to hang outside, but there's an air-conditioned section that way." He gestured vaguely toward the building behind us. "I much prefer hanging outside."

"I can see that." I licked my lips and debated how to broach the subject of the dead girls. "I don't suppose you know a woman named Savannah Billings?" The question felt forced, but I didn't want to linger in this environment longer than I had to. The testosterone was starting to make me uncomfortable.

"The name doesn't ring a bell," Liam replied. "Am I supposed to know her?"

"No. She frequented this bar, though."

"And?"

"And she's dead. She was killed inside her apartment and she's not the first in the area to succumb to the same killer."

Liam sobered instantly. "That news has been spreading fast," he acknowledged. "Everyone is talking about it. Are you saying one of the dead women hung out here?"

"Apparently this was one of her favorite haunts."

"The name doesn't mean anything to me. Do you have a photo? Maybe I saw her and didn't realize it."

"Um ... sure." I dug for my phone and searched through the file information Chris emailed us until I came up with what I was looking for. "That's her."

He stared at the screen for a long moment, stroking his chin as he searched his memory. "She does look familiar," he replied finally. "I don't think I ever talked to her, but I'm guessing I saw her here. She would fit in. Once seven hits, this place starts hopping. You can barely cut through the crowd."

"Do you know any other regulars here?"

"A few." He leaned back in his chair and regarded me. "What is this about? Are you a cop?"

"No, but I am part of the investigation. I work with a private group out of Boston."

"A private group that does what?"

I shrugged, purposely noncommittal. "What can you tell me about the dead women? There must be rumors."

"Oh, there are rumors." Liam turned serious again. "That's all people talk about. Women with dark hair are dying it blond so they don't make enticing targets and people are sticking together in groups even though Charleston is considered a safe city. My friends have made a pact not to let the women go anywhere alone."

I thought of Jack and his overprotective stance. "That's probably smart," I said after a beat. I would never admit it to Jack, but I understood why he was worried. "Have you heard anything else?"

"Well, I did hear one thing." He looked uncomfortable relaying the gossip, which meant it was probably good.

"What's that?"

"Someone said three of the victims worked at the aquarium."

I was taken aback. I didn't remember reading anything of the sort in the reports. Of course, we weren't privy to all the information because there were multiple police departments working on the case and apparently they weren't sharing information. "What aquarium?"

"The South Carolina Aquarium. A lot of people work there, It's a huge draw for tourists. I have no idea if it's true, but people are saying a number of the women worked there. You might want to check it out."

"I definitely will. I ... ." My eyes went wide when the waitress returned with our drinks. The glass she handed me was huge. "I'm not sure I should drink this," I hedged.

"Why not?" Liam's smirk was flirty. "Give it a try. I went out of my way to buy it for you, after all."

"Oh, well ... ."

"What's going on here?" Jack pushed his way through the crowd and stopped in front of me. He didn't look happy when he saw the cocktail. "Are you drinking?"

"Liam bought it for me," I volunteered.

"Who are you?" Liam asked, looking Jack up and down. It was clear he was sizing him up ... and the way he swallowed made me realize he was intimidated by what he saw.

"I'm Jack Hanson. This is my girlfriend. Any more questions?"

I shot him a dirty look at the proprietary nature he was putting on display. It wasn't attractive. "He gave me a good tip about the aquarium," I volunteered. "He said he heard three of the victims worked there."

"Then I guess we'll have to check it out." Jack plucked the drink out of my hand and sniffed it. "This smells good. What is it?"

"A Painkiller," Liam volunteered weakly. "It's one of my favorite drinks."

"Well, I do have a headache." He smiled at Liam before glancing at me and taking a sip. "Let's keep making the rounds, shall we? I don't want to be here all night."

He obviously wanted me to go with him. I couldn't blame him. The crowd was overwhelming and it was swelling. Still, I felt I owed Liam something. "Thanks for the information," I offered warmly. "The drink is great, too. I appreciate it."

"Yeah, well ... come back around if you're ever on your own. Leave the chaperone behind, though, huh?"

I grinned. "I'll do my best. Thanks again for the tip."

SIX

The rest of our group was at the villa when we returned. The leads generated were weak, but that didn't bridle Chris's enthusiasm.

"We're definitely dealing with an incubus," he announced. "It's the only thing that makes sense."

I risked a glance at Jack and found him — to my amusement — gritting his teeth as a muscle worked in his jaw. He wanted to call Chris on the declaration, but somehow managed to fight the instinct. I felt bad, as if I'd somehow changed his entire outlook on life, and made a vow to talk to him about it.

There was something else I wanted to talk to him about, but it would have to wait until we were alone. For now, I decided to help him out.

"I'm confused about how you can be so sure it's an incubus," I offered, earning a surprised look from Jack. He clearly wasn't expecting me to take up his usual position of group skeptic. "I mean ... what evidence do we have?"

Chris blinked several times in rapid succession. "What evidence do you need?" he asked finally.

"I would take any evidence at this point," I admitted. "We have several dead women with no marks on their bodies, who appeared to have had sexual contact before their deaths, and who might've had open bedroom windows. From the police reports I saw, law enforcement officials agree the windows were open but in two of those reports it's not known if a responding officer opened the window to get some air in a stuffy room or if it was already open when they arrived."

"That's true," Chris hedged, clearly uncertain. "I thought you were with me and agreed that it made sense for it to be an incubus."

He almost sounded hurt, which made me feel like a real jerk given the fact that he'd taken a chance on me when I was fresh out of college. I owed him a great deal. If it hadn't been for Chris I wouldn't have met Jack. "I think it's quite possible it could be an incubus," I said hurriedly, loyalty winning out. "I just want to know what proof we have." It was a lame response, but I couldn't think of anything else to say.

"She's trying to help me," Jack announced, catching me off guard. "I was teasing her earlier that she always jumps in with both feet without having proof and she took it to heart. She believes it's an incubus."

Chris looked relieved. "Oh, well ... that makes sense." He grinned at me. "Don't let Jack dampen your enthusiasm. You're a dreamer, Charlie. That's what we all like about you."

"Speak for yourself," Laura muttered.

Jack shot her a look before focusing on Chris. "I'm the one who doubts this is an incubus ... and that's not only because I didn't know they existed until this case. We don't have any concrete evidence that we're dealing with anything paranormal."

I was glad to see he was at least partially back to his former self. He didn't have to believe simply because I did.

"Well, that's what we're here to prove," Chris noted. "Speaking of that ... what did you find, Hannah?"

Hannah, who had been watching the interplay with a blank face, finally smiled. "You're probably going to like what I have to tell you." Her eyes sparkled when they locked with his. They had a flirty way of interacting that only they understood. It made them adorable.

Chris grinned indulgently. "Lay it on me."

"The coroner is baffled. He can't find any reason for these deaths. They all appeared relatively healthy. None had heart problems ... or blood clots ... or died of strokes. The bodies seem to indicate they all simply stopped breathing for no apparent reason while in bed."

"Which is unlikely," I mused.

Hannah nodded. "Very unlikely. They're running toxicology results — and put a rush on them because they're worried it could be some environmental factor they're not aware of — but right now they're simply stumped."

"See." Chris shot Jack a knowing look. "It's an incubus."

Jack shook his head. "Of course you would go there. Everyone else heard, 'We have no idea what it is,' but you heard, 'It's a demon.' Did anyone else find anything of note?" He glanced between faces, receiving nothing but head shakes in response. "Well, for now I think we should break up for dinner and take a few hours downtime. We'll hit this again in the morning."

Laura, who had been mainly silent since returning to the villa, stirred. "What about dinner? Aren't we all eating together?"

"I have no idea what you're doing," Jack replied. "I'm taking Charlie out for seafood and a walk on the beach. That's a two-person outing. The rest of you are on your own."

And just like that, Jack had cleared the evening for us. I was relieved because we had a few things to discuss.

JACK LET ME PICK THE RESTAURANT. Folly Beach was a seafood community, which appealed to me, but there was no limit to the places I could've selected. I finally opted for the Folly Beach Crab Shack because it looked kitschy and fun ... and who doesn't love crab?

We settled in a corner booth that allowed us to sit next to one another without looking like idiots. The menu was so overloaded with options I didn't know where to start.

"Have you ever had oysters?"

"I have," he confirmed, his nose wrinkling.

"I take it you're not a fan."

"That depends. I don't mind them fried, but they wouldn't be a first choice even that way. Raw oysters taste like snot dipped in seawater. Frying them adds some texture to the mix."

I made a face. "Seriously?"

He chuckled at my reaction. "Try them and decide for yourself. I don't want to inform your food choices. Besides, oysters are supposed to be an aphrodisiac. I'm never going to suggest that's a bad idea."

My cheeks colored as he winked, and I went back to the menu. "I don't know. I need to think."

"They have a Major Cluster Shuck," he offered. "That sounds funny enough to order."

I found the option on the menu and frowned at the price. "I'm not ordering a meal that costs a hundred and fifty bucks."

"I'm paying."

"Then I'm definitely not ordering it."

He made an exasperated sound. "Charlie, I need you to stop worrying about money. I know you want to be self-sufficient, but there are certain things I want to do for you and making sure you're fed is one of them. I don't want you going hungry."

That was a hilarious statement on the surface. "I don't think turning down a hundred-and-fifty-dollar dinner means I'm going hungry. Besides, I don't want to eat sea snot anyway."

"Fine." He held up his hands in capitulation. "I'll make sure you have a pile of seafood in front of you before the night is over, so don't even try picking a cheap entree. It'll cause a fight."

I knew something else that was going to cause a fight and now seemed the time to broach the subject. "Speaking of that ... you know you can't act like an alpha dog and bare your teeth when I talk to other men, right?"

His expression was incredulous. "Where did that come from?"

"The bar earlier." I refused to back down. "I was getting information from Liam, not trying to date him. You acted as if ... well ... like I was your property."

His frown was pronounced. "That's not what I was trying to do. I ... ." He trailed off and then pressed the heel of his hand to his forehead. "You're right and I'm sorry. I won't do it again."

I wasn't expecting the quick turnaround. "Just like that?"

He nodded. "I knew it was wrong when I was doing it. I was on edge because I lost you in the bar and that filled me with fear because. You look like the victims. It makes me uneasy."

I rested my hand on top of his. "I get that you're worried, and that actually fills me with this giddy girly feeling that I should be ashamed of because I fancy myself a proponent of female empowerment. I'm glad that you care enough to act like an idiot."

"There was a compliment buried in there, wasn't there?"

"Maybe not a compliment but certainly emotional reinforcement. I'm glad I have you in my life. But you can't hover. I know you don't want to hear it, but I'm capable of taking care of myself. I've been doing it for a long time. I, more than anyone else in our group, need constant protection the least. I have a few weapons in my arsenal."

He let loose a grim sigh. "I know. I've seen you in action. I'm betting that's only the start of what you can do. This might make me sound weak, but I don't like that you don't need me. I mean ... you never needed me. I convinced myself you did because you were young and naive when you started with us.

"It turns out you were never any of those things and I only told myself that was the case," he continued. "I'm the head of security. It's supposed to be my job to protect you. Knowing you don't need it leaves me feeling adrift."

I'd already come to the same conclusion. The surprise was that he was self-aware enough to see it. "I don't need you to protect me, Jack." I kept my voice low so there was no chance of the other diners hearing me. "That doesn't mean I don't need you. You offer much more than muscles and a smart mouth."

He smirked and leaned closer, briefly resting his forehead against mine. "Thank you for that. I'll do my best not to embarrass you when you're grilling a suspect from here on out. I can't guarantee I won't act like an idiot again, though. You bring it out in me."

"I kind of like it when you act like an idiot, even if I find it irritating. It proves you're mortal. Dating a superhero isn't always easy because you make the rest of us look like dolts."

The charming smile he mustered took over his entire face, making him even more handsome than usual ... if that was even possible. "That was very smooth. You're getting better at bolstering my ego."

"Your ego doesn't need bolstering." I sat back and considered the next thing I wanted to say. "You also don't have to change who you are, what you believe, because of me. I know finding out what I can do threw you, but your natural inclination is disbelief when it comes to the paranormal. Don't change simply because you think it's what I want."

He worked his jaw. "I don't know if I can give you what you want on that one," he said. "I assumed all paranormal things were bunk when I took this job. Now I know that I was wrong, so it opens the door for me to question things. I don't know that I can go back."

That seemed fair. "Okay." I squeezed his hand and went back to looking at the menu. "I just wanted you to know that you won't hurt my feelings if you go back to thinking I'm full of crap when I get excited about the possibility of Bigfoot ... and the Chupacabra ... and ghosts."

He snorted. "Bigfoot is still crap."

"If you say so." I furrowed my brow as I stared at the menu. "I want the Charleston Steamed Seafood Tray. There are a few oysters, so I'm going to try them ... but ask for them to be fried just to be on the safe side. Maybe they'll make me jump you, huh? That might be fun."

"Sounds like a plan." He pressed a kiss to my temple and lingered a moment before pulling back. "We should get some key lime pie, too. That's a favorite of mine."

"Sounds good." I shifted my eyes to the middle of the table, where a hole containing a bucket rested. "What's that for?"

He laughed at my confusion. "The shells. Seafood is a messy business."

"Oh." I brightened considerably as realization dawned. "That's genius."

"It is." He grabbed one of the plastic bibs from the center of the table. "So are these. I expect you to use one so you won't be wearing your dinner for our walk on the beach. I have specific plans for you."

That sounded intriguing ... although wearing a bib wasn't high on my fashion list. "Are you going to laugh at me if I wear it?"

"Yes. And you can laugh at me for wearing one. We're in this together, right?"

"Yeah. We're in this together."

For better or worse now, there didn't seem to be a way around that.

MY SHORTS FELT UNCOMFORTABLY TIGHT when we hit the beach an hour and a half later. I ate my weight in seafood — Jack was right about the oysters, which seemed like a non-entity in all the batter — and a walk was exactly what I needed to alleviate the feeling.

"That was really good." My fingers still felt greasy from cracking the crab legs despite the fact that I'd gone through four packages of the wet napkins provided. "I don't think I'll be able to eat again for a week."

He laughed as he swung our joined hands. "I bet you rally in time for breakfast. They have crawfish omelets in the hotel dining room. I saw them on the menu."

"I thought crawfish was a New Orleans thing."

"It's a Southern thing, and I happen to love a good crawfish omelet."

The mere thought of food was too much to bear, so I turned my attention to the water. It was picturesque, the breeze strong enough to ruffle my hair, and the setting sun made the water look as if it was on fire.

"It's pretty here," I noted. "It feels ... magical."

"It does," he agreed, sliding his arms around my waist from behind and pressing his chest to my back so he could kiss my neck. "I like Charleston a great deal."

"Is this where you would choose to live if you could pick anywhere?"

He hesitated. "I don't know," he replied after a beat. "I haven't given it much thought. I mean … I love the city, but there are a lot of places I love. Where would you choose to settle?"

"I don't know that I'm ready to settle anywhere." That was the truth. "I like traveling and seeing new places. It's still exciting."

"Fair enough. You don't want to travel forever, though, do you?"

It seemed a roundabout way to ask a question, and it made me smile. "I'll want a home of my own eventually. I enjoy traveling, but there's joy to be found in claiming something for yourself."

"There is," he agreed, kissing the ridge of my ear. "I know you haven't traveled much, but if you were forced to choose right now where would you want to live?"

"I really liked New Orleans. The city had an energy that I've never felt anywhere else. I liked the music … and the architecture … and the food. I could see living there."

"I like New Orleans, too," he said. "I think you fit there. Your personality meshes well with the city."

"What about your personality?"

"I'm happy wherever you're happy." It was a simple answer, and I melted into him as he began to sway. "We have time before we have to decide on any of that. For now, we should just enjoy a fantastic sunset on a beautiful beach."

I couldn't argue. My eyes were heavy-lidded thanks to the glare of the sun when I raised them to the water. It really was breathtaking. I enjoyed the view for a few moments before something on the water caught my attention.

"Is that a boat?" I squinted to get a better look.

"What?" Jack sounded distracted, his nose buried in the crook of my neck. "After the shark incident, I prefer we not get on a boat for the foreseeable future."

My heart skipped as I focused my full attention on the water.

"That's not a boat." Slowly, I separated from Jack and moved closer to the water. "I thought maybe it was a sailboat, but ... that's not it."

He frowned, his gaze following mine. "I don't see anything, Charlie."

"No?" That made me even more uncomfortable. My stomach twisted as I shielded my eyes with my hand and stared. It took me a moment to adjust to what I was seeing, and when I did, I inadvertently let out a gasp. "No way!"

"What?" Jack was instantly alert, his body going rigid. "What do you see?"

It was hard to explain. I wasn't even sure what I was seeing was real. It had to be, though. There was no other explanation. "There's a woman standing on the water. I mean ... like standing, as if she's walking across the waves."

"That's not possible, Charlie." Jack's voice took on an edge. "I don't see her."

There was a reason he couldn't see it. The woman was most definitely there, but she was no longer alive. She was a ghost ... and she was somehow anchored to the water and staring at the shore. It wasn't difficult to make out her dark hair and slim frame. She was clearly one of our victims. The question was: What did she want?

"It's a ghost," I said finally, swallowing hard. "I think it's one of our dead women."

Jack was bewildered. "Why is she out there?"

"I think we need to find out."

"Um ... yeah. That's the understatement of the year."

SEVEN

The ghost never moved. She didn't speak. She didn't come when I beckoned. She simply remained in her spot, staring at the Folly Beach landscape.

Jack finally insisted we return to the villa. He never caught sight of the ghost and I'd lost her in the darkness. She was still out there, though. I could feel her.

Laura was in the living room watching television when we entered, her eyes narrow slits as we crossed in front of her and headed for the stairs. "How was dinner?" she asked.

"Good," I replied. "I tried fried oysters." It was an automatic response. I barely registered who I was talking to. I also didn't give enough thought to how she would take the statement.

"Oh, well, how great for you guys," she drawled. "I was forced to eat alone because everyone else went out on dates."

"There might be a lesson in that," Jack countered, putting his hand at the small of my back and prodding me toward the stairs. "If you were a nicer person we might care that you had to eat alone. But you're miserable, so we don't care if you're miserable."

"Well ... thanks for that," she said. "You know, you used to be much nicer before Charlie came into our lives. I'm starting to think she's a bad influence on the group. I wonder if Myron would like to know how she's screwed up our chemistry."

Myron Biggs was Chris's uncle and the head of the Legacy Foundation. He was also Millie's ex-husband, although they didn't interact all that often. He'd been at the center of several kerfuffles the past few months. Almost all of them had been initiated by Laura, who was feeling out of sorts because she believed I supplanted her in the group dynamic. Er, well, at least that was what I deduced.

"Do what you want," Jack shot back, his temper bubbling close to the surface. "If I were Myron, I would definitely do something ... about the only individual out of all of us who is constantly complaining. That's up to you. We're going to bed."

"I don't need your attitude," she sneered.

"Then don't pick a fight." Jack was still fuming when we stepped into the bedroom. He immediately shut the door and kicked off his shoes. "I really can't stand her. This group would be so much better without her. She's like the seventh wheel that makes all our lives miserable."

I didn't want to see anyone — not even Laura — lose a job. "I don't think she means to be the worst person in the world," I said as I sank onto the settee and kicked off my sandals. "She's unhappy and lashes out as a result. Getting her removed from the team won't make things better for anyone but us."

"I only care about us."

That was bold talk, but I knew better. "I feel sorry for her."

"That's because you have a good heart."

"So do you."

"Not where she's concerned. I'm not going to pretend to care about her feelings when she goes out of her way to make you miserable. I don't have it in me, so don't ask."

I blew out a sigh and nodded. He wouldn't budge on that subject, so it seemed a waste of time to push him. "You know what would be good? We should get a hot guy to be the eighth member of the team and she can switch her attention to him."

Jack snorted. "He would have to be evil, just like her, to even look in her direction."

"I don't know. The right man might do wonders for her personality."

"You only believe that because you're an optimist." He stripped out of his shirt and shorts, revealing a ridiculously buff body that belonged on the pages of a beefcake magazine. He was silent for so long I had to wonder if he'd asked a question that I'd somehow missed.

"Did you say something?" I asked after a beat, raising my eyes.

Amusement flitted across his handsome features as he shook his head. "You keep looking at me that way and we're going to spend the entire night testing the oysters theory."

I couldn't stop myself from laughing. "Maybe tomorrow night. I ate too much. If you try a complicated maneuver I might puke on you."

"It could be worth it."

I had my doubts. "I'm tired." I moved to the sliding glass doors to look out at the water. I couldn't see the ghost, but I knew she was still there. I felt her. "I need to think about what I saw. Maybe I imagined it."

"I don't think so." Jack lifted the covers and let loose a low whistle. "You need rest. Into bed. We'll talk about the ghost in the morning. If she's still there when we wake up ... ." He left it hanging. I had no doubt he was struggling with what he should say.

"We'll deal with it tomorrow." I slid out of my clothes and pulled an oversized T-shirt over my head. It was shapeless and far from sexy, but Jack didn't seem to mind. "You shouldn't have let me eat so much," I complained as we rolled in together and his arms automatically came around me. He tugged until we were both on our sides, facing each other, and my cheek rested against his chest.

"Sleep," he murmured as he kissed my forehead. "We'll figure it out."

"You keep saying that."

"Because it's the truth."

That's all I needed to hear. I drifted off within seconds, although my dreams were of the dark variety.

I WOKE WELL-RESTED. I didn't feel draggy or overfed. Jack was just stirring when I opened my eyes and the first thing he saw was me staring at him. He probably thought it was creepy, but I didn't care. He was an absolute masterpiece in the morning with his stubbled chin and sleepy eyes.

"Morning," I said, grinning as I stretched.

"Morning. Is there a reason you were staring at me?"

"You're pretty."

"I was just going to say the same about you."

"Except when I wake up with bedhead I look like Medusa. You look like a really hot guy with perfectly-tousled hair. It's not fair."

"I happen to think you look cute in the morning." He gave me a quick kiss before engaging in a stretching routine of his own. "How did you sleep?"

"Hard."

"Dreams?"

I hesitated before answering, but the quick gleam that flashed through his eyes told me lying was a terrible idea. "I dreamed about the ghost on the water a bit," I admitted, rolling away from him so he couldn't see the guilt cascading through me. I focused on the sliding glass doors, and before I even realized what I was doing I was on my feet and unlocking them.

"Where are you going?" Jack called after me.

"I just want to see."

I could hear him muttering and wasn't surprised when he appeared on the balcony next to me. "Anything?" he asked in a low voice.

I nodded. Now, with the early-morning sun offering a hand, it was even more difficult to make out the astral figure on the water. But I knew where to look. "She's still out there."

"Can you give me a basic location?"

"That way." I pointed. "It's not like there are any landmarks. I'm sorry."

"Don't apologize." He was terse as he moved his hands to my shoulders. "How far out do you estimate she is?"

That was a difficult question to answer. "I don't know. I'm bad with distances. I guess ... um ... half a mile? Does that make sense."

"None of this makes sense. I have faith in you, though. If you say you see a ghost out there, I have to believe you do. We'll have to find a way to get a closer look, which won't be easy because I can't see where you need to go and I'll be the one driving."

Something occurred to me. "Only if we take a boat."

"Are you suggesting we swim out there?" His eyebrows hopped. "There's probably sharks out there, and after the last time ... ."

He was never going to let that go. He was convinced I'd almost died — something he blamed on Laura — and complained whenever the subject arose. I certainly didn't want to dwell on it now. "I'm not talking about swimming."

"Then what are you suggesting?"

I pointed at a large sign on the beach. His forehead wrinkled as he read it.

"Kayaks? Seriously?"

I shrugged. "Why not? It shouldn't take us that long to paddle out there and I can control our destination."

He didn't look convinced, but he didn't argue. "I'll think about it. We have other things to do first."

That was as good as he was going to give this early. I had to take it.

WE BROKE INTO TEAMS AGAIN. This time Jack and I were tasked with going to the aquarium to question the manager, an interview Chris had already set up. It seemed like a long shot, but I wasn't in charge. Besides, I happened to love a good aquarium, so it wasn't much of a hardship.

Brock Wilson was waiting for us at the gates. The facility didn't open for another two hours, so it was just the three of us as we made the rounds. There were very few employees on site, something I found interesting and filed away for later consideration.

"This is the Great Ocean Tank," Brock volunteered as we stood in front of the open tank that contained so many species of colorful fish I had trouble keeping track of what I had and hadn't seen. "We have a special educational program in which locals can come and learn about the marine life in our waters … and then feed them."

I was intrigued by the notion. "Feed them?"

He grinned at me and retrieved a bucket from the ground. "Go ahead and throw some in."

"Really?" I looked to Jack to make sure it was all right, but he was already nodding.

"Go ahead." He looked amused by my excitement. "I kind of want to watch."

I needed no further prodding. I dug my hand into the bucket and grabbed a handful of the food, enthusiastically tossing it over the water. The fish close to the surface immediately starting sucking in the nuggets of goodness, causing Brock to laugh delightedly as I leaned over the edge of the tank for a better look.

"Cool, huh?"

I nodded in agreement. Despite the fish, I knew we were at the aquarium with a specific agenda, though, and I directed the conversation toward something important. "We're actually here for a reason."

Brock sobered. "That's what I understand. You're investigating the dead women, including Savannah Billings, Jenny Fields, Megan Louden and Freya Debney."

Jack's expression was hard to read, but I could tell Brock's ability to rattle off so many names — we're talking half of our dead girls — was enough to make him suspicious. "You knew them. How is that?"

"They all worked here."

I was taken aback. "That can't be right. I saw the files. Megan Louden was a legal secretary and Jenny Fields was a student at the local culinary school. I can't remember what the others did for a living, but I think I would remember if they all worked for you."

"Let me rephrase that," Brock offered. "They all volunteered here. We have a thriving volunteer community and all four women were a part of it."

"How does that work?" Jack asked.

"We focus on conservation," Brock explained. "We have a special program that brings in injured sea turtles. We try to rehabilitate them. If they can be released into the wild after their treatment, we do that. If they can't, then we find a place for them here."

"That's all well and good," Jack noted. "That doesn't explain why the women were volunteering here."

"I'm getting to that." Brock flashed a tense smile. He seemed to be chafing under Jack's pressure, which made me believe he was used to being in charge. "The volunteer program involves a variety of things, including ritzy parties and fundraisers.

"Most of our volunteers are genuine animal lovers," he continued. "They want to help the animals above all else. There is a small contingent, however, who care about the glitz and glamor associated with the parties more than they do the animals."

"Ah." Jack nodded in understanding as I kept tossing handfuls of food for the fish. "These charity events naturally draw the wealthiest benefactors in the area. Certain individuals — including some of our victims — were more interested in those donating money than the actual cause."

Brock cleared his throat, as if trying to remove something that was lodged there, and nodded. "I would never speak ill of the dead, but ... I was under no illusion that these women were volunteering their time because they cared about the animals. In fact, all four of them only volunteered to help with party events. They didn't want anything to do with the facilities or the fundraisers that were geared toward the general public."

"That's too bad," I noted as I added more food to the tank. I found the fish fascinating. "I would volunteer just to feed the fish every day."

Brock chuckled. "We actually don't have a shortage of people willing to do that. Our guests pay a premium to be able to feed the fish. The same goes for the ray tank. That one is even more of a draw."

I straightened. "You have a ray tank?"

Jack shot me a quelling look and shook his head, making me realize that if I wanted to feed the rays it would have to be at another time. "How well did you know the women?"

"Not well," Brock replied. "I know I'm supposed to say something about how tragic this all is — and it is — but I didn't know them well enough to mourn them.

"When word came down that one of our volunteers died — I believe the first one we were made aware of was Freya — I had to search for a photo just to know who the others were talking about," he continued. "Then when more began to fall ... it occurred to me there might be a tie, but the other women weren't volunteering here."

"That doesn't mean they didn't have ties to the four women volunteering for you through another group or charity," Jack mused. "Can you tell us anything about your four volunteers? I mean ... even if it seems mundane. We're looking for a tie that can lead us to a killer."

Brock's shoulders stiffened as he stood straighter. "I'm sorry but ... I didn't think a cause of death had been released. Last time I heard, there was a dispute whether it was natural causes or perhaps a pathogen of some sort. Either way, it was considered an accident, not something intentional."

Jack obviously realized he'd overstepped but he didn't react in a shady way. Instead, he kept his smile in place and remained calm. "We can't overlook any possibility. We don't want a single other person to die."

"No, of course not."

"We're simply looking for a tie between all the women. Anything you can tell us would be helpful."

Brock nodded, rubbing his hand over his chin as he considered the request. "I don't know that this will be helpful, but the one thing these women always talked about was a television show they were convinced they were going to get. Other volunteers and employees brought that up several times when the identities started becoming public."

I jerked up my head, tearing my gaze from the fish. "They were getting a television show?" Somehow that hadn't made the reports.

"No, but they were pitching the idea," Brock explained. "I'm not sure which company, but there was talk of driving to Atlanta because that's a big Hollywood production hub now. They actually put together something called a 'look book.' Supposedly you need one when pitching a television show."

"I'll have to take your word for it," Jack said dryly. "What was this show about?"

"It would've been a reality television show. A group of women living in Charleston, fighting with one another and living the high life while backstabbing their friends. You know ... like *Southern Charm*. I believe that was the basis for their show."

Jack looked to me for help, immediately causing me to raise my hands. "Don't look at me," I said. "I have no idea about reality television shows like that. I love true crime documentaries and those Animal Planet shows, but otherwise I prefer watching dramatic fiction."

"Me, too." He dragged a hand through his hair, his expression unreadable. "I don't suppose you know if they shared an entertainment lawyer or anything, do you?"

"I'm sorry." Brock was legitimately apologetic. "I don't know about the inner workings of their plan. The only thing I can tell you is that they went on regular wine tours because they thought they could meet rich men that way. That was the crux of their show pitch. They wanted to date rich men ... and ultimately find husbands. They were very vocal about their plans."

I was flabbergasted by the thought. "That sounds ... lovely."

Jack nodded in agreement. "Yeah, but it's another possibility to chase. Thank you very much for your time, Mr. Wilson. We greatly appreciate it."

"We do," I agreed, wiping my hands on the seat of my shorts.

"Feeding the fish was awesome, by the way. I totally want to come back and check out the ray tank."

Brock's smile was indulgent. "You're welcome any time. Just tell the individual at the front gates that I gave you clearance and he or she will allow you in without having to pay."

"Oh, I would totally pay to feed the rays."

"Even better. When you have a handle on your schedule give me a call and I'll arrange it."

EIGHT

"What do you think?"

As a very food-oriented person — actually, we rolled that way as a couple — Jack insisted it was time for an early lunch after we left the aquarium. I believed he wanted to absorb the news before making a decision on our next move. Honestly, I didn't blame him.

It was his turn to choose and he opted for a place called Fleet Landing, which someone had mentioned the previous day. It was on the water, had an outstanding view, and the menu gave me little chills because I was surprisingly hungry despite the amount of food I'd eaten the previous night.

"I don't know," Jack replied. "It's weird. I find the whole thing weird. I've never been one who wanted to be on television."

"I'm actually surprised Chris hasn't hired a cinematographer to follow us around on cases," I mused. "He figures it's only a matter of time before we see something that proves his theory about the paranormal. He'll want proof of that."

"Bite your tongue."

I giggled despite myself. "If he does that, it's going to put me in a weird position." I sobered as I considered it. "That's going to be a big risk. If I'm ever caught doing something … ." I purposely left it hanging. The possibility was too horrible to consider.

"Hey, we'll handle that if it comes." Jack leaned across the table and grabbed my hand. "I don't know that Chris would go that route. Even though he wants to prove the existence of — well, whatever paranormal creature he can — he values his privacy."

"Yeah, but … it feels like something he might eventually do if he gets desperate."

The look on Jack's face told me he believed the same thing. He didn't dwell on it, though. Instead he forced a smile and inclined his chin toward the menu. "The she-crab soup is supposed to be amazing."

I had no idea what that was. "Why is it she-crab soup? Why are the men not killed for it?"

He laughed. "I don't know. You might want to ask the waitress. I only know it has a solid reputation."

"I do love me some crab."

"You do."

We lapsed into amiable silence for a few moments, both of us studying the menu. Eventually, I couldn't stop myself from focusing on the most important tidbit we'd gleaned from the conversation with Brock. "They all knew each other."

Slowly, he lifted his eyes until they snagged with mine. "We don't know that yet," he cautioned. "We know that four of them knew each other."

I waited because I knew he wasn't finished.

"It is quite the coincidence," he admitted, leaning back in his seat. He placed his feet so they were on either side of mine. It was an unobtrusive way to touch me during the meal and I found comfort in it even as I tried to wrap my head around what we were dealing with. "Have you ever watched the show? The one he mentioned, I mean."

For some reason I found the question insulting. "Do I look like the type of woman who sits around watching shows about women who just want to find a man because then their lives will be complete? I'm a *Stranger Things* girl … or *The 100* … or even *The Walking Dead*. I don't watch reality television unless it involves documentaries on serial killers."

He stared at me for a long moment and then broke into a hearty guffaw. "Is it any wonder that it was basically you from the second I saw you?" He shook his head and snickered. "Geez. You're never going to be normal. I love that about you."

The tone in his simple sentiment caused heat to rush to my cheeks. "Most people think that I talk too much, that I speak before I think, and that's not a good thing."

"I won't pretend that you always say the exact right thing at the right time, but you speak your truth and you're not a liar."

I lifted my eyes. There was something about the declaration that set me off. "I did lie to you, though." That was true. I lied about who I was and what I could do from the beginning. I'd planned to tell him the truth, but he found out in the middle of a fight. He hadn't really lambasted me for being a liar since. While I was grateful, I was also eager for him to get it out of his system. "You haven't really said anything about that."

He leaned back in his chair and crossed his feet at the ankles as he regarded me. He was about to open his mouth and say something when the waitress arrived to take our orders.

"I'll have the she-crab soup and the signature burger, medium, ketchup on the side. I'll have an iced tea, too."

The waitress nodded, flashing him a flirty smile, and then focused on me. "And you?"

"I'll have the soup, too." I quickly scanned the sandwiches. I'd been paying more attention to talking than selecting. "I'll also have the fried green tomato BLT. I'll just have water to drink."

"Sure." The waitress collected our menus and disappeared back into the restaurant. We were early for lunch, so we were pretty much alone on the outdoor deck. That was probably good given the conversation I'd kicked off.

"We haven't really talked about it," Jack hedged when he spoke again. "I'm sorry for that. It's on me. I wasn't sure what to say."

"You don't have to say anything. I just thought you would feel something more about the situation."

"I have a lot of feelings," he said. "The thing is ... after it happened, I was in shock. So were you. I could tell. I didn't know what to say to make you feel better, so I did the only thing I could do and not make you feel worse. I had questions, but ... you were really upset."

"I was afraid," I corrected. "I let the fear consume me."

"You were afraid I would tell Chris," he surmised, frowning. "I never would've done that."

I couldn't hide my surprise. "I never thought you would tell Chris. That's not who you are. You would've let me go right then and there if I felt the need to run and requested silence from you. You're the protective sort, and I appreciate that."

His eyebrows drew together. "Then what were you afraid of?"

"That it would be too much for you and ... you would just pull away." I felt like an idiot giving voice to my fears. Only a high-schooler would worry about her boyfriend breaking up with her despite the things we were dealing with.

"Were you honestly worried about that?" Jack's expression was hard to read.

I nodded. "You don't believe. Up until then, you just didn't want to see it. I figured you would think I was a freak and walk away. I was going to tell you because I knew you needed to know, but I was certain you would break my heart in the end. I'm sorry about that, too. I should've had more faith in you."

"You should've," he agreed, rubbing his cheek. Something that looked like anger flashed in his eyes. "But I get it. You've kept this to yourself for a really long time. Have you ever told anyone?"

It seemed like a weird setting to get the nitty-gritty out of the way, but I was so relieved it was finally happening I didn't argue. "My parents knew. My adopted parents, I mean. When I was a kid I managed to do a few things that set off alarm bells at school."

"Well, that sucks, but you were a kid. I'm sure they stood with you."

"No, I mean I literally set off alarm bells. I once got in a fight with a kid and I was so annoyed my anger set off the sprinkler system. I was standing next to it but didn't touch it and it just went off. The kid I was fighting said I pulled it, but when I told my parents what really happened they said I had to make sure nobody ever found out about what I could do.

"I was confused because I was young and didn't know what was happening," I continued. "Then one day there was a fire down the street and I knew about it without looking through the windows. I knew one of our neighbors was in trouble. That's when my parents really started taking notice."

Jack was calm as he regarded me. "What did they do?"

"They wanted to take me to specialists. They figured I might be mentally disturbed though they never came right out and said it. They were afraid to do it in case I was deemed dangerous. They'd wanted a child for so long ... and then they got me. I was an inferior model, but they didn't want to disappoint me or risk losing me because they might not get a second chance."

"Don't say that!" Jack's eyes flashed. "You're not an inferior model. I don't want you thinking that."

His vehemence took me by surprise ... and warmed me all over. It was something I needed to hear even though I was mostly comfortable in my own skin. "Thanks, but I didn't mean that the way it came out. I'm not feeling sorry for myself as much as ... they were good people. I loved them. They took care of me. They just wanted a normal kid, but I was pretty freaking far from normal."

"You're special," he countered, unruffled. "Every parent wants a special child. They got you and I guarantee they were happy about it. On the flip side, I'm betting there was fear there, too. If you were discovered ... ."

"I might've been taken away," I finished. "They warned me to be very careful. I wasn't allowed to have sleepovers until I was old enough to understand the ramifications if I manifested in front of someone. They were careful to keep me out of sports – except for track when I was in high school – because I'm so competitive they thought I might do something to draw attention to myself. They loved me, but were terrified of the things I might do."

He picked up my hand and flipped it over to trace lines on my palm with his fingers. "I don't want you to be afraid." His voice was low. "I want you to be mindful and careful ... and it's probably best if we keep this to ourselves for a bit. You don't have to be anything other than what you are with me. I like you the way you are and I don't want you to change.

"But I need you to be careful," he continued. "Because you're special, you're going to draw attention from certain individuals if you're too overt with what you can do. I'll protect you to the best of my ability, but I won't always be with you ... ."

I understood what he was saying. "I've been keeping this secret for a long time," I offered. "I was going to tell you because I thought it was important for us going forward. I didn't want everything we have to be based on a lie. Millie found out because I didn't have a choice if I wanted to save us during that whole Chupacabra thing. As for the rest ... I have no intention of telling any of them what I can do."

"Good." He lifted my hand and pressed a kiss to the palm, causing my heart to stutter. "We'll figure this out."

There was his mantra again. It made me smile. "I know. If you have questions, though, I want you to ask them. It's okay to be curious."

"I have questions, but I don't think this is the right place to ask them." He glanced around the patio. It was starting to fill up with people. "We have plenty of time to go over all of this. I want to see what you can do. I want to hear the stories. It doesn't all have to be in one night.

"It wasn't that I wasn't interested in that stuff," he continued. "I just didn't want to push you. There was a fragility about you that made me want to wrap you in bubble wrap to keep you safe, shut out the rest of the world. That was probably a mistake, but I can't help wanting to protect you.

"From the moment I met you, I felt this overwhelming need to take care of you." He was earnest as he held my gaze. "I get that you're an adult and can take care of yourself. I won't try to take your independence from you. I'm hoping that you'll see there's a benefit in us taking care of each other. That's what I want."

Emotions I didn't even know I felt bubbled up and grabbed me by the throat. "I want that, too. I just ... I don't want you getting overwhelmed. I couldn't help but feel you were getting frustrated last night with the ghost deal. I don't want that."

"I don't want that either. And for the record, I wasn't getting frustrated with you. I wanted to see what you were seeing. You can help. I just need to figure out how."

"I'm telling you the kayaks are the way to go."

"And I will consider it." He flashed a smile that made me go weak in the knees. "For now, let's enjoy our lunch. I need to figure out if there's a way to tie those other four women to the ones who served as volunteers at the aquarium."

"I think it's unlikely that they all volunteered at the exact same place. That would limit their options and creature competition," I offered. "I think it's far more likely that they volunteered at different places. That doesn't mean they didn't meet up at the same place. I think that's the location we need to suss out."

"That's a good idea." He squeezed my hand extra hard. "Just one more thing and then we'll take a break from this. No matter what happens, I need you to promise me you'll always trust that I'm doing my absolute best for you. You don't have to hide things from me. I want to know, and even if I don't understand I promise that we'll figure it out."

Tears pricked the back of my eyes. That was exactly what I needed to hear.

"We'll figure it out," I agreed, swiping at my cheeks as I lowered my eyes in embarrassment. "Thanks for that."

"Oh, you make me want to buy you ice cream when you act all stiff-upper-lippy like that. Don't cry, baby." He moved his thumbs to my cheeks and attacked the tears. "We're in this together. You're not alone, not ever again."

I nodded through a watery smile. "You have no way of knowing how much that means to me."

"It's only going to get better. I promise you that."

. . .

THE CRAB SOUP WAS SO GOOD I figured I would be talking about it for weeks. I'd already done ten minutes on it when Jack led me away from the restaurant and toward the docks.

"What are we doing here?" I asked, pulling up short.

"Brock said that his volunteers were going on wine-tasting cruises to meet men," Jack replied, firmly tugging on my hand to drag me forward. "One of the boats is down this way, and I want to grab a flier in case we want to arrange an outing."

"Oh." That made sense. "I forgot he'd mentioned that part."

"Yes, that's why I'm the brains of this operation and you're the looks," he teased, tapping the side of his head with his free hand.

"I think you might be the looks and the brains."

"No, we're equal partners." He was in no mood to listen to me wax poetic about my feelings of inadequacy … even if they only popped up in weak moments. "Here are the fliers."

While he selected the ones he wanted from a kiosk, I turned my attention to the end of the dock. There, two scantily-clad women — they wore bikini tops and short-shorts — waved and flirted with anyone who passed in their direction. Even the women weren't off limits.

"Are they going to be on a cruise with us if we go this route?" I found the idea annoyed me.

Jack followed my gaze and grinned. "Probably. I think they look fun. You don't like them?"

"I think they look ... cold."

He snorted. "They're there to keep the men happy because it's assumed the men have the money. Notice that Savannah and the others weren't looking for true love. They were looking for rich guys. They didn't even pretend to be looking for the real deal, which makes them unbelievably pathetic in my book."

My gaze was weighted when it landed on him. "Tell me how you really feel."

"That is how I really feel. I'm not interested in anything superficial. I want the real deal or nothing at all. Why do you think I couldn't stay away from you even though I tried ... really hard?"

I couldn't stop myself from laughing. "We're quite the pair. I yelled at you for getting territorial about Liam and now I'm judging those women because I know they're going to be all over you if we head out on that boat. I'm a hypocrite."

"We'll worry about that if it comes to it. We're not there yet." He slid a brochure into his pocket and grabbed my hand again. "I want to see if I can get us out to see that ghost. It seems to me that's our best play right now. We'll worry about the wine cruise later."

"Did I mention how good the bisque was? I might want to reward you for suggesting that later if we have time for a break. Just food for thought."

His eyes gleamed. "I like the way your mind works."

"Right back at you."

NINE

Jack made some calls about securing a boat — something he wanted to do without Chris finding out — and while we were waiting to hear back he phoned the Charleston Police Department. He expected to run into a dead end. Instead, the detective in charge agreed to meet with us. He was at the Charleston City Market, which was close to our location, so Jack set up a meeting and we were on our way.

We had forty-five minutes to burn so Jack suggested checking out the booths at the market. I'd never seen anything quite like it. Sure, I'd been to open-air markets a time or two, but this one had personality, and I had a great time wandering around.

It constituted four city blocks and included area crafts, maps, restaurants and even sweetgrass baskets, which were being woven directly on the premises.

"That's kind of neat," I enthused as I watched the women work. Their deft fingers almost became a blur. "They're really good."

Jack shook his head. "Leave it to you to be excited over basket weaving."

"It's a skill. I've always wanted a skill."

"You don't think what you do is a skill?"

"I was born this way."

"And you work hard to control what you do. You have a gift that you've honed. That's a skill, baby."

I couldn't hide my smile. "That's possibly the sweetest thing anyone has ever said to me."

"That makes me sad, but I can get sweeter. Later, when it's just the two of us, I'll whisper sweet nothings until your toes tingle."

This time I rolled my eyes. "That's not sweet. That's sexy. They're entirely different things."

He stilled. "Which one do you prefer?"

"It depends on my mood. Right now, I like when you're sweet."

"Fair enough." He took me by surprise and swept me close, hugging me tight. "You're the prettiest girl here," he whispered, causing the hair on the back of my neck to stand on end. "I like spending time with you and I want to go for a romantic walk on the beach with you later because I like the way the wind blows your hair and how the moon illuminates your smile. How's that for sweet?"

I thought my heart might pound out of my chest. "That's pretty good, but now I'm feeling sexy."

He laughed and gave me a quick kiss before pulling back. "Do you want one of the baskets?"

The question caught me off guard. "Oh, well … ." I wasn't sure how much they cost and didn't want to admit that would inform my choice.

As if reading my mind, he arched an eyebrow. "I'm buying one for you."

"I don't need one." The sentence slipped off my lips before I thought better of it. "They're very cool, but it will be difficult to get home."

"We have a private plane. You're not limited to how many bags you can bring, and all you have to do is keep it separate so it doesn't get crushed."

He had a point. "Um … ."

"Yeah, you're getting one." He gripped my hand and pulled me closer to the selection. "Tell me which one you like, and it better not be the smallest one because that will tick me off."

I heaved out a sigh. He was adamant when he wanted to be. Still, it was a sweet sentiment. A sweet sentiment with sweetgrass. The concept made me smile. "I like that one." I pointed. "You really don't have to do this, though."

"I'm doing it. Don't give me grief."

"Thank you." I pressed a kiss to his cheek. "I really appreciate it."

He slid his eyes to me. "The fact that you get legitimately touched over a basket is one of the many reasons I adore you."

"Really? What are some of the others?"

His lips spread into a sly grin. "Are you fishing for a compliment?"

"Maybe."

"Okay, I like the way you eat."

It wasn't the answer I was expecting. "Really? Why?"

"Because you do it with enthusiasm. You're not one of those women who spend all their time counting calories and checking the nutritional value of certain foods online. You made yummy noises every time you had a spoonful of soup over lunch. How is that not awesome?"

I wasn't sure how to answer. "There might come a time when I have to watch calories," I said finally. "I'm in my twenties. My metabolism is still revving. One day that might change."

"We'll cross that bridge when we come to it. For now, I like that I don't have to talk you into dessert and that you get excited at restaurants because they have big buckets in the center of the table for shells."

"I do enjoy the little things in life."

"And you're going to enjoy the basket, which is exactly why I'm buying it for you. It will be a nice decoration for your place."

"The place that you're helping pay for."

"Don't start on that again. You're safer there and I don't want to hear another word about it."

I let loose a sigh. "Okay. Thank you for the basket."

"You can thank me later."

"Are you back to being sexy?"

He winked. "You know it."

FORTY-FIVE MINUTES LATER, I had my basket and we were sitting in a small coffee shop. Our table was in the shade, which was welcome given the Charleston sun, and I was happily sipping my green tea as I stared at my new gift.

"It's pretty cool, huh?"

Jack arched an eyebrow and merely shook his head. "You might not be like a normal girl, but you still have girlish tendencies. Just for the record, men can't get worked up over baskets. It's not humanly possible."

Detective Rick Carter picked that moment to join us. Jack had given him a description, so he headed straight for our table. His smile was friendly, but there was curiosity lurking in the depths of his green eyes. He looked between us for a moment and then focused on the basket.

"I see you've been shopping. Those things are great, aren't they? I have, like, five of them in my house. They're versatile and look great on tables."

He'd been too far away to hear Jack's admonishment about men and baskets, so I knew it was an off-the-cuff remark. Still, it made me smirk. The look on Jack's face was straight out of a sitcom and I had to break eye contact to keep from laughing.

"Jack Hanson." He was on his feet, his hand extended. "Thank you for coming. This is my associate Charlie Rhodes. We appreciate you taking time out of your day."

Rick nodded as he sat, glancing back and forth for a moment before signaling the waitress. "I'll have a sweet tea and a blueberry muffin when you get the chance."

She nodded in acknowledgment.

"I'm a regular here," Rick explained. "I haven't had lunch. As for you two, I think it's clear you're more than associates."

I shifted on my chair, uncomfortable. I didn't want to be seen as unprofessional. It was hard enough for me to be taken seriously because of my age. "Oh, no. We're totally associates."

Jack rolled his eyes. "She's my girlfriend. She says goofy things sometimes. Ignore her."

Rick chuckled. "It must be nice to be able to work together. I would guess, given the logistics of your job, you spend a lot of time traveling. It's nice you have someone you care about with you on the road."

"It *is* nice," Jack agreed, leaning back in his chair. "What do you know about the Legacy Foundation?"

"I know more than you probably think," Rick replied. "News that you guys were joining us spread fast. I didn't understand why some people were so worked up ... until I did a little research on your boss. Chris Biggs has quite the reputation."

"He's a good man," I interjected hurriedly. If Rick was going to start badmouthing him, I was going to put up a fight.

"I didn't say he wasn't a good man," Rick reassured me quickly. "It's just ... some people think he's nuts."

"And how do you feel?" Jack asked, his expression unreadable. There were times Jack thought our boss was nuts, too. That didn't mean he wasn't loyal.

"I feel as if this is one of those cases that's going to haunt me forever." Rick was matter-of-fact, something I liked. "We have eight dead women. Three of the murders are being handled by outside communities — something I'm not thrilled with — but I can't exactly wrest control from them, much as I would like to."

"Why does it matter who is investigating?" I asked. "As long as everyone is working together ... ."

"That's just it. Not everybody is working together. The smaller communities sometimes get their backs up when they feel we're poking our noses into their business, which I understand. I don't want to take anything from them. I want them involved. It's just ... well ... ."

He didn't finish. I was confused and looked to Jack for help.

"Charleston has more experience when it comes to things like this," Jack explained. "The smaller communities don't investigate murder as often, and when they do it's not of the serial variety."

"It's not as if we've had a lot of serial killers," Rick said. "We had Lavinia Fisher, who was reportedly the first female serial killer. She was active in the 1800s. In the 1960s we had Lee Roy Martin, who turned himself in after strangling two women. Pee Wee Gaskins was executed in 1991 for killing his cellmate. He killed a bunch of women in the 1970s and buried them in shallow graves. He had fourteen victims — all acquaintances. He even killed his own niece.

"Then there's Susan Smith, the woman who claimed her kids were carjacked but drove them into the lake while they were still strapped in the car," he continued. "We had Larry Bell, who was a sick psychotic, and Richard Valenti, who went after young teenagers. I say this so you know we're not unfamiliar with high-profile killers. But this one has me terrified."

"Because you can't find a cause of death?" I asked.

"That and the precision with which these crimes are occurring," Rich replied. "The thing is, the front doors on all these homes were locked, seemingly indicating the women should've been safe inside. As far as I can tell, a window was open in each home, but I have to think there was some sort of coercion involved in getting the women to open the windows."

"I don't understand," I said, shifting on my chair. "Why do you think the women opened the windows to allow their killers in? Doesn't it make more sense that they had their windows open to allow in fresh air and someone took advantage of the situation?"

Rick immediately started shaking his head. "Not in this weather. You guys are from Boston, right? I'm guessing in the summer months it's not unheard of for you to sleep with the windows open. Down here, with the heat and out-of-control humidity, that's rarely done."

That hadn't even occurred to me, but it made sense. I flicked my eyes to Jack. "Did you think of that?"

He shook his head. "I assumed our killer took advantage of an opening. Well, at least at first. I didn't realize a lot of the victims had ties to each other until this morning. I've been re-thinking my earlier assumptions since then."

Rick's eyebrows drew together. "What ties?"

"At least four of the victims volunteered at the aquarium."

"Really?" He rubbed his chin. "I wasn't aware of that. Where did you get confirmation on that?"

"Brock Wilson. One of the managers at the aquarium. He was very helpful."

"It sounds like it. I'll have to stop by and have a conversation with him. What else did he tell you?"

"Apparently the four women were pitching an idea for a television show," Jack replied. "They wanted it to focus on them working for various charities while trying to land rich husbands. Apparently they were very open about their intentions.

"I can't confirm the other women were involved in this, but ... it seems a little too convenient to be a coincidence," he continued. "I'm guessing that someone knew about the plan and that's how this individual got close to them."

Rick leaned back in his chair as the server delivered his iced tea and muffin. He smiled at her, offered a mock salute, and then returned his focus to us. "We don't have the Hollywood ties that a place like Atlanta does. That said, the show *Southern Charm* has put us on the map for reality show wannabes."

"You're the second person to bring up that show," Jack acknowledged. "I don't know anything about it."

Rick's chuckle was dry. "So you don't want to watch socialite women belittle one another and focus on the trivial things in life? I'm shocked."

"I'm a sports fan, and Charlie spends all her time watching old science fiction and fantasy shows," Jack supplied. "I've watched old shows that I never knew existed because of her — like there's this submarine show from the '90s that has a talking dolphin and is all kinds of crazy that she makes me watch — but reality television … ," he shook his head.

I balked. "*Seaquest* was awesome. I can't believe you're badmouthing it."

He shot me a look. "I watch it because you like it. Don't push it."

Rick snorted. "I've never heard of that show, but it sounds amusing. As for reality television, I'm a little more familiar with it than I would like. I have a twelve-year-old daughter who is obsessed. Trust me, these aren't the sort of values I want her embracing. She has a mind of her own, though, and all the kids talk about this *Southern Charm* show and aspire to be like the characters."

"And you think that our dead women modeled their plan to snag a reality television show on this particular show," Jack mused. "What can you tell me about the show?"

"Not much. I find it tedious. I tried to watch with my daughter — her name is Ava — but she got annoyed with all my questions, so that died a quick death.

"Basically it focuses on several people — I think there are, like, seven of them, both men and women — who run in socialite circles," he continued. "They go out for dinner and snipe at each other and attend events and snipe at each other. It's the worst thing you've ever watched."

"Sounds like it." Jack was thoughtful as he tapped his bottom lip. "Do these people have much of a following in the area?"

"Oh, they're pretty much considered gods here. We don't have many Hollywood starlets in the area. The *Southern Charm* cast is revered here."

"Which is why our dead girls wanted their own show so badly," I mused. "They thought it would give them a leg up on society functions."

"And finding husbands," Jack added. "Brock stressed that they were intense about not only finding mates, but rich ones. They wanted someone to fund a certain lifestyle and they clearly thought the combination of the show and their reputations would pave the way."

"I didn't know about the show," Rick said. "I'm glad I met with you because now I have a different angle to pursue. If I find out the other four victims had ties to this show that will be a definite place to focus our efforts ... although they could've been in contact with any charlatan south of the Mason Dixon Line who they thought might be able to get them a show."

"It doesn't even have to be a real person," Jack noted. "They might've thought they were dealing with a real individual, but it's possible we're dealing with a chameleon, someone who made up an identity to get close. Our victims might not have realized who they were dealing with."

"Rick nodded. "It's a good lead, though. As for the window thing ... I can't figure out why any of these women would purposely open a window to a stranger. I know you guys have a paranormal bent in your investigations. Do you have any ideas as to how our killer managed that?"

"Technically we can't even confirm we have a killer," Jack pointed out. "I mean ... you don't have a cause of death."

"No, but there's no way eight healthy women just dropped dead in their beds during the overnight hours. It's not possible."

"I agree. As for the paranormal world ... well ... I'm not the one you should talk to. I'm always the skeptic. My boss is the believer."

"And me," I added.

"And Charlie." Jack shot me a fond smile. "She always believes."

"And what do you think it is?" Rick shifted his attention to me. "If you're a believer, you must have a theory."

I was uncomfortable being put on the spot but saw no reason to lie. "My boss thinks it's an incubus. That's a demon that enthralls women and then kills them with sex. All our victims had sexual contact right before their deaths. That's our hunch. We have no proof for or against it right now."

"I appreciate your candor." Rick looked troubled. "I don't think I can go to my boss and say a demon killed our victims. He'd probably have me committed."

"Probably," Jack agreed. "Even if it is a demon, I'm guessing it has ties to the show those women wanted to do. If we find the common thread to that show, then we'll have a culprit."

"That's more than I had a few hours ago. I appreciate the information. I'll check on the other victims and try to tie them to the four who volunteered at the aquarium. As soon as I have any concrete information, I'll give you a call."

"We appreciate it," Jack said. "We'll keep digging, too."

TEN

We returned to the villa once we'd finished with the detective. Jack had some computer work he wanted to do. I dropped off the basket so it wouldn't be damaged and then moved out to the beach.

The ghost was still there. I hadn't expected her to disappear. What was really frustrating was she'd been joined by two others. Both had dark hair, were seemingly anchored somehow to their spots, floating on the water like ethereal buoys.

It was disheartening.

"I think I managed to get a line on a boat for tomorrow, Charlie," Jack noted as he walked out the rear sliding glass doors, pulling up short when he realized I was sitting on the sand rather than in one of the chairs. "What are you doing?"

I'd been resting outside for at least an hour, watching the ghosts. I'd lost track of time, forgotten that I wasn't alone, and jolted at the sound of his voice. "Just watching."

His gaze was sharp when it pinned me. "Are you okay?" He abandoned all pretense of talking about work and dropped onto the sand next to me. His fingers were gentle when he tipped my chin back so he could study my eyes. "Do you feel sick?"

The question caught me off guard. "Why would I feel sick?"

"I don't know. You're really pale and a little sweaty." He put the back of his hand to my forehead. "Anyone else who looked like you, I would assume they were sick."

I wasn't sure whether to be touched by his concern or insulted. "I'm okay."

"Then why are your fingers shaking?" He gripped my hands and squeezed. "Tell me what's going on."

There didn't seem to be a way around that and I figured it was better to get it out of the way before the others returned. "There are two more ghosts out there now."

He stilled, his hands ceasing their fervent motions over my face. "Just like the first one?" he asked finally.

I nodded. "They're just floating on top of the water and staring at the shore."

He stroked his hand over my hair and stared at the water. He couldn't see what I saw, but he obviously believed me because the concern etching into his face was profound. "Well, I have a call in to a guy about a boat. I'm hopeful it will work out. If not, we'll have to check with other locals. I know you thought a kayak was a good idea, but that sounds like a lot of work and it's not exactly easy on the ocean. A boat would be better."

I hadn't considered that. "Whatever you think is best." I rubbed my forehead and blew out a sigh. "Did you get anywhere with the reports?"

"Not yet," he replied. "I don't have all of them. Rick forwarded what he has, but he's obviously missing the ones from the outlying communities."

"What are you going to do?"

"I've already drafted formal requests for each department and sent them. I'm hoping they don't give me too much grief. If going through official routes doesn't work I'll have Chris contact Myron to go through unofficial routes. You'd be surprised how well Myron works when he gets to bend the rules."

"I'll have to take your word for it." I drew my knees up and rested my cheek on them as I returned to the ghosts. "I've never seen anything like this, Jack. I know you probably think I'm a crackpot because you can't see what I'm seeing, but ... it's weird."

"Hey, I don't think you're a crackpot." He was earnest as he got comfortable next to me, sliding his arm around my back and tucking me in at his side. "I have no doubt that you see what you claim to see. The difficulty is helping you figure out why."

"Yeah, well ... ." I rubbed my forehead. "We obviously can't go out searching on a boat tonight. We're going to lose the sun. Dwelling on that won't do me any good."

"No, but you're allowed to dwell on whatever you want to dwell on." He kissed my temple and rested his forehead there for a moment.

"This is a nice moment," I murmured.

"It is."

"I don't want to ruin it for you."

"You rarely ruin things ... unless you put yourself in danger and try to give me an aneurysm."

I smiled at the lame joke. He deserved a reward for the attempt. "Thanks for your kind words."

"You're welcome." He poked my side and grinned before turning serious. "I booked us on the wine tour."

I turned, surprised. "We're going on the wine tour?"

"Our victims were using it as a way to pick up men. Maybe one of those men is our culprit. At the very least there's a chance one of those men might know where to point us next."

"That's true." I dragged my fingers through my wind-swept hair. "I've never been on a wine cruise. Do I need to dress up? Are we acting like a couple? Does that mean we get to be romantic in public?"

He laughed at the cascade of questions. "Shorts and a T-shirt are fine, but I'd bring your hoodie in case it gets cold as the sun sets. As for acting like a couple ... ."

The way he hesitated told me that was not on the agenda. "I was only teasing you," I reassured him. "I know we're on the clock."

"That doesn't mean I wouldn't like to play the 'we're a simple couple on a romantic wine cruise' game," he supplied. "Under different circumstances I'd be all over that. But we're not going alone."

"Oh." Realization dawned on me. "I didn't realize the others were going with us."

"Laura overheard me making the arrangements. She's inside, by the way. She pitched a fit and now everyone is going because Millie interrupted us and actually took Laura's side for a change. She said she didn't want to miss out on a booze cruise."

I had to bite the inside of my cheek to keep from laughing at Jack's obvious annoyance. He was one of those guys who couldn't hide his real feelings. It was one of the things I liked best about him. "It's okay. There's no harm in going as a group."

"I can think of a few ways that I feel harmed. It doesn't matter, though. The reservations are already set."

"I didn't realize the others were here." I craned my neck to look inside. "Did they see me out here? I probably look like a loon staring at the ocean for so long."

"I don't care how you look."

"So ... I definitely looked like a loon. Good to know."

He heaved out a sigh. "You didn't look like a loon. Millie asked where you were and I told her you were enjoying some downtime outside. She poked her head out but didn't join you. I think she realized you were busy with other stuff. She's good like that, even though she's often a pain in the behind."

"What about Laura?" I asked. "There's no way she doesn't think I'm a loon."

"We don't care what Laura thinks. She's a horrible person and we're happy to pretend she's not part of the group."

"She's going to be upset when she's the odd woman out again on the cruise."

"I don't care. Although ... take it easy with the wine. It's the job of these sommeliers to keep your glass full because if you're tipsy you're likely to buy wine. That's what they want. You'll think you only have one glass of wine, but because they're refilling it you'll get drunk very quickly. I want you to have fun, but you should probably be mindful of that."

"Oh, you don't have to worry. I don't even like wine."

"That's even better." He glanced at the villa to make sure nobody was watching us and then lowered his voice. "I want you to watch the water very carefully. If there are more ghosts out there, even though it's a different area, I want to know. We need to see if we can get you in contact with them."

"I'll be on the lookout." I glanced at the three ghosts, who really did look like me from a distance. "This is getting creepier by the minute."

"We'll figure it out."

"Do you ever get tired of saying that?"

His grin was lightning quick and full of charm. "No. I mean it. We'll figure this out. I don't want you to worry."

That was easier said than done.

THE WINE CRUISE BOASTED A full contingent of passengers. At least fifty enthusiastic guests were on the large sailboat, which glided slowly around the bay. Our small group was seated on one side so we had a clear view of the setting sun.

"This is kind of nice." Laura wedged herself between Jack and Chris before we left the dock. She was determined to be part of the action. "It's beautiful, isn't it?" She shifted closer to Jack. "A sunset like this can give a person ideas."

He didn't bother to hide his scowl. "Give it up," he muttered before turning to focus on me. "There are a lot of older gentlemen here," he noted. "I think we should try talking to them."

"Because you think that our victims were trying to hit on some of them?" Millie asked. She was on the other side of me, Bernard on her right, and she looked flushed with excitement and somehow serious at the same time. "By the way, I probably get this mentality better than the rest of you because I spent decades in a world where this regularly happens."

I hadn't thought about that. "You probably saw it all the time;

young women trying to entice older men just because they had money. Did any of them ever try to get a reality show deal out of it?"

Millie snorted. "No, but I managed to extract myself from that world before reality television became big."

"It feels as if the Kardashians have been around forever, though."

"That's true." She patted my shoulder and then turned to study the group. "See those five guys down there." She inclined her head. "That's where we should start. They're clearly here to ogle the women — and, seriously, could those bikini tops be any skimpier? They would've been the sort of men our victims targeted."

"I don't want to be overt," Jack said. "I want to question them, but I don't want them to be suspicious. We have to be smart about this."

"Then you should send me over there instead of going yourself," Millie noted.

Jack's face was blank, which made me want to laugh.

"No offense, Millie, but I've never believed that it's better to send you to question people rather than doing it myself," he said finally, clearly choosing his words carefully. "I don't want to give you grief, but you tend to spout off despite your best intentions."

"I know how to read a room better than you," she persisted. "No, seriously. In this particular case, I can handle those men a great deal better than you."

Jack heaved out a sigh. "Whatever. How about we both go check them out?"

Millie made a face. "You're only saying that because you feel you need to keep an eye on me. It's annoying."

"Welcome to the real world. There are numerous things that can ultimately turn annoying. That's my offer. Take it or leave it."

"I'll take it." The look on Millie's face told me she wasn't happy. "You'll be begging me to take over the conversation. I understand these stuffy, rich dickweasels," she continued. "You're the straightforward type. These guys will play games. You'll be glad I'm with you."

"I guess we'll just have to wait and see." Jack shifted his eyes to me. "Do you want to come or stay here?"

It felt like a loaded question even though I knew there was no hidden meaning behind it. "I'll stay." I'd been watching the water closely for signs of ghosts and, so far I'd come up empty. "I don't particularly like dickweasels."

Jack's lips quirked. "Fair enough. Remember what I said about the wine, and be careful when walking close to the sides. There are rope lines keeping you safe, but it would be easy to slip between them."

I could see that myself. "I'll be on the lookout for sharks if something happens and I fall overboard."

"That's not funny."

"It's kind of funny."

BECAUSE SHE COULDN'T TOLERATE BEING left out, Laura insisted on going with Jack and Millie. As much as I hated watching Laura try to flirt with Jack, I was relieved she'd opted to move away from me. That allowed me to watch the water without her prying eyes invading my space. As a gadget guy, Bernard was more interested in the nautical equipment, so he made his way to the steering column and started talking to the crew. That left me alone ... although not for long.

"Nice night, huh?"

A blonde in skintight capris, her hair pulled back in a long ponytail, plopped down in the open spot next to me. She wore a tank top that put all her assets on display and a pair of six-inch heels that couldn't possibly have been considered safe on a sailboat.

"I ... ." My mouth went dry when I lifted my eyes and scanned her face. I recognized her.

"Harlequin Desdemona Stryker," she offered. "You can call me Harley."

Like I could ever forget that name. "What are you doing here?" I took a moment to glance around, to see if any of the guests were acting weird. They didn't seem to be paying us any attention. "Can they see you?"

The question made her laugh. "Yes. I'm not a ghost. You don't have to worry about that. Speaking of ghosts, though, you know you have a situation, right?"

Harley was a crossroads demon. She made deals with people for their souls. We'd met in New Orleans a few weeks ago, to my utter surprise she'd helped Jack and me out of a tight jam. I wasn't sure I would ever see her again. Apparently I was to be graced with her presence on any number of occasions.

"You know about the ghosts by the hotel on Folly Beach," I noted, my interest piqued. "Can you see them?"

She nodded. "I have an interesting skill set. Of course, you do, too. The ghosts are the talk of the paranormal world in this area."

"And what are you doing here? I thought you were stationed in New Orleans."

"That's the thing. When you do what I do for a living, you have customers all over the world. I don't stay in one specific place. I hop around."

"You must have a home base."

"I do." She didn't offer up a location, instead barreling forward. "Do you know why the ghosts are doing what they're doing?"

I was taken aback. "Why would I know? Why don't you know?"

"Because I'm not omniscient. Everyone is trying to figure it out. The ghosts are anchored here. They're essentially being tortured. Their souls cannot move on unless they're freed."

A sneaking suspicion stole over me. "One of the souls belongs to you, doesn't it? I mean ... you made a deal for it."

Her petal pink lips curved. "You're smarter than you look. I'll give you that." She patted my arm and glanced out at the water. "One of the dead women did sell her soul for fame and fortune."

"Technically none of these women achieved fame and fortune."

"In local circles they did. That's a semantics argument anyway. I can't claim her soul until it's freed and, try as I might, I can't free the soul myself. I think you're going to have to help me."

"I don't know how to free the souls."

"You'll figure it out." Harley sounded sure of herself as her busy eyes landed on Jack. He stood on the opposite side of the boat, his arms folded over his chest, glaring in our direction. Millie stood somewhat in front of him, engaging one of the older men in conversation, and Laura was to his back talking nonstop. It was obvious she was trying to get his attention. "Your boyfriend doesn't like me."

"He doesn't know you," I countered. "To be fair, I can't decide if I like you either."

She chuckled, genuinely amused. "You're funny. I like that about you. And, don't even bother denying it. You like me and we both know it."

She was right. I did like her. "I don't know what I'm supposed to do about the ghosts," I insisted. "It started out as one and now there are three. I've never seen anything like it."

"I haven't either and I guarantee I've been around longer than you. The fact that the ghosts are showing up anchored to this plane in such a specific way makes me think your killer is doing it on purpose. Do you know what you're dealing with yet?"

I shook my head. "My boss thinks it's an incubus."

"What do you think?"

That was a good question. "I don't know. It's hard for me to wrap my head around. I don't feel as if I know enough about incubi to even be certain they're real."

"Oh, they're real." Harley's lips curved as Jack slid around Millie and started in our direction. He looked to have fought his instincts for as long as possible and was now giving in to his baser urges. That meant he couldn't leave us alone to converse in case Harley wanted to cause trouble. "I figured he wouldn't be able to stay away."

"Don't give him grief," I warned, my voice low. "He's doing the best he can. This is all new for him."

"No promises." Her eyes sparked as she glanced at me. "Did I mention how much I love messing with guys who are as tightly wound as Jack? This is going to be fun."

That was not the word I would've used to describe our predicament.

ELEVEN

Jack managed to plaster a smile on his face, but it was hardly pleasant. He immediately positioned himself so he could act as my personal security guard, something I found mildly amusing given the fact that Harley was a demon. She could've taken him out without batting an eyelash.

"Good evening." He greeted her tersely. "I didn't realize you lived in Charleston."

Harley grinned. "I'm a world traveler at heart."

"Yeah, well ... ." Jack glanced around. No one was paying us any attention as far as I could tell. Well, that wasn't entirely true. Laura was watching from the other side of the boat and it was obvious she was curious.

"You mustn't worry, Jack," Harley offered in a low voice. "I'm not here to hurt you."

"I don't care about me."

"I'm not here to hurt Charlie either," she promised. "I happened to be in town for something else and discovered her presence. I thought we might compare notes, nothing more."

Jack didn't look convinced. "How did you find out she was here?"

"She has a certain presence. I'm certain you know exactly what I'm talking about."

Jack didn't look amused by the statement. "I think you should go."

"Oh, really?" Harley arched a challenging eyebrow. "How should I do that? Do you want me to throw myself over the side and swim for the shore? I'm guessing that would draw attention, which is the exact opposite of what you want."

Jack scowled. "I don't think you should be here. People will talk."

"What people?" Harley was enjoying herself far too much. "None of these people have any idea who I am or why I'm here. If I suddenly disappear into thin air, that might cause some talk. You need to chill out."

Jack glowered at her. "Why are you here? What do you want from Charlie? You don't want to ... take her ... do you?"

The question caught me off guard. Was that what he was worried about? "Jack, I'm not going anywhere. You don't have to worry about that."

His gaze never left Harley's face. "You can't take her."

Even though she was the sarcastic sort — she could've majored in it at college she was so good — she took pity on him and sighed. "I'm not here to take her from you, Jack. I don't operate under parameters of that sort."

"Charlie told me how you operate. You steal souls."

"I barter for souls. There's a difference. Charlie isn't stupid enough to trade her soul away. Besides, she already has everything she wants — well, almost everything — and she's not stupid enough to trade away her future for answers on a past that will become clear without me at some point."

It took me a moment to sort out what she'd just said. "You know about my biological parents?"

Harley hesitated before sliding her eyes to me. "No, but I could find out if you made a deal. That's how it works. You don't want to make that deal, though."

"Definitely not," I agreed. "I want answers, but I'm not willing to trade my soul for them."

"So we understand one another." She flashed me a winning smile before focusing on Jack. "I understand that you're gripped by fear at the notion someone you don't recognize or understand — or rather some *thing* — will someday take her from you. If you constantly live life looking over your shoulder, you're going to lose out on the joy she brings to your life. Is that what you want?"

He hesitated before shaking his head. "This is new for me."

"I know. You'll be fine." She patted his arm and grinned as she caught my chastising gaze. "Don't look at me like that. I get my kicks where I can. This isn't always an uplifting job."

"Is that why you're here?" Jack asked. "Are you on a job?"

"She's here for one of the women," I supplied. "You haven't told me which one."

"I can't tell you. It ultimately doesn't matter. I've asked around, stopped in to chat with the local reapers. They all say the same thing. None of the souls were present to be gathered. Whatever creature is doing the killing is somehow restraining the souls as well."

"And what sort of creature does that?" Jack asked, his hand automatically moving to my back so he could lightly rub his knuckles up and down my spine. "I mean ... do you know what's doing this?"

Harley shook her head. "No, and don't think I'm not interested. I'm stuck in this place until I can claim my soul. I was hoping Charlie would have an idea — and I am intrigued at the notion of an incubus — but I can't say with any degree of certainty that we're dealing with a demon. It could be something else."

"Like what?"

"Not all creatures are one thing," she explained. "Like Charlie here. She's magical at her core, but she's also a good person firmly anchored in a human world. I can't get a true sense regarding her blood. I think she's a hodgepodge of things. There's some witch in there, maybe a little mage. It's ... weird.

"I've done a little research since meeting you in New Orleans," she continued. "What I've found makes you even more intriguing. It's been suggested that you're the culmination of several lines of little magic, meaning that all those tiny magic genetic markers somehow erupted into a big line ... and you're something new."

"And who suggested that?" Jack demanded.

"People in the trade," Harley answered, waving her hand. "I'm not providing you with that information, Jack, so you'll have to let it go. All I can tell you is that Charlie is garnering interest. Before you freak out, you should know that doesn't mean people want to take her from you. They will, however, want to tap into her magic. It's a simple reality when you're as powerful as Charlie. You'll have to get used to it."

"I won't let anyone hurt her." Jack's tone was icy. "That includes you."

"I have no interest in hurting her." Harley smiled as she turned back to me. "He's kind of alpha, isn't he? That can be a turn-on or a turn-off depending on when he decides to unleash that power. You need to keep him under wraps. If he mouths off to the wrong entity ... ."

She left it hanging in such a manner that it sent chills up my spine. "Jack will be fine." I would make sure of that. "We need to focus on whatever is taking out these women. I doubt it's going to simply stop because we've arrived in town."

"The thing is, if it's an incubus as you suggest, then it's already sensed me ... and you," Harley said. "That's part of their makeup and how they've managed to survive for centuries even though they've been hunted by humans and other paranormals from the start. Incubi aren't regarded well in any circle as far as I know.

"They keep to themselves and generally try to hunt in secret so they don't tip off law enforcement," she continued. "It's not like before when cities were removed from one another and local police departments didn't talk. Everyone is aware of what's going on here, which makes me believe that this particular incubus — if that's what we're dealing with — had some other issues. He's clearly succumbing to his bloodlust, which means he'll get worse before he gets better."

"So ... how do we stop him?" Jack asked. "There must be a way."

"We have to find him first. When we do, I find a simple beheading works as well as anything else."

Jack scowled. "I can't just walk up and behead him when we find him. There has to be another way."

"He'll be susceptible to magic," Harley said, her gaze laser pointed on me. "But we're not even certain we're dealing with an incubus. I'll keep my ear to the ground and try to get some confirmation. If I get any leads, I'll funnel them to you."

"Maybe do it by phone," Jack suggested. "That way I won't be tempted to throw you off a sailboat because you just show up out of nowhere."

Harley snorted. "My phone is for playing Pokemon Go. I don't like talking to people on it."

He shook his head. "You're annoying," he muttered.

"So are you." Her eyes sparkled as she glanced around. "I need to be going. I'll be in touch."

Jack opened his mouth to say something else — I was convinced he was going to question how she planned to disappear in the midst of a crowd — but it was already too late. One second she was there and the next she wasn't. She simply popped out of existence. It was just the two of us.

"I don't like her," Jack announced when she was gone. "She's going to be trouble."

I had no doubt he was right. But it also was obvious she was going to be helpful. "We'll worry about that later. We need to question those rich, old dudes. That's why we're here."

He sighed. "Okay, but I'm still keeping an eye on her. She says the right things, but she could be lying. She's a demon, after all. They lie."

"I'm glad to see you're getting into the spirit of things," I drawled. "We don't have to worry about her. We have much bigger problems."

We tabled our discussion on Harley and went back to what we were doing. It was all we could do because we were caught in a holding pattern.

It wasn't a feeling I enjoyed.

. . .

THERE WAS ANOTHER GHOST ON the water when I woke the next morning.

"That's four of them," I noted as Jack joined me in front of the sliding glass doors. He was still sleepy, his eyes clouded with confusion, and he wrapped his arms around me from behind and kissed my neck.

"Why do you think they're showing up this way?" he asked. "I mean ... why didn't they end up out there right from the start? Why the delay?"

That was a very good question. "I don't know. I think, at this point, we have to assume that the ghosts of all the women are going to end up out there. I think the location is key."

"Why?"

"Our incubus — or whatever it is — wants the souls close to him. It's no fun for him to torture them if he can't have regular access. That means he's somewhere on Folly Beach."

Jack stilled. "I hadn't actually put that together. That makes sense."

"There were no ghosts on the bay last night. This location means something to our killer. We have to figure out what."

"Well, there's nothing we can do about those ghosts right now, so let's focus on the important stuff."

I cast him a sidelong look, legitimately curious. "Like what? Did you have an idea?"

He nodded solemnly. "There's a restaurant on the main drag that supposedly has the best omelets in Charleston. I'm starving."

I choked on a laugh. Leave it to Jack to focus on food. Of course, my stomach picked that moment to growl, causing us both to grin. We were a food-oriented couple. There was no getting around that.

The rest of our group was already in the living room when we arrived, and there seemed to be some sort of argument going on.

"I don't think I'm being unreasonable," Laura snapped. "Everyone on this team is paired up, which leaves me feeling uncomfortable and isolated. That's not fair. It makes for a hostile work environment."

Millie rolled her eyes as Chris adopted his best "what do you want me to do about it" look. "What do you suggest?"

"We need to add another member to the team," Laura replied without hesitation. "I don't want to be an afterthought. I want to be at the forefront. I want to be a contributing member. I don't think that's an unfair request."

Chris hesitated before answering, and I could tell he was legitimately considering the suggestion. "The truth is, we've been considering adding another team member," he admitted. "I want someone good with computers and technology."

"You have me," Jack pointed out.

"Yes, but your attention is split these days."

"Because of Charlie," Laura muttered.

Jack scorched her with a look. "If you're not careful, I'll suggest we add a dog to the group and make you his keeper."

Chris brightened considerably. "Oh, I read about those ghost-detecting dogs in the magazine you gave me. Apparently you can train certain dogs to be able to detect ghosts. I'm considering getting one."

I pressed my lips together and averted my eyes when Laura turned hostile. I found her reaction funny rather than fearsome, which only proved that I was getting used to her.

"I want an actual person," she hissed. "I don't think I'm asking for too much. You guys all have your little office romances to fall back on. I have nothing."

"Perhaps that's because you're a genuinely disagreeable person," Millie suggested.

"Or perhaps it's because you guys are all jerks," Laura shot back. "I'm going to make a formal request at the office when I return – or maybe even before – whether you like it or not. I just thought I would at least pretend to go through proper channels first."

Chris heaved out a sigh and shook his head. "I'm not opposed to the idea. We'll need to advertise when we get back."

"Actually, I happen to know a guy," Laura countered. "He'll be a perfect fit for our group."

"Oh, well, if Laura is suggesting him that means he's probably a total tool," Millie countered. "I don't know about anyone else, but I would like to respectfully veto this idea before it goes too far."

Chris shot her a look. "Nobody is being vetoed. Laura, if your friend wants to forward his application and paperwork to Human Resources, I'll take a moment to look things over as soon as this case is in the rearview mirror. How does that sound?"

"I'll email him this morning," Laura replied primly. She seemed happy, although I didn't miss the predatory smile she shot in my direction. It made me understandably nervous. "Now, with that out of the way, what are we doing today?"

"I have assignments for everybody," Chris replied. "Although I'm not sure who I should send Laura with. I hadn't gotten that far this morning before she brought up adding another team member. Um ... hmm. Let me think."

Laura's eye roll was pronounced to the point I had to lower my head to avoid eye contact with her if I even wanted to pretend to be professional. "And this is why we need another team member," he muttered.

"We could do Rock, Paper, Scissors," Millie suggested. "Loser has to take Laura for the day."

Laura's mouth dropped open. "Excuse me?"

This situation was spiraling out of control ... and quickly. "We'll take her," I offered, resigned. Even though I disliked her a great deal, I couldn't help feeling sorry for Laura. She was being treated like a leper and it wasn't entirely her fault. Of course, it was mostly her fault.

"No, we won't take Laura," Jack countered, firm. "Millie can take her. They're a better fit."

"Puh-leez!" Millie's reaction was pronounced. "Putting us together is like trying to squeeze a Kardashian rear end into extra-small panties. It's going to chafe."

I turned so fast I accidentally smacked into Jack's chest because I was laughing so hard. He didn't miss my expression and looked to be as amused as I felt.

"Rock, Paper, Scissors won't be necessary," Chris offered. "Millie, you're going back to the docks because you've already built a rapport with the individuals there. I think it would be best if Laura went with you."

"Yes, because she will be a big hit with the guys on the docks," Jack drawled.

Chris shot him a quelling look. "As for you two, I have something special in mind. It's geared toward Charlie's interests. I think she's really going to like the assignment."

I was already sold. "I'm all in. Just tell me where you want me to go."

TWELVE

Our assignment was to visit the Old Charleston Jail. It was supposedly haunted and one of the most notorious parcels of land in the city.

I had no idea why it was important to this case.

"I don't understand why Chris insisted we come here," I admitted as Jack paid the tour guide standing on the steps. We were still twenty minutes from showtime, so we could talk ... and commiserate about our bad luck. "I thought we were going out on a boat."

"I'm going to get you out on a boat," he promised. "As for this ... you know Chris. He heard this place was haunted and figures it's worth a shot. As if we'll somehow stumble across a ghost who will have all the answers."

His poor attitude was on full display and it chafed a bit. "You don't have to go inside," I suggested. "I can do it without you. There's a coffee shop just down that way. Why don't you head over there and wait for me? I promise not to dawdle."

"Um ... no." He immediately started shaking his head. "I'm in this with you. You're not wandering around by yourself."

"I doubt the incubus is in there."

He glanced around to make sure nobody was listening and then dragged me several paces away so we could talk more freely without risk of anybody eavesdropping. "Don't say that word when someone might overhear. We don't even know that we're dealing with a ... monster."

I had to laugh. "I'm glad you're getting back to your old self. I happen to be fond of Professional Denier Jack."

"Ha, ha." He lightly flicked the spot between my eyebrows. "I'm not saying it's not possible. The first rule of conducting a successful investigation is to remain open to everything and only dismiss a possibility when there's no other choice. I think I forgot that rule at some point, and I'm trying to be responsible about this."

Something occurred to me. "Because Laura and Chris said your focus has been on other things of late, right?"

He frowned. "You're still my focus. They're not wrong about me shirking my duties, though. I need to be better about it because ... well, just because. I like to think of myself as a diligent employee, but I've been distracted."

"I can see that." I smiled and patted his arm, my eyes going to the ornate building serving as a backdrop. "This place is really supposed to be haunted?"

"That's what they say."

I plucked the tour brochure from his hand and gestured toward a bench in the shade. We had time to kill. "Let's see what we've got." I started reading the brochure. "The jail was operational from 1802 to 1939."

"So we're dealing with really old ghosts," Jack muttered.

I ignored him and kept reading. "It's four stories with a two-story octagonal tower. Back in the day there was a hospital, workhouse and poorhouse here. The property was designated for public use."

"A workhouse is where runaway slaves were punished," Jack noted, leaning closer. "I don't get the feeling this was exactly a happy place. No wonder there are ghosts here."

I smiled to myself at his change of heart. He talked big but had a good heart and he loved history ... just like me. Sure, he was more likely to shut down paranormal possibilities immediately, but that would change as his world expanded. I didn't have a single doubt about that.

"Some 19th-century pirates were housed here, which is kind of cool," I offered.

"I doubt they looked like the hot pirates in *Pirates of the Caribbean*."

"Slaves were held here after Denmark Vesey's planned slave revolt," I noted. "He sounds interesting. I don't know why I've never heard of him before. He bought his own freedom and was accused of planning a rebellion. He supposedly was going to organize a bunch of people — obviously slaves and former slaves — to kill the masters and then they were going to escape Charleston and sail to Haiti.

"He was arrested before the uprising and executed, even though no one died," I continued. "They say his ghost haunts the hallways, still looking for the wife and son he couldn't free from slavery. That's kind of sad."

When I risked a glance at Jack, I found him watching me with a cocked eyebrow. "What?"

"I think there are very few happy slave stories," he said. "You're right, though. That is a terrible story. What else do we have in store for us?"

"That woman that Detective Carter mentioned was housed here," I volunteered. "Lavinia Fisher. She's considered one of the first female serial killers … although there's an argument that she didn't kill anybody, so her execution might've been a mistake."

Jack pursed his lips and slid his arm around my shoulders. "What's her story?"

I settled in at his side. It was a comfortable moment — even though we were talking about murder and mayhem — and I wanted to enjoy it. "She reportedly invited travelers into the Six Mile Wayfarer House — I'm assuming that's where she lived — and asked them questions about their occupations to determine if they had money.

"If she felt they did, she sent them up to their rooms with a cup of poisoned tea," I continued. "Once they were asleep, her husband supposedly stabbed them to death. There's a wild legend that says

Lavinia would wait until they were passed out to pull a lever to drop the contents of the bed into a pit under the house."

"I'm guessing that wasn't a real thing," Jack said dryly. "That sounds like something straight out of a *Scooby-Doo* episode."

"Right?" I grinned. "But it's interesting to think about. They say she roams the halls of the jail, too."

"What for?"

I shrugged, thinking back to what a Michigan witch once told me. "I have no idea. As far as I can tell, most ghosts stay behind because they were either ripped so abruptly and violently from their lives that they don't know they're dead ... or they want retribution. That's just a hypothesis. I've never been able to prove it. I haven't always been able to see ghosts. At least . . . I don't think I have. I wanted to. Now, apparently, I can."

His fingers were gentle as they moved my hair away from my neck. "It's as good of an explanation as anything. Does it frighten you to see them?"

It was an honest question so I thought it deserved a well-thought-out answer. "Not really. Maybe when I was younger. They're not really a focus for me. I've known other people who fixate on seeing ghosts. I see them only some of the time, but maybe it's all of the time and I'm not always looking. I'm not sure why it is the way it is for me.

"I mean ... like Bay," I continued, reminding him of the blond witch at the heart of all this. That was our first case together. We were looking for Bigfoot but met witches instead. Of course, I kept the family secret for them. It wasn't something I felt comfortable sharing. "She's been able to see and talk to ghosts her entire life, and I think they take over at times. It's not comfortable for her. I've never had that problem."

Jack shifted on his seat. "You mean Bay who lived in the witch town? I didn't know she could see and talk to ghosts."

I realized my mistake too late. "Oh, well ... ."

Jack cocked his head. "There was real magic in Hemlock Cove. Of course there was. I should've seen that. You covered for them."

"I didn't cover for them," I said hurriedly. "I just ... I wouldn't want anyone else sharing my secret. They're good people. I really liked them. They offered me help, and I still talk to Bay every few weeks. She calls to make sure I'm okay. I promised to go back one day so we could explore our magic a little more."

He massaged the back of my neck. "I'm curious. How many other magical creatures have you found and covered for?"

The question made me distinctly uncomfortable. "Um … ."

"You don't want to say."

"It doesn't feel like I should. Going forward, obviously I would keep you in the loop. I made a promise, though."

"To the Winters family?"

My stomach heaved and I didn't answer. He'd been knocked unconscious at the home of Aric and Zoe Winters. He hadn't witnessed Aric and his daughter Sami turning into wolves and chasing after the bad guys. He wasn't present when Zoe showed off her mage powers. All he knew was that something weird had happened.

"You don't have to tell me," he said finally, grabbing my hand and giving it a squeeze. "It's okay. I get it. I knew something happened that night. I should've followed my instincts."

"I'm sorry."

"You have nothing to apologize for." He leaned closer and kissed the corner of my mouth. "Go back to the jail. What else should we expect?"

"Just a bunch of ghosts, according to this. I still don't understand how this is supposed to help us."

"That makes two of us. At least we can act like a couple on the tour. If this place is haunted I'm going to want to hold your hand."

"So you can protect me?"

"No. So you can protect me."

A giggle bubbled up. "I think that can be arranged."

THE TOUR LEADER WAS A BEAUTIFUL brunette with an infectious smile. Salem Taylor claimed to be a local witch. Her mother had named her for the city in Massachusetts, and she was thrilled to share her knowledge of all things Wiccan.

"Do you think she's real?" Jack asked as he trailed behind me. He seemed more annoyed than enamored with the woman.

"I don't know. I'm guessing no. The eyeliner is pretty impressive, though, huh?"

He wrinkled his nose. "I prefer it when you go natural. You don't need makeup."

"Oh, you're so sweet." We stood outside an old cell as Salem told the story of Lavinia Fisher. It was obvious she'd told the story so many times she could've done it in her sleep. It was still entertaining.

"There are a lot of rumors about Lavinia," she intoned gravely. "So many I can't even count them all. The one I tend to believe is that she was a witch."

"Because of the potions?" I asked, briefly running my fingers over the bars. There was a dark energy in the jail. I didn't know if it was really haunted — I'd yet to see a single ghost — but the blood spilled on the land had definitely tainted it. There was no doubt about that.

"The potions are a big part," Salem agreed, casting me a sidelong look. "Are you a practitioner of the craft?"

"Not really. I'm just a paranormal buff. I'm no witch."

"Except when she first wakes up in the morning," Jack countered, earning an appreciative chuckle from the men in attendance and dark glares from the women. "I'll just be standing over here being quiet again," he offered, causing me to laugh.

"It's good that you're open to different things," Salem offered. "There's nothing worse than the negative energy of a non-believer." Her gaze was pointed when it landed on Jack. "Doubt ruins it for us all."

"I don't doubt Charlie," Jack replied. "As for the rest ... I love little more than to learn something new."

"That's true," I offered helpfully. "Just this morning, in fact, we were discussing what happened to all those women who have been in the news. He says it makes the most sense for a paranormal entity to be involved because otherwise it's too fantastical to believe."

Jack slid me an appreciative look but didn't comment. It was clear he was impressed at the way I'd managed to turn the conversation.

"I've been thinking that myself," Salem admitted. "Everyone in the city is terrified that some creature might come after them. Nobody wants to be out alone at night. I guess, if something good had to come from this, it's that."

"Nobody should be walking alone after dark as it is," Jack offered. "You should always have a friend with you. Even during the day, if you can manage it. That's the smart way to go."

Salem snorted. "I think it's impossible to have someone with you twenty-four hours a day. If you have enough friends to cover all those shifts, more power to you."

"I just have Jack." I jerked my thumb in his direction. "He likes to act as my personal bodyguard."

Salem's smile was legitimate. "It's nice to see two people so obviously devoted to one another. In this day and age, when technology divides us all, the simple act of bonding with another human being is more impressive than ever."

That was a weird way to phrase things. It was obvious Salem was riding high on the "peace, love and magic" train. I had no intention of diminishing her spirits. "I think it's great, too," I agreed. "What are people saying about the deaths? You guys have your finger on the pulse of the supernatural community. Do you have any ideas?"

I didn't think Salem had enough real magic to stifle a sneeze. She was the enthusiastic sort, probably prayed to the Goddess on a nightly basis and burned a lot of sage, but she wasn't the real deal. I couldn't feel even a hint of power emanating from her.

"There are whispers." Salem looked over my shoulder, clearly gauging the interest level of the other tour participants. Finding sufficient enthusiasm, she barreled forward. "The thing is, Charleston is home to more than one sort of creature. Witches are prevalent. Obviously ghosts are here. But there's more than that."

I exchanged a quick look with Jack. He was obviously annoyed at the theatrics, but kept his opinion to himself. That was wise. We didn't want to alienate Salem. I honestly wanted to hear what she had to say.

"What are the whispers saying?" I asked.

"It's a vampire."

That wasn't the answer I expected. "Um ... I don't think so. I read in the newspaper that there were no marks on the bodies. Vampires kill by draining blood. They need puncture wounds, however small, to do that."

"Maybe it's like the show *True Blood*," one of the women volunteered from the back. "Maybe they heal the marks with their saliva right after so you can't tell it happened."

That was a gross thought. "Perhaps, but that's fiction. We're talking reality."

"I'm not talking about the gothic representation of a vampire," Salem volunteered, her enthusiasm building. She clearly loved being the center of attention. "I'm talking about a different sort of dark king of the night."

Jack grimaced and growled and I jabbed him with my elbow to keep him quiet. I wasn't a fan of Salem's ridiculous flowery language, but I wanted to hear what she had to say.

"What sort of vampire do you think it is?" I prodded.

"It's an energy vampire. Instead of drinking blood, they suck the life force from individuals. It's a quiet death, more dignified. We obviously have an insatiable killer in our midst."

On that we could agree, but I'd never heard of an energy vampire. "And where does the energy vampire hide during the day?"

"There are plenty of places." She gestured toward the cell directly in front of us. "There are parts of this building we're not allowed to visit. I think it's entirely possible that he could be living here, amongst the ghosts. I mean ... it's possible."

Whispers fluttered behind me. She'd hit the perfect mark for her group and she knew it.

"Now let me tell you about a reported vampire who lived in the jail for two years before his execution," Salem started. "Both the capture and ultimate death are tricky on this one, so listen closely. This way."

. . .

TWO HOURS LATER, JACK BOUGHT us iced teas from a corner food cart, muttering a bevy of undecipherable complaints. I was used to it, so I let him vent and instead turned back to study the jail from afar.

Protected under the shade of a huge willow tree was a familiar face ... and it was staring directly at us.

"Isn't that Brock Wilson from the aquarium?"

Jack jerked up his head and followed my gaze. "Yeah. What's he doing here? Was he on the tour with us?"

When Brock realized we were staring at him, he turned and ambled in the opposite direction. Jack looked as if he was going to give chase for a moment, but we both knew that would be hard to explain if Brock started questioning him ... or called the police.

I glanced around. "I don't think he was, but I was only paying attention to you and Salem. I tuned out everybody else."

"Let's follow him," Jack suggested. "We'll act like we're doing touristy things. I just want to see."

I was uneasy enough to agree. "It could be a coincidence," I said as I followed Jack.

"Maybe, but I've never been one to believe in coincidences."

We had that in common.

THIRTEEN

We never got a chance to talk to Brock. He disappeared down the sidewalk and when Jack tried to trail him, he was long gone in the crowds of tourists.

"What do you think?" I asked as we headed back to Folly Beach. "Was he following us?"

Jack shrugged, his eyes on the road. He was an excellent driver, but traffic was heavy and he was always cautious when driving a rental under the auspices of the Legacy Foundation. "I don't know. He might've been there on a date or something. That's always possible."

"He looked alone."

"Why do you think he was there?" There was an edge to Jack's voice I couldn't quite identify.

I was having trouble even scraping up feasible ideas. "Maybe he's the gossipy sort and wants to know what happened to his former volunteers. He might look like a big shot to the money folks if he tells them what's going on."

Jack cocked an eyebrow, clearly unconvinced. "Do you really think that?"

"No, but it's possible. Maybe the other donors believe they're in danger."

"Unless they're brunettes in their twenties that would seem a ridiculous conclusion."

"Fear motivates people in strange ways."

Slowly, even though traffic was wretched, his eyes slid to me. "It does indeed. Fear can freeze you in your tracks if you let it."

"I try not to let it."

"Me, too."

"Sometimes I forget."

His lips curved as he turned back to the road. "Me, too."

We drove in silence for a bit, Jack reaching over to collect my hand once we were free of the worst of the traffic. After hitting Folly Beach, he parked at the hotel and then inclined his head in the opposite direction of the villa.

"Let's get lunch before we head back."

I didn't even realize I was hungry until my stomach growled in unison with his footsteps. "I could eat." I moved to his side and started studying the restaurant signs. "What do you want to try today?"

"I was about to ask you that."

"It's your turn to choose."

"I chose Fleet Landing."

"Yeah, but ... that was really good. You can choose again."

"Uh-uh." He shook his head and made a tsking sound with his tongue. "You choose."

I pursed my lips as I gauged my options. "I like tacos." I nodded toward a place called Taco Boy.

"Are you sure that's what you want, or are you only choosing it because you think it's cheap?"

"I like tacos," I repeated.

He frowned. "That's what I thought." His gaze was steady as he scanned the restaurants. "I know I said you could pick, but I think you're trying to placate me — or at least make it so I spend very little money. How about Loggerheads? I saw a billboard yesterday. It's near the water."

"Why is that important?"

"I'm looking for boaters."

"Oh." Realization dawned. "What kind of food do they serve?"

"Typical American fare. Wraps, burgers, the like. They also have shrimp tacos."

I frowned. "Call me crazy, but I prefer my tacos made with beef, chicken or pork. Shrimp and fish aren't supposed to be in tacos."

"Oh, really?" His grin was quick and sly as he slid his arm around my shoulders. "I didn't realize you were so militant about food. Tell me all about it."

Because he seemed so amused on my stance, I did just that.

LOGGERHEADS WAS THE SORT OF restaurant with a welcoming ambiance that made me want to eat three courses instead of one. We picked a spot on the patio, under a large umbrella, and ordered iced teas before reading the menu.

"Do you really think you're going to be able to get someone to take us out on a boat?"

He shrugged. "I really think that wouldn't be a problem if I could use the Legacy Foundation's influence to secure a boat. Since I can't, it's been more difficult."

"I'm sorry."

"Why? You didn't cause this."

"If I hadn't seen the ghosts ... ."

He rested his hand on mine. "We need to know about the ghosts. Whatever is happening here is far from normal. The tour today actually made me wonder a few things ... but I want to wait until after we order to talk about them."

He was essentially saying he wanted to minimize chances the waitress could overhear us. I was with him on that. "Good idea." I focused on the menu ... and immediately started laughing. "They have something called a 'Build Your Own Big-Ass Burger.'"

Jack smirked. "That sounds good. Is that what you're getting?"

It was tempting, but I wanted to try something with a more regional flair. "I don't know. I was thinking I might get the scallops."

His grin widened. "You love seafood."

"I do. I didn't get many options in the Midwest. It was Red Lobster or bust. We had great Middle Eastern, though. I liked that, but there don't seem to be as many options in Boston. Even when you find it, it's not as authentic."

"If we go back to the Midwest, you can take me for Middle Eastern food," he promised. "You can choose all the food in Detroit if we ever get lucky enough to land there."

"Oh, that's a dangerous proposition," I countered. "You'll be eating coneys until they come out of your ears, and I won't listen to a thing about it because you think they're cheap. Just because they don't cost much doesn't mean they're not delicious."

He shook his head. "I'm sorry. I shouldn't have made the offer for you to pick the restaurant and then change my mind after the fact. I thought it might be easier for us to find someone with a boat here."

"You should've just said that."

"Sometimes I say and do completely idiotic things. I can't seem to help myself around you."

We had that in common, so I let it go. Once the waitress returned to take our orders, the conversation turned to a heavier topic. Jack was serious when he delved in. "Do you think it could be witches?"

I wasn't expecting the question. In hindsight, I should've. He'd been attentive at the jail, but his suspicious eyes had been pointed at Salem the entire time. That was probably why we didn't notice Brock was on the tour with us.

"I guess I'm confused about why you believe that," I said. "Is it just because Salem irritated you?"

"She did irritate me," he agreed without hesitation. "And there's no way that's her real name. I know she said her parents named her that because they were hippie moon children, but she's full of it. She chose that name. I bet her real name is Jane or something."

He was so animated I had to press my lips together to keep from laughing. "Does it matter? I mean ... we have no reason to suspect her. We invited ourselves to her jail tour. She didn't seek us out."

"I know that. She tried to point us in the direction of vampires really hard, though. I can't help but wonder if that's because she wanted us to focus in a different direction."

"Or she's a little nutty," I countered. "She didn't say it was normal vampires. She said it was energy vampires. That's something she obviously took from a book ... and not a history book. She's a believer, like Chris. She doesn't need facts because she enjoys letting her imagination run wild."

He was quiet for a moment and when he started talking again his tone was more measured. "Back when we first met, you let your imagination run wild. You've been more ... quiet, I guess is the word ... the past two weeks."

And here I thought our deep conversations — at least about our personal relationship — were behind us. Apparently I was wrong. "What are you worried about, Jack?"

"I don't know. Usually you would jump all over the witch possibility. Now I'm the one suggesting that and you're being a pragmatist. It's like up is down and left is right. It's freaking me out."

His response made me smile. "You're afraid I'm trying to change to appease you."

"Maybe a little," he hedged. "I don't want that, for the record. I want you to be you."

"I want you to be you, too," I shot back. "You don't always have to be careful about stepping on my toes. You never used to worry about that. In fact, you bossed me around and told me I was an idiot."

He frowned. "I don't want to call you an idiot. You're smart. I've always believed that ... even when I thought you did idiotic things."

"I don't particularly like being called an idiot. But if you think I'm doing something idiotic you should probably call me out on it. You're not doing that. Instead, you're bending over backward to make sure I'm okay.

"I appreciate that, but I'm stronger than I look and I don't want you constantly worrying about hurting my feelings, because that's not who we are," I continued. "It's okay to yell at me occasionally. I mean ... I don't want you turning into an abusive boss or anything, but our relationship was founded on arguments. I don't want to lose that."

He blew out a sigh and gripped my hand. "Me either. I just ... I don't want to push things too far. You've been through a lot. *We've* been through a lot. I want a little peace before we got back to sniping at one another."

"I can live with that." I meant it. "I just want to make sure that we do get back. We'll lose something bigger if we can't be ourselves with one another."

He nodded. "Fair enough. I still think witches are a possibility."

I had to laugh. He was just too funny. "Well, I don't particularly think that. An incubus makes more sense."

"How do you figure? You said a spell was anchoring the souls of the victims to the water. That screams witch to me."

"Except witches are usually female," I argued. Even though it wasn't a weighty discussion, it felt relatively normal to debate a topic like this with him. I liked it. "I'm not being sexist and saying that there are no male witches — New Orleans is filled with male brujos, for example — but most witches are female."

"What does that have to do with anything?"

"There was sexual contact with all our victims," I reminded him. "We have to be dealing with a male."

"Huh. I hadn't considered that." He leaned back in his chair and stroked his chin. "Still, it could be a male witch."

"It could," I acknowledged. "The thing is, everything I've read about witches — and it's a lot — seems to suggest their magic is rooted in the four elements: earth, air, water, fire. There's rarely a sexual component to it."

"Your ghosts are anchored in the water," he pointed out. "That's water magic, right?"

I tilted my head, considering. "Maybe, but ... no." I shook my head. "I don't think that's what we're dealing with. Obviously I can't know with absolute certainty, but I don't believe that's the sort of magic we're dealing with.

"Those souls aren't anchored to the water," I continued. "They anchored to the creature that killed them. He clearly has an affinity for water. That's the tie."

"Are you sure?"

"No, but it's what I feel."

"That's good enough for me." He planted his feet on either side of mine and grinned at me over the table. "It was a minor fight, but that should make you happy, huh?"

I returned the smile. "It was a start."

"We'll get back to where we were," he promised, earnest. "I just don't want to push things too fast and too hard right now. It feels wrong."

He didn't have magic at his disposal, but his instincts weren't something to be ignored. "That's good enough for me," I supplied. "Even though I know I'm stepping on your line, I truly believe we're going to be okay."

"That we are." He was silent for a beat and then changed the subject. "So ... what's the deal with you and fish tacos? They're awesome. I think you should give them a try."

"I don't like fish unless it's cod."

He made a face. "That's not real fish ... and I've seen you eat a pile of crab legs bigger than your head."

"Ah, but that's different." I wagged my finger in a chiding manner. "I love seafood. I like all kinds of seafood, in fact. Lobster, mussels, clams, scallops, shrimp and crab. I could eat those every day for the rest of my life and be happy. But fish is gross."

"Fish is brain food."

"Well, you said I was smart, so I obviously don't need brain food. I'll leave that to you."

He scowled. "I won't forget you said that."

I shrugged.

We held each other's gazes and grinned like idiots. Slowly but surely we were getting back to where we were. It was a rclicf.

AFTER A FILLING LUNCH, JACK led me down to the water's edge, to a small bar where the locals kicked back and enjoyed beers while watching television and commenting on the state of commercial fishing.

Jack pointed me toward a table and I obediently sat. He seemed determined to find someone with a boat even though I believed kayaks were the perfect solution. He'd vetoed that idea relatively quickly, and I was still saucy about it.

He ordered iced teas at the bar and carried them to the table, relaxing in a chair across from me so he could survey the crowd.

"See anyone you want to hit on?" I asked dryly.

He shot me a look. "You're so funny." He poked my side and then turned back to the crowd. "Those guys." He inclined his head toward two men who were whooping it up near the bar as they drank and enjoyed a basket of fries. "They're the ones we want."

"How do you know that?" I was genuinely curious. "I mean ... how do you know they even have a boat?"

"Because they're wearing boat shoes and the one closest to us has an anchor tattoo."

"I've always wanted a raven tattoo," I argued. "That doesn't make me an ornithologist."

The look he shot me was withering. "That right there was the most pain-in-the-ass thing you've said since New Orleans. Under normal circumstances I would give you grief for it. I'm happy to see it today."

"That's all well and good, but it doesn't change the fact that you can't possibly know they have a boat just by looking at them."

He rolled his eyes and then cleared his throat to get the men's attention. "Excuse me, my girlfriend and I were just talking about hiring a boat to take us around for a bit. I don't suppose you're for hire."

I had to give him credit. He didn't even ask if they had a boat. He simply pushed forward as if it was a foregone conclusion.

"We might be," one of the men replied, turning serious as he glanced between us. "What did you have in mind?"

"Just a trip around Folly Beach," Jack replied. "In fact, if you're busy here, I wouldn't mind renting your boat and taking her out myself. I'm willing to pay whatever you're asking."

That's when I realized what he was doing. He wanted to come to a bar because he thought he could bamboozle drunken guys — the sort of guys who got plowed in the middle of the day — and convince them to hand over the keys to their boat. It was a bold move, but it wasn't going to work.

"We're not just going to let you take our boat," the second man said on a snort. "We're not idiots."

Jack faltered. "I'm willing to pay whatever you're asking."

"Perhaps you should buy your own boat then. Ours isn't for sale. If you want a ride tomorrow morning when we're sober, we'll take you. We don't go out while we're drunk. And we certainly don't hand over our boats to people we just met."

I tried to keep my smugness in check as I slid Jack a look. "So ... how do you feel about kayaks again?"

His expression was dour. "We'll go down to the beach and ask. The thing is ... I'm a little nervous about the kayaks. What if you fall in?"

"I'm good on a kayak."

"Yeah, but you're a trouble magnet. If something bad is going to happen on a kayak, it's going to happen to you."

Sadly, he wasn't wrong. "It will be fine." I was almost positive that was true. "Or, well, it might be fine. Let's give it a shot anyway."

FOURTEEN

We ended up renting kayaks after all. I was excited, but Jack was a nervous pile of goo after we changed and prepared to head out.

"Don't fall in," he warned as he gave me a light shove to get going.

I cast him an amused look over my shoulder. "I've kayaked before. I'll be fine."

"In the ocean?"

"No, but ... I'll still be fine." Something occurred to me. "Have you never kayaked before?"

Annoyance, quick and fast, colored his features. "I'm good."

"That wasn't really an answer." I struggled to keep my kayak in place as he settled into his. "If you don't want to do this because you're afraid ... ."

"I'm not afraid," he practically barked. "I'm athletic. How hard can this be?"

I pressed my lips together and faced forward. "Let me know if you need help."

He grumbled something under his breath that I couldn't make out, but within a few minutes we were well on our way. True to his word, his athletic ability helped him catch on fast. There was just one thing.

"I don't want to nitpick," I said when he drew even. "I really don't. I'm not one of those women who feels that's ever the way to approach things."

"But?"

"But you're using the paddle wrong." I felt like a jerk for pointing it out. "Flip it around. You'll get blisters on your hands if you keep using it that way."

Jack studied the paddle for a bit and then flipped it over, testing it. Instead of being angry about the shift in the effort he had to expend, he was subdued. "This is better."

"I'm glad."

"I'm also sorry for giving you grief. I just ... I'm not used to being the one who has to be taught something."

That was probably hard for him to admit. That didn't mean I was going to let him off the hook. "I bet there are loads of things I can teach you."

I didn't realize the statement could be construed as dirty until his lips curved and he shot me a flirty wink. "I'm looking forward to those lessons."

I was mortified. "I didn't mean ... um ... ."

"Oh, no." He shook his head, firm. "You can't take it back now. You said it. I expect a proper lesson this evening. I hope you have a good lesson plan ready."

My cheeks were on fire and it wasn't because of the sun. I forced my attention on the water and tried to pretend I hadn't said something so embarrassing. "The ghosts are this way."

Jack caught on quickly and within a few minutes, he was taking the lead. He definitely had athleticism on his side and I tried not to be bitter about the fact that he was suddenly better than me despite this being his first outing.

The brilliant sunshine made it difficult for me to find the ghosts. There were few landmarks — a few buoys here and there and the pier — but they weren't much help. After thirty minutes of fruitless searching, my frustration erupted.

"I don't understand."

"Calm down," Jack ordered as we took a moment to rest. He reclined in his kayak, his feet resting on top of the vessel, and closed his eyes. "This is nice. I love the smell of the ocean. I know that probably sounds weird, but I totally do. I think I would want to settle close to the ocean eventually."

The conversational shift threw me. "Are you planning to leave the Legacy Foundation?"

"No. I'm happy where I am right now. I don't foresee this being a forever job, though. I mean ... I like the travel for now. I especially like it now that you're with me, but I wouldn't mind a house of my own instead of a condo or apartment one day."

I hadn't given it much thought. I worked as hard as humanly possible while in school because I knew I had only one shot at getting everything I'd ever wanted. The Rhodes were hardly poor, and when they died they left enough money for me to attend school, but if I screwed up there would be no second chance. That meant my education was the most important thing. Once I found out about the Legacy Foundation that became my primary focus. I wanted to enjoy my accomplishment. But now Jack was making me think about other things.

"What would you do?" I asked finally, my eyes focused on the water as I tried to make out an ethereal form to direct us toward. "You probably have a lot of options. I'm not trained for much else than this."

When he didn't immediately respond I turned my head and found him watching me in such a way that I felt self-conscious. "What?"

"We'll figure it out," he said finally. "If you want to stay with the Legacy Foundation forever, we'll make it work. But don't sell yourself short. You're the most talented person I know. You can do whatever you want."

The sentiment in his eyes made me go warm all over. "That's a nice thing to say."

"I'm a nice guy."

His delivery made me laugh. "You are, even though when we first met you went out of your way to hide that fact. You put on a big show about being mean and brusque, but you're really a big marshmallow."

"I think I'm only a marshmallow for you. Everyone else who is terrified of me has earned it. Like Laura, for example. I don't think she believes I'm a big marshmallow."

That brought up another interesting topic. "Do you think she's trying to bring in a specific person to make our lives miserable? I mean ... she was pretty adamant when she made the request for another team member."

"Since it's Laura, I doubt she has good intentions. That said, if we had another team member we wouldn't ever have to deal with her. I've been trying to get Chris to fire her, but he won't consider it because of the number of complaints she's filed with Human Resources. He says it could lead to a lawsuit ... and nobody wants that."

"It's too bad she won't quit," I mused, something on the water catching my attention. I had to shade my eyes to get a better look.

"That would be the ideal outcome," Jack agreed. "She's smart, though. She knows how to play the game. She won't quit because then she won't get unemployment. In addition to that, she can't make our lives miserable if she willingly walks away and her whole reason for being these days seems to be to torture us."

He wasn't wrong. "I think I see something that way, over by the lighthouse. Can we check it out?"

He nodded. "We have the kayaks for another two hours. If this doesn't work, we'll have to arrange something on a boat even if it puts us in a precarious position. I don't see a way around that."

"You have the business card from those two guys," I pointed out as I started paddling. "They said they would take us out once they were sober."

"Yeah, but explaining what we're looking for — and why you're going to talk to thin air — is bound to make them suspicious. It would be better if we could just rent a boat."

"And why is that a problem again?"

"Because I need to use the Legacy Foundation insurance to cover us, and to get access to it I have to tell Chris what we're doing. That's not exactly high on my to-do list."

I could agree with him on that. "Well, maybe we'll luck out here."

We navigated the kayaks to the small island surrounding the lighthouse because it was too hard to keep them even in the current. When we beached on what was essentially a large square full of rocks, I immediately turned in the direction of where I thought I saw the ghosts ... and wasn't disappointed. "There." I pointed. "She's right there."

Jack moved to my side, his eyes alert as he scanned the area for signs of other people. "I think we're alone out here. Try talking to her."

"She's, like, thirty feet from the shore."

He shrugged, noncommittal. "She's a ghost, right?"

"Um ... yeah."

"Then she should have superhuman hearing."

"How do you figure that?"

"It's a fact ... that I just made up." He grinned as he prodded me forward. "Try. I don't know how we're going to get the kayaks to the spot they need to be and I'm not keen about swimming out there."

"The current is too much," I agreed. "We might get battered in the process. Unless ... maybe the water isn't that deep."

"What do you mean?"

"Does your phone work out here? Can you look up the history of the lighthouse? Maybe we'll get lucky and the water isn't that deep. We might be able to walk right out there."

Jack didn't look convinced, but he was game to try. He retrieved his phone, which he'd wisely wrapped in a plastic bag for the trip in case we tipped, and started searching.

"Sit down for a few minutes," he suggested, motioning toward the uncomfortable looking ground. "We can at least be comfortable while we look this stuff up."

I dropped next to him, pressing close to his side so I could see the phone screen. It wasn't cold, but the wind was strong enough it felt a good ten degrees cooler than it had when we set out. "Anything?"

"Hold your horses, baby." He grinned when I made a face and kissed my cheek. "Just let me look. I have service, but it's only one bar so it's taking a while."

That was to be expected, so I forced myself to feign patience.

"It's called the Morris Island Lighthouse," he started. "This base is timber piling and concrete, which could explain why it's so uncomfortable."

Ugh. That was such a man thing. "I'm more interested in the history of the lighthouse," I prodded. "Building supplies don't exactly blow up my skirt."

"Oh, is skirt blowing going to be part of the lesson you teach me later?"

And I was back to being embarrassed. I had no doubt he said it to shut me up so he could read. Frankly, I had it coming, so I kept quiet ... just barely.

"This was originally a much larger island," he said, suddenly all business. "It was constructed in 1876 and was approximately twelve-hundred feet from the water's edge. Further construction to protect the shipping lanes changed the current, though, which resulted in rapid erosion.

"It hasn't been manned since 1938 and was replaced in 1962," he continued. "Hurricane Hugo took out all the surrounding buildings in 1989, leaving just the tower." He glanced up. "That's kind of sad. I hate it when old buildings are basically abandoned."

And that was also a guy thing. "How shallow is the water?" I felt as if I was asking the question into a void.

He laughed at my response. "You are the most impatient woman." He playfully pinched my flank. "It says there's shallow water surrounding the island but it doesn't say how deep it gets or how fast. The only mention of the water depth I can find is from kayak enthusiasts."

"That means it's worth a shot." I was already on my feet and moving toward the edge of the structure. "I'll check it out. You wait here."

"Absolutely not." He caught me around the waist before I could plunge into the water. "Look around, Charlie," he chided, his lips directly next to my ear. "There's a bunch of marine life around here."

I followed his finger as he pointed. "Those are dolphins." My heart stuttered at the sight of the fins but I settled quickly. "They won't give us grief."

"No, but if dolphins are here, other marine animals probably are, too. I know you're not a fan of sharks. After what happened in Florida, neither am I."

My heart gave a small heave, but I held it together. "South Carolina hasn't had a fatal shark attack in a hundred and seventy years."

He pulled back to give me a long look. "How can you possibly know that?"

"I looked it up this afternoon when it became apparent we were going to have to take kayaks. I might come across as brash and stupid sometimes, but I most certainly don't want to be eaten by a shark."

"Well, that's at least something." He rolled his neck and stared at the water. "Do you know what kind of sharks are in the waters off Folly Beach?"

I didn't want to answer that question, but had no choice. "Blacktips, hammerheads, bull sharks, tiger sharks and lemon sharks."

He waited, as if testing me.

"And the occasional Great White," I added, sighing. "The odds of getting bitten by a shark are astronomical. Besides, I've already escaped one shark frenzy. It's not likely to happen again."

"Probably not," he agreed. "Some might say the odds of finding a girlfriend who can move things with her mind while psychically invading people's brains are slim, too."

He had a point. Son of a ... ! "I need to try, Jack." I couldn't back down. Not when we were so close. "It will haunt me — no pun intended — if I don't at least try."

"I wasn't suggesting we not try. I just thought there might be a better route."

"And what's that?"

"We'll go out on the same kayak."

I was confused. "How will that help?"

"I can keep us balanced and fight the current while you talk to the ghost. That way you don't have to split your focus and I don't have to worry. If something happens and I feel we're in too much danger I'll move us back to the island. Those are my conditions."

I wanted to argue, but he made sense. "Okay, but I don't want to hear any grief when I try to talk to her."

"I guarantee I won't give you a hard time about it."

IT TOOK US A MINUTE TO FIGURE OUT the logistics, but once we were on the water, my back pressed firmly to Jack's chest and his legs on either side of mine, it wasn't all that uncomfortable.

"To the right up here just a bit," I ordered as we closed in on the ghost. She didn't as much as look at me, her gaze fixed on the beach. As far as I could tell, she wasn't aware that I was even sharing the same world with her. "Excuse me?"

She didn't look down. Ah, well, it was probably time to go for it. There was nothing to lose.

"Um ... hi. I'm Charlie Rhodes. I'm with the Legacy Foundation and we're trying to figure out who killed you. I'm kind of curious about how you ended up stuck out here and I was hoping you would be able to explain it to me. You know ... help me help you."

Behind me, Jack shook with silent laughter and I had to tamp down my agitation.

"We want to help," I insisted. "There has to be a way for you to communicate with us."

The ghost continued staring at the beach. She was the paranormal entity and yet, to her it was as if I was the one who wasn't there.

"Anything?" Jack asked.

"No. She doesn't even look at me."

"Do you know which one she is?"

"I ... ." Honestly, that hadn't even occurred to me. "No. I can look her up when we get back."

He rested his chin on my shoulder and waited. "What do you want to do? We can wait here a bit longer if you want."

I didn't see where that would make much difference. "No. We can go back and get my kayak. I don't think this is going to work."

"I'm sorry."

I shrugged, doing my best to put on a brave face. "At least I tried. I … ." Whatever I was going to say died on my lips as the sound of a boat engine — extremely loud and close — assailed my ears.

Jack gripped me tighter as he looked to the east. There, a sleek speedboat had come to life from behind the lighthouse and was speeding in the opposite direction. It moved so fast I barely had a chance to register it before it was gone.

"Do you think it was there the whole time?" I asked.

"I don't know." Jack glanced over his shoulder to make sure we weren't about to take on any other surprises and then shook his head. "Did you catch the name? It was Knot something. Like Knot Sure or Knot Pure."

"I didn't. Sorry."

"It's okay." He rubbed his hand over my stomach. "We need to get you back to your kayak and then head to shore. I want to see if I can start a search for the boat name. I don't feel safe out here."

"Whoever that was might have nothing to do with us," I reminded him.

"Then why take off like that?"

"Maybe they were illegally fishing or something. They might not have seen us until just now and panicked."

"Maybe." He didn't look convinced. "We're going back anyway. You can't communicate with the ghosts and we need to think up a new plan."

I was a little shaky so I readily agreed. "Yeah. Let's get out of here. I'm sorry to have dragged you out for nothing."

"It wasn't nothing." He flashed a smile. "We spent a few hours together and you're going to teach me something fun tonight. How can I complain?"

I frowned. "You're not going to let that go, are you?"

"Nope."

I was afraid of that.

FIFTEEN

We showered and changed our clothes upon returning to the villa. When we made our way downstairs, the rest of the group was already assembled. One look at Laura's face, the smug smile tugging at the corners of her lips, and I knew I wasn't going to like what was to come.

"We thought we'd all eat together tonight," Chris announced. "That will allow us to catch up and share information."

I slid my gaze to Millie and found her scowling. She obviously didn't like the idea.

"Fine," Jack volunteered. "There's a barbecue place about two blocks away. We were thinking of that for dinner."

That was news to me, but I wasn't about to argue. The way my stomach growled I could've eaten just about anything.

"That sounds good." Chris nodded, obviously relieved. He must've assumed that Jack was going to argue. When it didn't happen, Chris was ready to agree with anything.

We walked to the restaurant because it was easier than navigating Folly Beach traffic. Once the sun started to set, the streets came alive with revelers.

"This must be a party town," I noted as I walked with Millie.

"Everyone is out drinking every night as if it's spring break or something."

She laughed. "It's a beach town. The bulk of the money coming in is from tourists. When they're on vacation, they want to cut loose and have a good time. That bar right there, it has a rooftop spot and serves alcohol in fish bowls. I mean ... what's not to like about that?"

She had a point. "Fish bowls?" I glanced over my shoulder, to where Jack and Bernard were walking and talking. He'd obviously overheard because he nodded. That meant there was a fish bowl in my future and I was looking forward to it.

"They're good drinks," Millie enthused. "Bernard and I had several last night."

THE BARBECUE PLACE WAS one of those wooden tables, open windows, wonderful smells places that beckoned me from the street. My stomach gave an appreciative growl and I practically skipped through the door.

It wasn't difficult to find a table because it was mid-week and I had a menu in my hand within two minutes. There was a moment of potential static when Laura tried to wedge herself between Jack and me to sit, but he edged her out with his hip and then pretended nothing had happened.

"I want ribs," he said without hesitation. "There's nothing better than southern ribs. I swear I dream about them sometimes."

I snickered in genuine amusement. "I don't know what to get."

"Ribs," Jack and Bernard said at the same time.

"It's considered rude if you don't get ribs at a barbecue place," Jack added.

I furrowed my brow. "Is that true?"

Mille snorted. "They're messing with you. Men like meat on bones. They can't help it. That's the caveman in them."

Jack growled, as if he was a caveman and grinned. He was in a surprisingly good mood. Of course, that was probably because he was about to eat barbecue.

"There's a sampler plate," I noted. "I think I might try that so I can get a little of everything."

From across the table, Laura wrinkled her nose. "They only have corn and beans for side items. That's not very healthy."

"No, but it will be fragrant," Bernard offered.

I couldn't stop from laughing as Laura made a face. "Who doesn't love beans?" I asked no one in particular.

"I don't," Laura snapped. "I hate all this food. I don't see why we couldn't have gone to the hotel restaurant. They had a bunch of good stuff."

"I saw what they were offering," Millie countered. "It was all tiny portions and expensive prices. I don't care about the cost, but I like bigger portions."

"Anyone who has ever seen your hips could attest to that," Laura muttered loudly enough that no one could miss the overdose of derision.

Millie shot her a dirty look as Chris cleared his throat in an attempt to rein in the conversation.

"Why doesn't everyone tell me about their day?" he suggested. "Let's start with Hannah."

It didn't surprise me that he went to her first. She really was the level-headed sort. She rarely participated in group meltdowns and she was the professional in the group.

"I got to go over the autopsy results for each of our victims," she announced. "There was a lot of interesting stuff in there, but I had to dig. They probably thought I wouldn't notice, but once I picked up on it I searched each file and it was definitely there."

"What are we talking about?" Jack asked, leaning back and stretching his legs out in front of him. "Were they poisoned? I thought there was no discernible cause of death."

"There isn't. That hasn't changed. It's not that organs failed as much as these women simply stopped breathing. It happened fairly quickly. The lungs didn't look taxed. The skin under the fingernails didn't turn blue. I've never seen anything like it."

"And yet you found something," I prodded. "What?"

"There's an unidentifiable compound in the blood of each woman," Hannah replied, leaning closer and talking in a conspiratorial whisper. "I'm not sure what it is, but I've sent samples to the lab in Boston. An extra set of eyes can't hurt."

"You must have an idea what we're dealing with," Jack pressed. "You wouldn't be this excited if you didn't have a hypothesis."

"I do," she confirmed. "From what I've been able to see under a microscope, it seems to have the same properties as a sleep aid ... not the ones you can buy over the counter. We're talking the narcotic type."

"They had narcotics in their blood?" I was beyond confused.

"As I said, I can't identify it ... at least not yet. I just know it has a lot in common with a narcotic sleep aid. That's all I can say with any certainty right now."

I ATE TO THE POINT I hated myself. Again. I didn't have much control over my hunger when faced with something delicious. Jack and Bernard had been right. The ribs were delightful. As was the brisket ... the steak ... the corn ... the beans ... and the slice of chocolate cake that was as big as my head.

We split up after dinner even though Laura had her full pout on. She suggested we go to the bar as a group but nobody was keen on the idea. Chris and Hannah went straight back to the villa. They weren't much for drinking. Bernard and Millie went to the Irish pub because they were having karaoke and Millie liked to get her sing on. Jack and I went to the rooftop bar so I could drink out of a fish bowl. And Laura? Well, she took off on her own. She didn't look happy when she disappeared.

"I kind of feel sorry for her," I admitted as I sipped my drink. It was huge and I didn't have the best tolerance. I couldn't even remember what I ordered. I just knew it was blue and tasted delicious. "She's cut out of the action and nobody wants to spend time with her."

Jack, who opted for a beer rather than a fish bowl, grinned as I stuck out my tongue and tried to catch my reflection in the mirror on the wall. "That's because she's not any fun."

"Lots of people aren't fun. Maybe she can't help herself."

"It's not just that she's no fun," Jack countered. "She's also mean and vindictive. She goes out of her way to hurt people in our group ... especially you. I won't put up with it."

"Yeah. She's a butthead sometimes." I pursed my lips, which were also blue, and regarded him. "I liked the barbecue. That was a good choice. I don't remember talking about it before you suggested it."

"That's because it didn't happen. I suggested it because I knew Laura wouldn't like it. She's the reason we all ate together in the first place. She demanded it and Chris felt caught."

I'd picked up on that myself. "You don't feel even a little bit sorry for her?"

"If she were a nicer person, maybe. She's brought all this on herself, and there's absolutely no way I'm going to sit around and let her torture you. I won't have it."

"Aw. That's kind of sweet."

His smile widened as I sipped again. "Are you drunk?"

I scoffed at the notion. "I haven't even finished one."

"But it's huge and you rarely drink. The few times I've been around you when you're drinking have involved some raging hangovers if you over-imbibe. I'm just looking out for you."

And because he was telling the truth it gave me pause. "I should probably only drink the one."

"It's up to you."

"You'll have to carry me back if I drink two."

"You're light."

"I need my wits about me tomorrow if we're going to figure out how to communicate with the ghosts."

His smile slipped. "Yeah, well ... I'm searching for boat names. I'm hopeful that will point us in the right direction. We need a break here because we're spinning our wheels trying to force the information we already have."

I leaned back so I could move my feet to Jack's lap under the table, causing him to arch an eyebrow. "I'm feeling pretty good. I'm thinking we should take advantage of the magical blue drink and head back to the villa."

His smile was impish. "Are you ready to teach me something?"

"Are you ready to learn?"

"Bring it on."

I WOKE IN A DREAM THAT somehow managed to be dark and sparkly at the same time.

I was self-aware. When I looked over I found Jack sleeping in bed, his arms wrapped around me, and I was dead to the world in his embrace.

I didn't know what to think as I stood next to the bed and watched us sleep. It felt somehow invasive even though that was ridiculous, at least on the surface. An uneasy wave washed over me as I tried to come to grips with what was happening ... and failed.

"You guys are kind of cute," Harley announced, appearing at the end of the bed. Her blond hair was a bright splash against the darkened room. "I was wondering if you were going to take the invitation I kept shoving into your mind. I was about to give up when you finally walked through the door I opened."

"You opened a door?" I was beyond confused. "Where are we?"

"We're one plane over from your world. That's why you can see yourself. This is the death plane. Souls often move on to this plane before dispersing. Your souls are still on your plane even though their minds are elsewhere."

"I don't understand."

"I'll show you." She gestured toward the sliding glass doors. "Come on. I promise you'll be safe."

I glanced back at Jack, an irrational bolt of fear coursing through me. "He'll be okay, won't he?"

"He'll be fine," she reassured. "So will you. There's absolutely nothing to worry about. Everything is under control. I promise."

I decided to take her word for it and followed her through the doors. She vaulted over the railing, causing me to race behind her and peer over the edge. She waved from the ground and prodded me forward. "Come on. You can't be hurt here because your body is back there. Just your consciousness is here. Trust me."

Because I did — I could see the truth written on her features whenever we crossed paths — I sucked in a breath and jumped over the railing. I didn't fall as much as float, landing on the ground without as much as disturbing the sand under my feet.

"That was weird," I noted, looking down. It was only then that I noticed I was wearing nothing other than one of Jack's shirts. "Oh, geez." I tugged on the bottom to make sure it was covering my rear end. "You could've let me get dressed."

Harley snorted. "Nobody cares what you're wearing. There's no reason to get worked up."

"Just show me what you want to show me. If Jack wakes up and I'm not there ... ."

"He'll freak out," Harley finished for me. "You are there. You're sleeping in his arms. He won't wake."

I watched as she kept striding toward the water, her feet moving on top of the waves as she trudged out to sea. She was walking on water. That was ... impossible. And yet I was intrigued enough to attempt the feat myself. It wasn't difficult in the least and the water felt solid under my feet.

"Well, this is ... neat."

Harley's laugh was light but loud enough to retain form over the breeze. "This way, please. We don't have much time."

It took us a full ten minutes to hike across the water. We didn't stop until we were in front of one of the ghosts. I recognized this one as Freya Debney. I'd looked at the photos when I got back to the villa. Just like the other woman close to the lighthouse, the one I later identified as Jenny Fields, she stared at the beach without acknowledging our presence.

"I need you to understand what's happening here," Harley started. "Even I wasn't sure until it was explained to me. This is a spell of some sort, dark magic from a different time. Somehow a creature managed to bring back magic that we all thought was dead."

I was taken aback. "How is that possible?"

"I have no idea. It's ... difficult to fathom." She poked at the ghost, her fingers going through the entity's transparent body. "From what I've been able to ascertain, only those who are magically strong can see them."

That didn't surprise me. "Isn't that how it normally is?"

"Sometimes," she hedged. "There are humans who live close enough to the line that they can see the dead. In fact, there are more of them than you might realize. You can see them because of your magic. It doesn't matter how sensitive a 'normal' human is when it comes to these women, though, because they're anchored here by a powerful totem."

"You mean that whatever creature did this managed to tie the fate of these women to a talisman of sorts," I mused. "That's actually good. If we manage to find the talisman we can destroy it and free them. The creature himself could be the talisman."

"In theory, that's true. I'm not sure how true it is in practice. I've never seen anything like this. My brethren are the same. Everyone I talk to is stymied."

"Could it be an incubus?"

She hesitated before answering. "Initially I thought you were looking in the wrong place. Now I have a different opinion. It's important that you realize there are two types of incubi. The first fell from the heavens and became demons. They're the most powerful. What we crossed paths with after were only half-blooded at best, monstrosities. They weren't pure of blood, so they weren't as powerful and were easily eradicated."

Slowly, what she was trying to say clicked into place. "You're saying that only one of the original incubi would be powerful enough to trap the souls of these women into a totem and anchor them here."

She looked relieved that I understood and she didn't have to delve deep into the mythology of a forgotten demon. "The creature doing this doesn't have a soul. I don't know if trapping these souls is an attempt to create one — it's happened in the past — or if we're simply dealing with a garden-variety sociopath who gets off on torturing them. If forced to choose, I would lean toward the latter."

"That makes sense." I studied the ghost. "Why can't she see us?"

"That's also part of the spell. She's essentially been trapped in a dark box. If you wish to communicate with her, the box must be removed."

"Any suggestions on how to do that?"

"I'm sorry, but ... no. That's out of the realm of my expertise."

"Well, great." I pressed the heel of my hand to my forehead. "This is just ... not good."

"Not at all," she agreed. "This isn't the first time this individual has done something like this. He's too powerful and his movements have been too deliberate. You might be able to track him down if you find previous incidents of mass death like this. He's too prolific to be a newbie."

"He has to be killed once we find him, right? There's nothing else that can be done."

"He definitely needs to be killed." Harley was firm. "You still have the coin I gave you?"

I nodded. "I carry it in my pocket."

"Good. If you find this creature, call me. I can have reinforcements to you in a matter of seconds. It's going to take a concerted effort to take him down. You can't do it yourself unless you pour absolutely everything you have into him. You need to know that's not necessary."

"You don't want me sacrificing myself for the greater good."

"I don't want you sacrificing yourself at all. It's a waste from where I stand because you have help. Think of that man back in your bed and how he'll feel if you fall. Be smart about this." She rapped my forehead, causing me to jerk back. "I like you. I think we're going to be good friends. But you have to survive to see that day."

"I won't do anything rash."

"That would be a nice change of pace."

I laughed, the sound low and ragged on the water. "You sound like Jack."

"There are worse people to emulate. Keep him close. He will try to sacrifice himself for you if he feels it becomes necessary. Call for help instead of taking it on yourself. You might seriously regret it otherwise."

Those were the last words she uttered. With a snap of her fingers, I was back in my bed, Jack snoring lightly beside me. The world was back as it should've been ... except for the tortured souls I saw glowing through the window. They were still out there and needed to be saved.

SIXTEEN

I slid into wakefulness in the morning. Jack was already up, his eyes on me, and he smiled when I managed to open my eyes.

"Morning," he murmured, pressing a kiss to my forehead. "How did you sleep?"

It was a standard question and yet the answer was anything but obligatory. "I had a visitor."

"In sleep?" He stretched a moment and then smiled. "Wait ... are you saying I stopped by for a dirty visit after hours? Good on me."

The things I had to tell him were serious, but I couldn't stop myself from smiling. "It wasn't that sort of dream. You were kind of there. At least at the beginning."

He listened with patience as I launched into the tale. When I finished, the smile flirting with the corners of his lips upon waking were completely eradicated. "Well, I don't like that," he grumbled, making a face. "Don't you think it's rude that she just took over your dream?"

I wasn't sure it was a dream. "She said I was one plane over. Maybe ... ." I couldn't finish the sentence.

His frown only grew more pronounced. "That's worse," he

muttered, running his hand over the back of my hair as he pulled me close. "I don't like that she can come in whenever she wants and take you from our bed."

Oh, well, that was a bit much. "I think that's kind of an exaggeration," I said. "She had something she needed to show me."

"The ghosts on the water."

"Yeah. They're trapped, too."

"You figured that out yesterday," he noted. "You didn't need her stealing into your head and taking you away when you were supposed to be resting."

His attitude was all kinds of surly. "Jack ... ." I squeezed his arm to offer reassurance. "I never left your side all night."

"Your head did."

"I guess it did in a way," I admitted. "In general, I wouldn't be okay with someone climbing into my brain and taking me for a ride. But in this case I think she was trying to do me a favor."

"What favor? If she knows what's going on, why doesn't she take this creature out?"

At least we were getting somewhere. Until recently, Jack would've dug his heels in and declared there was a human to blame until the bitter end. He'd obviously gotten over that. "They don't know what it is. They know certain things, but they don't have all the answers."

"Then they should stay out of people's heads."

He was adamant ... and kind of adorable. He had morning stubble and his hair was tousled in that fabulous way that men can carry off and women can't. My hair looked like bees had built a nest in it when I woke in the morning. He looked as if someone had spent two hours "messing up" his hair just so he could walk down a runway. It was a bit annoying really.

"I think she was trying to help," I offered. The last thing I wanted was to get into an unnecessary argument. He had a right to his feelings, but in this case I happened to believe they were misplaced. "She made me think about something."

"The fact that you left me behind?"

I ignored the dig. "Harley said that our killer was prolific and knew what he was doing. Every step this guy has taken has been a deliberate one."

"I would agree with that," Jack concurred. "What does that matter?"

"Because it seems to signify that we're not dealing with a novice. This is someone who has done this over and over. He's honed a system."

Jack stilled, understanding dawning on his handsome features. "Oh."

I grinned. "If you can find similar cases — and I'm assuming you can because you're a security wizard who amazes me on a daily basis — then we might be able to track specific names from area to area."

"That was a bit much." He tapped the end of my nose. "I only amaze you every other day. I need to rest occasionally. You're the one who amazes me daily. I mean ... you make up lesson plans and everything."

I offered up an exaggerated face. "That wasn't funny."

"It was a little funny." He grinned as he leaned in and kissed the corner of my mouth. By the time he relaxed his head on the pillow he was lost in thought. "It's a good idea. We need to put some parameters together for the search. I can start one before we head out for breakfast. I can also get the Legacy Foundation research team on it."

I balked. "Won't we have to tell them why we're looking if we do that?"

"No." He rubbed his thumb over the lines in my forehead, perhaps trying to smooth them. "We'll just say I came up with the idea. As you rightfully pointed out a few minutes ago, I'm a genius and probably would've come up with this idea eventually."

"Ha, ha, ha." I pursed my lips as I considered the conundrum. "You're probably right. I'm simply being nervous for no reason."

"You've got a right to be nervous. And just for the record, I think it's always a good idea for you to err on the side of caution when it comes to this stuff. The fewer people who find out the better."

"You don't think Chris would be excited to know?"

"Chris would be so excited he wouldn't be able to keep his mouth shut. He would want to parade you around like a science experiment on display. Chris is a great guy, but he doesn't always understand real-world ramifications. This is your life. Once that genie is out of the bottle, there's no putting it back in."

He had a point. "I don't particularly want to tell anyone else. Millie found out by accident and has been a good sounding board. As for you ... ." I hesitated a moment before continuing. "Well, as for you, I felt I needed to tell you because of what was happening between us, but I was terrified. I thought you might try having me locked up."

His eyes were filled with patience when they locked with mine. "I get you being afraid. In your place, I'd feel the same way. There was no chance I would've disbelieved you, though. I think, inside, I knew there was something going on from the start.

"Do you remember that night we camped together in Hemlock Cove?" he continued. "I thought there was something up with you then. I pushed it out of my mind. I told myself I was being ridiculous."

I chewed my bottom lip, unsure what I was supposed to say. Finally, I started. "Something did happen that night."

"I knew it!" He jabbed a finger in my direction. "Spill. Oh, and if you tell me you saw Bigfoot we're going to have a big problem."

I chuckled and dragged a hand through my hair. "I didn't see Bigfoot. At least ... I don't think I did. There was a shadow in the campground that night. I was terrified when I saw it because of the size. It could've been something else, like the human murderer we were dealing with.

"Anyway, I was so worked up by what I saw — you felt like you were a great distance away from me at that point and I was so afraid I couldn't find my voice — I used my magic and dropped a huge tree branch on whatever it was," I continued. "It took off into the woods."

"And then I woke up," he mused, taking on a far-off expression. "I knew something had happened, but I couldn't figure out what. You were flustered and didn't want to sleep by yourself. We spent the rest of the night in the same tent."

"And almost ended up in the same sleeping bag," I added.

He snickered in delight. "I remember. I was so embarrassed when I woke up and realized I was holding you. Now, looking back on it, I think it was always meant to be."

"That's sweet and a little weird to think about."

"It totally is," he agreed, leaning forward and giving me another kiss. "As for your visit from the friendly neighborhood crossroads demon, it's a good tip. I'll set up the search before we go to breakfast. If we're lucky, we might end up getting results in a few hours."

"What are the odds we'll get that lucky?"

He shrugged, noncommittal. "Never say never. I feel as if I've been getting lucky since I met you."

I laughed at his unintended double entendre. "Nice."

"Yeah. I thought you would like that."

CHRIS WAS IN THE KITCHEN FUSSING WITH his coffee. His hair was wet from a shower and he seemed unusually bright and alert for this time of day.

"You're up early," Jack noted as we moved toward the coffee machine. "Is there another body?"

That possibility hadn't even occurred to me and I found I was filled with dread at the prospect.

"No. At least not that I'm aware of. If another body is discovered while we're in town I've been promised a chance to be on the scene from the start. I haven't gotten a call, so I'm assuming that hasn't happened."

"Okay." Jack prodded me around Chris so I could grab two mugs. We were the sort of people who needed caffeine nearly as much as oxygen. "Then what's going on?"

"My uncle called," Chris replied, leaning his hip against the counter as he sipped from a generic plastic mug. "He's okayed the addition of another team member."

I was taken aback. "That was fast. Laura just suggested it and it's already been approved? That's ... wow."

Chris's smile was thin. "It's not the first time she's suggested it. She put in a formal request with Human Resources before we left town, even though she pretended otherwise. She's had this on her mind for some time."

"How do you feel about that?" Jack asked as he poured coffee.

"Listen, if you think I don't realize there's a problem with Laura, you're wrong." He lowered his voice. "She's not an easy individual."

"That's putting it mildly." Jack shook his head. "She's the most difficult person I've ever met ... and that's saying something because I served overseas for years and met actual warlords."

I shot him a quelling look. His disdain for Laura was growing with each passing day. I understood why he hated her. She went out of her way to make things rough for us and even threatened the foundation of our relationship. If one of us were removed from the team because of her complaints, things would shift dramatically in our personal lives.

The only one who wanted that was Laura.

"I think she's been having difficulty assimilating since I joined the team," I countered, choosing my words carefully. "She seems to have a specific problem with me."

Chris's expression was hard to read and then, out of nowhere, he started laughing. "Oh, that was a totally diplomatic statement. I see what you mean about her being unintentionally funny, Jack."

Jack arched an eyebrow when I pinned him with an accusatory look. "Right? She's hilarious." I tried to elbow him in the stomach but he was expecting it and easily sidestepped the attempt. "Calm down, Tiger. It's too early in the morning for wrestling."

I did my best to focus on the important topic. "Are you going to say something to Laura about going over your head?"

"I don't know." Chris looked troubled. For a guy who was always so happy and excited about the possibility of today being the day he proved the paranormal world existed, it was tough to see. "On one hand, I think that she should know I won't tolerate another instance of that. On the other, she seems to get off on attention, even if it's negative attention."

"I've noticed that, too." Jack carried his coffee to the table and sat. "Why can't we just fire her?"

"You know why." Chris's gaze was pointed. "We've had this discussion at least three times that I can recall. Human Resources is building a case, but doesn't have everything they need quite yet. It's important they be able to prove without a shadow of a doubt that Laura was in the wrong if the case ends up in court ... and with Laura at the center of things, it most certainly will end up in court."

I felt sorry for him. He looked momentarily lost as he considered the possibility. "This is my fault. If you hadn't hired me ... ."

I didn't get a chance to finish because Chris was already shaking his head and Jack was making a strange noise that reminded me of a feral cat.

"You're not the problem, Charlie." Chris was firm. "You've been a wonderful addition to this team ... and I'm not just saying that because you've managed to make Jack smile regularly. He was a real grump before you arrived and he often made life miserable for all of us, but you've offered much more than that to the team."

My cheeks colored with pleasure. "Oh, well, thank you."

Jack shook his head, amusement obvious as I tried to pull it together. "Do you know who we're bringing in yet?"

"Laura had someone in mind," Chris replied. "She already messaged the name to the selection committee. I haven't seen the specifics yet, but Uncle Myron says he doesn't have a problem with the hire. I just need to sign off on it."

"Do you think you will?" Jack asked. "I only ask because it seems to me that bringing on someone Laura sees as an ally might not be a good idea."

"I considered that," Chris admitted. "I've gone back and forth in my head. The thing I keep coming back to is that she might be easier to deal with if she doesn't feel so isolated. Either way, we can pair her with the new guy and not have to deal with her. I don't think that's necessarily a bad thing."

"I guess not." Jack didn't look convinced. "Does it make me petty that I simply don't want her to be happy?"

"Just a little," I teased. "When will you know about the new guy?"

"Not for a bit," Chris replied. "We have more important things to focus on right now. Although ... there is something I need to tell you, Charlie."

The change in his tone was enough to have my heart skipping a beat. The first thought that took over my mind, unbidden, was that I was being cut loose to make room for the new guy on the team. The mere thought made me sick to my stomach. "What's that?" I tried to sound relaxed, but my skin was practically vibrating.

"You'll no longer be the intern on the team with a new face coming in," Chris started.

Oh, geez. Here it comes. What was I going to do? How was I going to find another job? How would I manage to pay for the new apartment? Was I going to end up homeless?

"There's only one spot for an intern," he continued "You're being promoted to a full-time member of the team. The position comes with a significant raise, a 401(k), dental and a designated parking spot."

I stood there, rooted to my spot, and searched for the correct response.

"Charlie, now is the time to say 'thank you,'" Jack prodded.

That was enough to snap me out of my fugue state. "Seriously? I get ... all that?"

Chris nodded. "The raise goes into effect this week, so your next check should be a lot bigger. Human Resources is going to email all the specifics to you. I told them that was okay because we were out of town."

"That's great." My mouth was dry. "I ... um ... that's awesome."

Chris beamed at me. "I'm glad you're happy. I need to run upstairs and make sure Hannah is up. We have another full day ahead of us. I figured we would go to the hotel restaurant for breakfast and make plans for the day. Are you guys okay with that?"

"Yeah." Jack nodded, his eyes never leaving my face. "I have something I want to talk to you about anyway."

"Great. See you in a little bit."

I was still considering my good fortune when Chris left the room. Slowly, very deliberately, I focused on Jack. "Did you do this?"

He appeared surprised by the question. "What?"

"You were worried about me not having enough money. Did you pressure Chris into giving me a raise? If so, it's sweet, but I don't want a raise until I've earned it."

There was a momentary darkening of his eyes and I thought he was about to argue. Instead, he heaved out a sigh and shook his head. "I didn't bring it up. I'm not saying I wouldn't have brought it up eventually, but you didn't want me to get involved so I decided to take a step back."

"You maneuvered me into a different apartment," I reminded him. "That's not taking a step back."

"You're safer in that apartment, and I'm not sorry about that." His voice was firm. "As for this, I had nothing to do with it. You've proven your worth with this team. I wish you could just accept your accolades and enjoy it."

I let loose a shaky breath. "Do you promise you didn't have anything to do with this?"

He nodded. "I promise."

I thought my cheeks were going to split thanks to the wide smile taking over. "Then we should definitely celebrate. I can't believe I got a promotion." I threw my arms around his neck as he hugged me. "Is this the best day ever or what?"

"It's a great day. You deserve it."

I did deserve it. Things were definitely looking up.

SEVENTEEN

I was riding high on life after breakfast when Jack announced we were sticking close to the villa, at least for the morning. He had computer searches to run — multiple now that he had access to the Legacy Foundation researchers — and his morning was officially scheduled.

I wasn't great with computers, or searches for that matter, so my morning was wide open.

"I think I might run down to the street across from the hotel and check out some of the stores," I said. "There's one that has a big shark coming out of it."

He looked amused ... and also reticent. "You're going shopping? That doesn't sound like you."

"I don't really consider it shopping. I just thought I might look around. It's a cool area."

He pursed his lips. "You're not thinking of renting a kayak and going back out to the lighthouse, are you?"

Honestly, it hadn't even crossed my mind. That didn't mean I wasn't annoyed with the accusation. "Why would you assume that?"

"Because you have more guts than brains sometimes."

Well, I was officially offended. "Thanks for that."

He frowned. "Charlie, I don't want to start a fight. I just want you to be careful. I don't expect you to hang around the villa doing nothing today. That's not fair. I just don't want you finding trouble. After what happened in your dream last night … ." He left it hanging.

"I'm not going out on the water." That was the truth. "There's nothing I can do out there. It would be a waste of time and not nearly as much fun without you, despite the way this conversation is going."

The sigh he let loose was long and drawn out. It reminded me of my father, who often got frustrated when he thought I was being flaky or evasive. "Fine. Have fun downtown."

"I will." I grabbed my purse from the counter. "If you're lucky, I might buy you a souvenir even though you're being a butthead."

His lips quirked. "If it's a coconut bikini for you to wear, I'm all for it."

"Ugh. That's so perverted. Why does that turn men on?"

"It's built into our DNA." He leaned forward and gave me a kiss. "Do me a favor and try to stay out of trouble, okay? If you feel something is amiss or there's danger of some sort, call me." He gestured toward my phone. "I'll come running."

He always did. It was both a relief and annoying at the same time. "I'll be fine. It's the middle of the day."

"If we were talking about someone else, I'd agree. You, however, seem to draw trouble like laundry with a profound case of static cling."

It sounded like there should be an insult wrapped up in that, but I decided to let it go. "I'll text you regular updates of my movements. Will that make you happy?"

"Actually, it will."

"Then we're both happy."

"Absolutely."

DOWNTOWN FOLLY BEACH WAS A TOURIST'S wet dream. As far as I could tell, they had something of a system for the commercial development. Restaurant, bar, kitschy shop, coffee shop. Rinse and repeat. It made me laugh and I found I liked it.

Because the store with the shark going through the sign made me laugh, that was my first stop. I bought a shirt for Jack that featured a cartoon shark chewing on a sign and then moved to the Black Magic Cafe for coffee. The decor was right up my alley and I took my coffee to the back patio, where a sign warned (in no uncertain terms) that computers and tablets were not allowed.

"Well, that's welcoming," I muttered as I gripped my phone. "Can I text on this here?" I asked the waitress who was passing by.

She looked amused by the question. "Most people don't bother asking."

"I like to follow the rules." Mostly, I silently added. Oh, who was I kidding? I was just trying to figure out if I should be furtive when texting Jack with annoying updates.

"You're fine. It's a wi-fi thing," she explained. "We don't have a problem if you sit here and text while drinking your coffee. It's the people who try to take over the tables for hours after spending only five bucks who are the problem."

That actually made sense. "Thanks."

Once she was gone, I texted Jack my first update. I took a photo of my coffee and the cutesy little patio and sent it to him with the message, "Wish you were here." I didn't expect him to text back, but he did within a few seconds.

I already miss you.

I'm embarrassed to admit that I went warm all over. He had that effect on me. In fact, he was the one and only person who had ever had that effect on me. It was interesting to think about, which I didn't because my stomach occasionally reacted with uncomfortable butterflies when I did.

The waitress returned a few minutes later to check on me. "Do you need anything?"

I shook my head. "I'm good for now. Thank you."

"Sure." She moved to the far end of the patio and pulled a cigarette out of her apron. "Don't tell anyone," she warned with an admonishing finger.

I had to laugh. "Your secret is safe with me."

After lighting up, she exhaled in a way that told me she might very well enjoy the nicotine more than sex. "I'm Clara, by the way."

"Charlie." I watched her for a moment, debating. Ultimately, I decided to go for it. She seemed the sort of woman who had her finger on the pulse of the community ... at least the part of the community I was interested in. "Have you heard about the dead girls?"

As far as opening lines went, it wasn't my best. Clara struck me as the sort who preferred when people were upfront with her, though. I wasn't wrong.

"Yeah. That's all anyone talks about. Business owners want to bury the news, but the workers are afraid."

"What are they saying?"

Clara fixed her eyes on me, curious. "Are you a cop?"

"Do I look like a cop?"

"You look like your standard hipster. But there's something about you."

"I'm with a group helping with the investigation," I admitted, seeing no reason to lie. "But I'm not a cop."

"What sort of group?"

Most people didn't ask that question. Certain assumptions were made when you said you were helping with an investigation. Most people let it go at that point.

I hesitated ... and then remembered the name of the establishment I was visiting. "We look into the paranormal aspects of certain cases."

She barely blinked. "People have been talking about that, too. They say we have an evil creature on the loose."

"What sort of evil creature?"

"Vampire is what everyone is saying, but I think that's just because of the window thing. The cops say the houses were locked but the windows were open. That just screams vampire. Nobody's said anything about marks on the neck, though. I think that would've leaked."

I liked the way her mind worked. "There are no marks on the bodies at all."

"Is it true the women were raped?"

"Um ... ." Hmm. That was a trickier question. "It seems that sexual contact might be involved. I don't know too much on that front. I'm sorry."

"It's okay." She waved off the apology. "I get it. I don't believe it's a vampire."

"What do you think it is?"

"I don't know. Something else." She took another long drag on the cigarette. "People are afraid. Nobody is going anywhere alone after dark, especially those with dark hair." Her gaze was appraising when it slid back to me. "You should probably be careful."

I chuckled hollowly. "Oh, you don't have to worry. I have a bodyguard."

"Where is he today?"

"Running searches. He won't tolerate me being gone for long, though, no matter how he pretends otherwise. He's all for female empowerment ... unless he feels something bad is about to happen. I try not to take it personally. He means well."

"He sounds like a good guy."

"He is. I ... ." I trailed off, my eyes automatically moving to the other side of the street to track movement. There, to my utter surprise, Brock Wilson was cutting down an alley behind a restaurant. He seemed to have a clear destination in mind and didn't as much as glance in my direction

"Well ... that's weird."

Clara followed my gaze. "You know him?"

"Kind of. Do you?"

"He's a familiar face. I don't think he works here as much as lives down here."

Oh, well, that was interesting. I hadn't considered that. What if Brock was our culprit and he hunted in Charleston proper because he assumed it would be easier pickings and discarded his victims in Folly

Beach so he could enjoy his handiwork? It was definitely worth considering.

"I have to go." I was already on my feet. The gate leading away from the patio was closed but that didn't stop me from heading toward it. "The coffee was great. I'll definitely be back."

Clara watched me with a mixture of amusement and concern. "You might want to call your bodyguard if you're going to chase that guy. He's bigger than you."

I had no intention of doing that. "I'll be fine. Thanks again."

BROCK HEADED STRAIGHT FOR THE BEACH. He cut around the hotel and headed toward the pier, veering at the last second to a sandy spot where he had a clear view of a group of women spread out on a blanket and happily laughing about ... whatever they found amusing.

I studied them for a moment to see what had piqued his interest and immediately zeroed in on the brunette at the center of the action. Her hair was a dark, chestnut brown and she had a heart-shaped face. She was dressed in a relatively modest bikini, especially by today's standards, and she seemed to be having a good time with her friends.

I picked a spot in the shade of the restaurant balcony that happened to be located at my back and lowered myself to the sand. Given the brightness of the sun and my dark clothing, Brock would have to be really looking — or have superhuman sight, which wasn't out of the realm of possibility — if he wanted to see me. From there, I simply watched.

He was a fascinating specimen of a ... well, I had no idea. It was possible he was a simple man, of course. The fact that he kept showing up made me more suspicious. He had a blanket with him and he spread it out, as if he was simply a single man who wanted to enjoy a few hours of peace and quiet on the beach. He had a book, but I couldn't read the cover from my location. Finally, I used my phone to zero in and then almost choked when I realized it was a book about female empowerment. Obviously he was trying to use the book as a way to lure the women. Why, though? That was the question.

I settled in and texted Jack. I told him I was on the beach enjoying the sun. I didn't mention Brock, which made me feel slightly guilty, but I knew he would abandon everything and come running if I told him, and I still wasn't sure what I was dealing with. Besides, a quick glance up and down the beach told me there were plenty of people present. He wasn't going to attack out in the open like this. If he was an incubus, he hadn't survived this long by acting like an idiot. No, this had to be a scouting mission. It was the only thing that made sense.

He watched the women for a good thirty minutes before he even made an attempt to approach them. When he did, it was with a bright smile. Because of the wind, I couldn't hear what he said. In a surprising move, though, he directed his attention to the blonde on the corner of the blanket rather than the brunette in the center of things. I figured that was because he didn't want to make it obvious which woman he was stalking. Besides that, Clara had made it clear that everybody was on the lookout for a guy who paid an inordinate amount of attention to brunettes. He could simply be trying to ease their suspicions. It would be the smart way to go.

The blonde looked up with polite interest and said something back to Brock. There was no intrigue in her demeanor. Whatever he said didn't exactly flip up her skirt. She was calm and pleasant ... and utterly uninterested.

That didn't stop Brock. He plopped himself down on the edge of the blanket and started chattering away. He seemed animated, as if he was expounding on the nature of the universe and he had some unique knowledge. He used frequent hand gestures.

The women weren't impressed. There were five total, and two of them shot each other so many eye rolls they could've fueled a middle school for a full year. It was obvious they didn't appreciate the interruption. I had legitimate sympathy for their situation. They were trying to have a good time, just their little group, and they were being hunted. Did they realize? I had no doubt they understood that Brock was trying to hit on a member of their group. There was an underlying danger that they didn't seem aware of, though. To them, he was just an annoying guy who didn't have a shot. They didn't appear fearful.

Which left Brock. Did he realize they were disdainful? Did he really think he would be able to entice one of the women into isolating herself from the group and disappearing with him? Why did he even think that was a good idea? If something happened to that woman, he would be the first suspect.

I had so many questions and zero answers. It was frustrating.

Brock continued talking for a good twenty minutes. Most of the women stopped listening. The blonde, though, the one he first approached, continued to feign interest. It wasn't because she was attracted to him. Anyone could've picked up on the "stay away from me" vibes. Well, anyone but Brock. He simply kept talking.

And talking, and talking and talking.

I was growing bored when I noticed a subtle shift in the interaction. The other women remained uninterested in Brock. The one he focused his full attention on had turned her body so it was leaning toward him. Suddenly she was attentive and hanging on his every word.

My heart did a long, slow roll. Was this how he operated? Did he make initial contact, woo them with some sort of magic, and then cut them loose until he could enter their private domain under the cover of darkness? That had to be it. There was no other explanation for the change in the woman's demeanor. She'd simply been uninterested one moment and engaged the next.

He'd clearly done something.

Brock got to his feet and extended his hand. The woman didn't hesitate to take it. She was on her feet and staring into his eyes, her friends all but forgotten.

My heart pounded in my ears. Was he seriously going to remove this woman from the beach when there were so many witnesses? It certainly looked that way. And why was he changing his target now? Why go for a blonde when it had been brunettes? Was that just a coincidence after all? Was he willing to move on anyone who showed interest? Perhaps the pressure from law enforcement and women acting in their best interests to protect themselves had made it so he had no choice but to deviate.

I craned my neck in an attempt to hear what they were saying, but they were too far away. It was possible they were having a friendly conversation about the weather ... but I knew that was wrong. When Brock looked like he was about to lead the woman away, I made up my mind and hopped to my feet. I had to stop this from happening.

"Hey, Brock!" I yelled his name and vigorously waved my hand to get his attention.

He narrowed his eyes when he glanced in my direction and I didn't miss the look of absolute disgust that crossed his face. He was surprised to see me ... and less than happy.

"I thought that was you." I took two strides in his direction to let him know this wasn't a drive-by "how are you" conversation. I had a purpose and I wouldn't break from it. "I didn't realize you spent time out here, what with working at the aquarium and everything. I would've thought you would live closer to your place of business. The traffic must be murder for you during rush hour."

I was babbling. That was a regular occurrence for me, though, so I went with it.

"What are you doing out here?" he asked finally.

"Actually, I was hoping to talk to you." That wasn't true until he showed up out of the blue, but I didn't want to give him the chance to escape. "I have a few questions."

He nodded, as if in acquiescence, took a large step toward me and then veered to his left ... hard. Before I could even register what was happening he'd broken into a run and was racing away from me. More importantly, he was running away from the blonde.

She looked annoyed.. "What did you do?"

I ignored her and remained rooted to my spot for a moment. Then, like a total idiot, I gave chase. It seemed the thing to do. When a murder suspect — okay, possible demon — runs from you, it's necessary to give chase. Those are the rules.

Yeah. Jack wasn't going to buy it either.

EIGHTEEN

I could run. It was a habit I got into in middle school when my father drilled me about what I should do if someone unsavory approached me. He often couched the lessons with, "Look out for random perverts on the street," but I knew what he was really worried about. His fear was that someone would come looking for me, whether family or random evil doer. He was terrified of both and transferred that mindset to me.

So I started running track in middle school, made the varsity team as a freshman, and continued running throughout college. I didn't win any medals, but I could put on a good burst when I needed to ... and I clearly needed to today.

Brock had the benefit of knowing the area, but I had magic. I used it now, illuminating a trail to follow. All I had to do was keep my head down and run — the magical footfalls would guide me.

Brock didn't make it far. He cut down an alley, and I could see clearly where the footsteps ended. There was a large dumpster in that exact spot and I knew he was crouching behind it. I remained rooted where I was, debating, and then I whipped out my phone. I didn't want to be the idiot who got herself killed because she was chasing a lead and didn't tell anyone.

No way was that going to be me.

Brock showed no signs of moving — he probably thought I was confused and would turn around and leave — so I put a little thought into my text. I typed it three times, erasing each version before landing on something that I hoped would keep Jack if not calm, at least together.

I found Brock. He ran from me. He's hiding behind a dumpster in the alley behind Rita's. I'm waiting for you.

It probably wasn't my best literary effort, but it was better than my first try ... and the second. The third was arguably better, but it was a wall of text and I would've already taken down Brock by the time he'd finished reading it. At least this way he would be on his way before I beat the incubus to within an inch of his life.

I sent the message and pocketed my phone, sucking in a calming breath before speaking. "I know you're behind the dumpster."

He didn't respond, but I didn't miss the light shuffling of feet. He thought he'd outsmarted me. Obviously I wasn't going to allow that to happen.

"I texted Jack. He's on his way."

That did it. I knew it would. I might not be a formidable opponent — at least on the surface — but Jack was all alpha jock and it was obvious he could take down a full-grown man without breaking a sweat.

Brock poked his head out and glared at me, his distaste with the scenario evident. "Oh, hello."

"Seriously? Are you going to pretend that you were just hanging around behind that dumpster and I just happened to stumble across you?"

"I have no idea what you're talking about." He squared his shoulders and adopted a haughty tone. "I'm walking for exercise."

"Behind a dumpster?"

"I ... you ... I only came here because I was afraid for my life."

"You were afraid for your life?" This guy. Geez. "From who?"

"You. You were chasing me like a madwoman, waving a gun around and threatening my life."

I glanced down at my empty hands. "What gun?"

"That one over there." He pointed toward a spot behind my shoulder and started running again in the opposite direction.

I wasn't stupid enough to look — I hadn't fallen for that trick since I was seven, for crying out loud — and gave chase. This time he didn't have as much of a lead on me as before and I caught him at the end of the alley. Without thinking, I heaved myself at him and tackled him hard to the pavement. He absorbed the bulk of the blow, letting loose an unearthly screech that reminded me of an angry fourteen-year-old girl and then started whimpering.

"Get off me!" He tried to buck me off but I had him pinned with my weight. Jack had been teaching me self-defense moves for more than a month because he wanted to make sure I could take care of myself. He started before he learned the truth about me and then switched tactics when he realized I had magic at my disposal. It was the magic that came in handy now.

"I don't think so." I charged my elbow with a powerful magical bomb and slammed it into his back, causing him to yelp as I pressed him harder into the pavement. All of the fight went out of him when I pinned him. "I feel like a professional wrestler."

I was feeling proud of myself ... right up until the moment Jack arrived.

It took him only four minutes, which was fairly impressive. His hair was windblown, his eyes wild, his cheeks flushed with color, and there was mayhem etched across his handsome face. He pulled up short when he saw us ... and then took an involuntary step back.

"What ... ?" He didn't finish the sentence. There was no need.

"I caught him." I beamed at my boyfriend. "He tried to run and I tackled him. I used that elbow move you showed me and now he's crying. It was awesome."

Jack worked his jaw, clearly struggling with a bit of inner turmoil. Finally, he strode forward and nudged me away with his hip as he grabbed Brock under the arms and flipped him over.

It wasn't a pretty sight. Brock's cheek was marred from the pavement, his eyes wide and unfocused, and he was muttering something that I couldn't quite make out. It sounded a lot like, "Please don't hurt me."

"What did you do to him?" Jack asked finally, pushing his hair back from his eyes.

"Just what you told me. I tackled him, and when he tried to dislodge me I put my elbow in his back and pile-drived him to the pavement."

Jack's lips twitched and I realized he was trying not to laugh. "Did you do anything else to him?"

"Nothing worth noting." Even though Brock was clearly out of it I knew better than talking about magic in front of him. "I thought he would be harder to take down."

Jack was clearly thinking the same thing, because he nudged Brock's foot with his shoe and then focused his full attention on me. "Can you do me a favor and buy a bottle of water and maybe get some napkins so we can clean him up?"

"Sure." I started to move toward the street, but he stopped me by calling out.

"By the way, baby, excellent job." He flashed an enthusiastic thumbs-up, which caused the giddy feeling that had been washing over me earlier in the day to return.

"It was pretty awesome, wasn't it?"

"Definitely."

BY THE TIME I RETURNED, BROCK was sitting on a bench and glaring at Jack. He at least seemed somewhat aware of his surroundings, which was a bummer because I wanted to preen a bit longer for Jack's benefit without an audience.

Ah, well. I'd already had one heckuva day.

"Here." I handed the bottle of water and stack of napkins to Jack. "I stole the napkins because they said I had to buy food if I wanted them, but I'm not hungry."

"I should think not." Jack cracked open the bottle and wet some of the napkins before moving closer to Brock, who had the good sense to cringe and turn away. "I'm not going to hurt you unless you make me."

"Oh, really?" Brock drawled. "That one tackled me like a rugby player on steroids. She's a menace." He jabbed his finger in my direction. "I'm going to report this assault to the police. You're going to be locked up."

"You were the one running," I reminded him.

"Because you were chasing me!"

"Nuh-uh." Now it was my turn to wag a finger. "You knew I saw you preying on that woman and that's why you ran. Admit it."

Brock shook his head. "Preying? You make me sound like a killer, which is why I ran. I knew what you were doing, hiding in the shadows like that. You were looking for someone to pin these murders on and you decided on me. That's why you ended up on the same tour as me yesterday and that's why you followed me today."

I planted my hands on my hips, incensed. "I have news for you, buddy, I wasn't following you. I just happened to stumble upon you when you were hunting. Admit it."

"Whatever."

I adopted the expression my mother had used throughout my entire childhood to get me to fess up to a wrong even though I knew I would be punished in the aftermath. "Admit it."

Jack did a double-take and then quickly looked away. I had the distinct impression that he was trying not to laugh.

Brock, thankfully, had the opposite reaction. He jutted out his lower lip and burst into tears.

"Oh, man." Jack made a face and lifted his eyes to the sky. "Why are you crying? Dude, you're embarrassing all of us."

"She's mean," Brock complained, wiping his cheek with the back of his hand. "I thought she was cool, energetic and fun when she was at the aquarium. I was even going to ask her out until I realized she was with you. She's the sort of girl I dream about ... one who doesn't spend all her time looking in the mirror and trying to tear down others."

I flashed a small smile. "Oh, that's kind of nice."

His eyes darkened. "I'm starting to think the other type of woman is better."

"Whatever." I flopped on the bench next to him, internally laughing at the way he cringed from me. He wasn't exactly stalwart for a demon. I expected more. "Why did you switch up your hunting method? I would've thought for sure that the brunette with that group was more your speed."

"I wasn't hunting. Stop saying that."

"Oh, come on." I'd had enough of his denials. "You followed us yesterday because you wanted to know what we were doing, if we were close to catching you. Today you went hunting and I just happened to see you.

"I mean ... I watched you," I continued, warming to the topic. "Those women thought you were the dullest blade in the drawer. Then you fixated on the blonde. The rest tuned you out and rolled their eyes whenever they thought you weren't looking, but all of a sudden the blonde was all warm for your form.

"You're a demon and I know it." I folded my arms across my chest. "Just admit it."

Instead of owning up to his misdeeds, Brock's mouth dropped open. "A demon? I'm a ... demon?" He flicked his eyes to Jack. "Is she crazy? Is that why you keep her so close? It's because she's crazy, right?"

Jack looked hesitant to answer.

"I'm not crazy," I snapped. "You cast a spell on that woman today. I know it."

"I didn't cast a spell. Although ... I guess I kind of did. It was with words, not magic. I mean ... magic isn't real, you moron. It's make-believe. What I did today was skill."

I was about to land the insult to end all insults when Jack raised his hand to still me. "What was skill?" he asked.

"What I did with the woman. Her name was Jennifer, by the way, and she was totally hot for me. Do you want to know why? Because I lied about owning the aquarium.

"Look, I know I don't have game," he continued. "I'm not ugly, but

I'm not handsome like you. I can't land women just by taking off my shirt and flexing. I have to use other means. That's why I tell them I own the aquarium. I wait until they're already bored with the conversation to slip that in.

"Then, like magic, all of a sudden they're interested in me," he explained. "That's when I mention I can get them in to feed the rays. Women go freaking crazy for the rays."

Uh-oh. A sense of dread pooled in the pit of my stomach. I was starting to suspect I'd made a grave mistake. "But ... what about the jail yesterday?" I wasn't quite ready to let it go. "You were following us."

"No, I was there because it's easy to pick up tourists on that particular tour. The type of women who want to see ghosts at the jail are the same ones who want to feed the rays. I know it sounds unlikely, but I get a lot of action because of this story. I mean ... we're talking two to three women a week. They practically fall into my lap."

I looked to Jack and found him watching me with amused eyes. "I think I might've jumped the gun."

"I think so. Still ... you handled yourself well and nobody was hurt."

Brock gestured toward his face. "Nobody was hurt? Um ... hello!"

"Nothing important was hurt," Jack corrected, extending his hand for me. "As for you, Brock, go ahead and file a complaint with the police. When you do, Charlie will explain how the missing girls have gotten her worked up and she saw you acting oddly. The cops won't do anything in that scenario."

"Really? What about when I mention the demons?"

"What demons? I never heard mention of demons until you brought up the topic."

Brock's lips curved down. "You guys are kind of jerks."

"You're better off letting this go. Trust me."

JACK WAS QUIET FOR THE WALK back to the villa. I expected him to unload when we strode through the front door, but instead he returned to his computer.

"If you're going back to the beach, you should put some sunscreen on," he noted. "Your cheeks are a little pink."

I was stunned. "That's it? You're not going to yell?"

"Do you want me to yell?"

"No, but usually you can't seem to help yourself. I think it's part of your genetic makeup."

He chuckled and shook his head. "I'm not going to yell because, in this particular case, I think you handled yourself well. I wish you had texted me earlier, but you took care of yourself and that's the most important thing. I'm proud of you."

Well, that was just a kick in the keister. "Huh." I threw myself in the chair at the edge of the room and watched as he went back to typing. "I can't believe you're just going to let it go like that."

"I like to think I'm growing."

"I guess so." I watched him for a full two minutes before I spoke again. "Have you found anything?"

"A few things actually." His smile was firmly in place when he lifted his chin. "I've found three similar patterns, in Boston, Atlantic City and Virginia Beach."

I straightened. "Boston. How can that be? We would've heard about it."

"It was months ago, right around the time you joined the team, and in a city the size of Boston things like that get swept aside relatively quickly. It's not as big of a deal in a city with a denser population."

"But ... ." I ran the idea through my head. "Was that the order? Boston to Atlantic City to Virginia Beach?"

"Yeah."

"So, he's moving south."

"Yes. They're all coastal towns. I think the idea that our guy might work in the shipping industry is dead on."

"What about names?"

"I haven't gotten that far yet. It's going to take a lot of time to cross-reference people who were in those cities at the time of the murders and who are now in Charleston. We're not going to have change-of-address forms. This is a migratory individual."

"Right." It seemed daunting to think about. "Are you going to run Brock?"

"I am, but I'm guessing what he told us today is true. He's not a murderer. He's a tool."

"I'm not sorry I tackled him." Truthfully, I was a little sorry. He was going to be sore for days. "He shouldn't have run. Everybody knows that only the guilty run like that. It wasn't my fault."

"Of course not."

I pinned him with a glare. "You're laughing at me. Maybe not on the outside, but you're laughing."

"I happen to think you're adorable. What you did today ... it's a great story. I would prefer you not do it with the actual incubus, though. I'm glad you got it out of your system."

"You're still laughing."

"Only because you're adorable."

"Go ahead and stick to your story."

"I plan to."

We lapsed into amiable silence and then something occurred to me. "What about the ghosts? You said there were similar murders, but are ghosts anchored in the water there?"

"There's no way for me to check that, Charlie. I can't very well ask a law enforcement source about ghosts."

"No." I chewed my bottom lip. "Someone must know."

"I don't think there's anyone we can contact to check that for us. I mean ... who? We don't have anyone to ask."

I wasn't so sure of that.

NINETEEN

Because we'd been stuck in the villa for most of the day, Jack suggested it was a good idea to head downtown. Alone. I wasn't in the mood to explain to the others what had happened with Brock, so I was more than ready to escape.

Laura sneered on the couch as she read the report Jack filed with Chris right before our departure.

"Well done, Charlie," she sang out. "You beat the crap out of the town douche. Way to go." She shot me a sarcastic thumbs-up, causing my cheeks to burn hot.

"It's a great story," Mille countered, her gaze predatory when it pinned Laura. "She took down a full-grown man and potentially protected a woman in the process. How is that a bad thing?"

"He wasn't our killer."

"No, but he could've been. I'm proud of how Charlie reacted."

"So am I," Chris offered, his attention on the other reports Jack had provided. The moment Jack told him that he'd found a pattern of similar murders in coastal towns, Chris was enamored with focusing on that for the evening. "She did us all proud today. I'm going to make sure she gets a bonus."

Surprise rolled over me. "A bonus?"

He glanced up and nodded. "We have good citizen bonuses. You were trying to save an innocent woman. That's good PR for us when it works out. We won't get any public accolades for what happened today, but you put yourself on the line and I think that should be rewarded."

Seriously, I needed to buy a lottery ticket. This day was like the best ever. I slid my eyes to Jack to make sure this wasn't some elaborate hoax. His expression was full of annoyance rather than excitement.

"Charlie might've been a hero today and made all of us proud, but she still could've been hurt," Jack pointed out. "She deserves her bonus, but maybe it should come with a reminder that she's not replaceable and needs to be more careful."

My smile slipped. "I thought you weren't going to yell."

"That wasn't yelling. That was a simple suggestion."

"And a good one," Chris said. "Charlie, you're an outstanding citizen. Don't die on us."

"Unless you really want to," Laura groused.

Jack shot her a death glare and then prodded me toward the door. "We're heading downtown to eat. I don't know when we'll be back."

Chris offered up a haphazard wave. "Take your time. You did a lot of work here — both of you — and I greatly appreciate it. I'll be going through this information for hours. Hey, maybe we should order pizza and do it as a team."

The look Laura shot him was withering. "Maybe we shouldn't."

JACK WAS SEEMINGLY IN A GOOD MOOD for the drive downtown. We parked in a garage and then hit the sidewalk, a multitude of restaurants vying for our attention.

"What do you want?" I asked.

"I've done more than my share of picking the last few days. You pick. I'm open for anything."

That sounded like a trap. "Sure. How about sushi?"

He frowned. "I don't like sushi."

"So ... you're not really open for anything?"

He glowered at me and then shook his head. "I know you're annoyed about what I did regarding the bonus, but I'm not sorry. You were strong and brave today, Charlie. We got lucky. If something had happened to you ... ."

"It didn't. I can protect myself. I think I proved that today."

"With a little weasel who has to lie to women to get laid. You thought he was the incubus when you started chasing him. That could've ended badly. I doubt a demon would've gone down that easily."

He said the last part loudly enough that he drew the attention of a woman passing by in the opposite direction. I shot her a small smile, as if to say "he's crazy but I have to put up with him because he's my ride," and proceeded to push him down the sidewalk.

"I'm glad you're feeling more comfortable in my world right now, but you've got to take it down a notch," I insisted. "You're getting belligerent."

"How do you know this isn't my normal state?"

"Because I've seen you in action. You're usually calm and collected. Today you were a bit ... tattletale-y."

His eyes widened. "I'm not a tattletale."

"Today you were."

"I had to tell him what went down, Charlie. If Brock decides to file a lawsuit, Chris has to be made aware. I think the odds of that are slim because any lawyer worth his license will explain that's a losing proposition given the fear in this community right now, but it's still possible."

I hadn't considered that. "Oh."

"I wasn't being a tattletale."

"Okay. Sorry."

"Freaking tattletale," he muttered and poked my side. "I'll make you pay for that later."

WE SETTLED ON A RAW OYSTER BAR. The menu offered a wide

variety — including scallops and shrimp — and the ambiance was light and romantic. That seemed to be what both of us wanted.

"Shall I start you off with an oyster appetizer?" the waitress — her name tag read Blanche — asked with a cocked head. Her interest had been solely on Jack since she arrived at the table to take our orders.

"Why not?" Jack replied after a beat. "We'll have the oysters, the stuffed mushrooms and the mozzarella sticks as appetizers. I want the prime rib with a baked potato for my entree. You can skip the salad. What do you want, Charlie?"

"I'll have the scallops with rice," I replied. "Thank you."

She smiled as she took the menus from us, but her attention was still on Jack. "Any wine or beer?"

"Just iced tea," Jack replied. "We're keeping our wits about us tonight."

"Of course."

Once she left, I turned to ask him if he was really going to try the oysters. It was one thing to try the fried ones, which really did have little taste. The raw ones, however, made me leery. I never got the chance, though, because the spot next to me in the circular booth was suddenly filled with an extra body ... and it had seemingly appeared out of nowhere.

"Good evening, lovebirds," Harley trilled as Jack moved to drag me onto his lap as a protective measure. "Oh, don't do that. You'll draw unnecessary attention. People will think you're a pervert."

Jack scanned the other diners to see if anyone had noticed Harley's unorthodox arrival, but nobody was paying us any attention. "That was ... stupid."

"Oh, you're just jealous because you can't do it." She grabbed a breadstick from the basket at the center of the table and immediately bit in. "Oh, nice. They're warm." She said the second part around a mouthful of bread.

Jack made a face. "I didn't realize we'd invited you on our date."

"Charlie did." She patted my shoulder for confirmation. "She said you wanted a threesome and asked if I was open to it. I think the stick up your behind is far too large for me to work around, but nobody ever said I wasn't a team player."

Jack's mouth dropped open but no sound came out.

I was frozen in place. It took me a full ten seconds to find my voice. "I didn't tell her that," I said finally. "The threesome thing, I mean. I didn't ... there's no way ... never ... ."

My reaction was enough to snap Jack out of his trance and he actually smiled. "Don't worry. I didn't think you said that." He patted the hand that was resting on top of the table. "She likes to get a rise out of people. Apparently she's good at it."

"I'm the best," Harley agreed. "That's why I'm Papa Legba's favorite."

Now it was my turn to search the surrounding faces. Mentioning an ancient Haitian voodoo Loa in public was probably a recipe for disaster. Sure, technically he was Harley's boss and all, but he was also a freaky dude. I'd met him in New Orleans, too, but only in a dream. I'd yet to meet him in person. I didn't think I wanted to risk that.

"You should watch what you say."

Harley snorted. "Please. These people won't be able to pick me out of a lineup in ten minutes. Trust me. I have a way of flying under the radar ... despite how hot I am." She batted her eyelashes at Jack. "Don't you think I'm hot?"

Jack avoided eye contact. "Not really. Thanks for stopping by. If you don't mind, we're on a date. That's a two-person date."

Harley's smile was back. She was hard to rattle, something I actually liked about her. "You really need to see a doctor about that stick. I'm not here to ruin your date. I'm here because Charlie called me."

Jack shifted on the booth seat next to me as I fought the urge to wrap my hands around Harley's neck and start shaking. "You called her?" The question probably came out shriller than he intended.

"Technically I rubbed a coin," I hissed, indicating he should lower his voice. "I didn't use the phone or anything."

"Coins are better," Harley explained. "Nobody has to pay for roaming wireless with a coin. It's my favorite method of interaction."

"How great for you," Jack muttered before addressing his next question to me. "Why did you call her?"

"That's what I want to know." Harley grabbed another breadstick. "I'm not supposed to eat on the job, but this isn't exactly a sanctioned mission so I'm playing it by ear. If anyone asks, I was totally professional the entire time and you didn't see me pop a thing in my mouth." She paused. "Incidentally, that's the same thing I had my friends tell my father when I started dating in high school."

I was officially horrified ... and then my brain caught up to reality. "You didn't go to high school."

"No, I didn't," she agreed. "I just love that joke." She dipped the breadstick in marinara and pinned me with a look. "As fun as this is, I really am on the clock. What do you need?"

I felt put on the spot. "I expected you to come into my dreams again."

"Yeah, what's up with that?" Jack challenged. "She needs her sleep. Don't invade her dreams and drag her out to walk on water without me. If you're going to take her places, you'd better take me, too."

This time the smile Harley sent him was heartfelt. "I really do like you ... the stick notwithstanding. You're kind of a pain, but you have the absolute best heart." She fell silent for a moment. "I approve of this relationship. It's good for the both of you."

"Oh, well, I'm so glad you approve," Jack drawled. "Now we can change absolutely nothing about our lives."

"And there's that stick again." She winked at him — she seemed to like winking — and turned back to me. "What do you need? As for invading your dreams, I have other stuff going on. You're not the only person I visit when I'm in town."

"Okay. Sorry. I didn't mean to drag you away from anything important."

"Don't apologize to her," Jack ordered. "She's getting free food out of the deal. She's fine."

"The breadsticks are good," Harley agreed. "Seriously, though, what do you want?"

"I need a favor."

She stilled, the breadstick halfway to her mouth. "You want to make a deal?"

"No." I fervently shook my head. "I know better than to make a deal. That's the way to losing my soul. I never want to make a deal."

"Just for the record, there are different kinds of deals," she offered. "The soul is the big one, of course, but I take other things in trade." Her eyes were mischievous when they locked with Jack's serious blue orbs. "All different types of things."

"Stop it." He extended a warning finger. "I get what you're trying to do. You want to knock us off our game so we make a stupid trade. That's not going to happen. In fact ... we don't need anything from you. I don't know why Charlie called you in the first place."

"I called her because she can travel in a way you and I can't ... and she can see the ghosts," I explained. "We found a pattern, Harley. Women died in the exact same manner in Boston, Atlantic City and Virginia Beach. We've been able to confirm that. What we haven't been able to confirm is the ghosts."

Harley looked thoughtful as she considered the news. "That's ... interesting. That would seem to indicate a pattern. Somebody was traveling along the coast."

I nodded. "We think this is an important pattern. Jack is running searches, but they're massive because we don't have much to go on. If you could go to those cities — do that poofing thing you do and just check — we wouldn't expend unnecessary effort."

Harley pursed her lips. "You just want me to check for the ghosts?"

"Yeah."

"I can do that."

"You can?" I was so relieved. "Thank you."

"We still have to make a deal for it."

Ah ... so close. "A deal?" I swallowed hard. "I don't think I should make deals with you, Harley. Crossroads demons are tricksters. I don't want to sell my soul for an easy favor."

"I don't want your soul. Sure, Papa Legba might get off on the idea, but I'm not that cruel. I told you I do different sorts of trades. That's what we'll have to do."

I was instantly leery. "What sort of trade?"

"I'm thinking that one day you're going to have to take me to dinner in Boston — we're talking crab legs, all the breadsticks I can eat and a vat of that great butter sauce for dipping — and in exchange I'll check the other locations."

That sounded far too easy. "You only want dinner?"

"I don't want anything from you, but you engaged the coin. To give you something, I must get something in return. I don't make the rules, but I can't break from them."

"Oh." Well, that sort of made sense. I glanced at Jack to see what he thought, but his expression was unreadable. "We can do dinner. I'm getting a bonus at work so I'll be able to pay for it and everything."

Jack cleared his throat. "I'll pay for it. I'll be the one to make the deal with you."

Harley arched a surprised eyebrow. "Why?"

"Just to be on the safe side. If there's a trick in this, I want it to come back on me and not Charlie."

I balked. "No way. I called her."

"But you're the one who has something they really want. Your friend here is less likely to screw me because she knows they'll never get you if something happens."

My heart filled with dread. "No."

"There'll be no screwing," Harley promised. "I came to her first looking for help with whatever is happening here. If I could do this for free, I would."

"And I mostly believe you," Jack said. "But I can't risk her. I won't."

Harley shook her head and sighed. "Fine. I'll make the deal with you because that's the only way you'll feel safe. You're kind of a pain, Jack. Has anyone ever told you that?"

"A few people." He glanced around, uncertain. "What do we do?"

"I propose the deal and we shake hands. There's no trick involved. We can't have buyer's remorse in this business. Everything is laid out in a particular fashion for a reason."

"Then do it."

"Fine." She flashed her megawatt smile. "I, Harlequin Desdemona

Stryker, agree to travel to Boston, Atlantic City and Virginia Beach to search for similar ghosts as those plaguing Charleston. Now you have to say your part."

"I, Jack Hanson, agree to buy Harlequin Desdemona Stryker — is that seriously your name? — a crab dinner, complete with breadsticks and endless butter sauce, on a date of her choosing. Is that good enough?"

She nodded, apparently appeased. "It's great." They shook hands, a deal done, and then Harley got to her feet. "I heard you got the oysters. You should totally eat a pound of them and then frolic like bunnies until you pass out. One of you obviously needs a little less stress in his life."

I offered her a light wave as Jack linked his fingers with mine. "Thanks for helping."

"It's not a problem. Try to get him to lighten up."

"Oh, trust me. That's at the top of my to-do list."

TWENTY

Jack was feeling romantic after dinner so we took a walk. The streets were well lit and the bars hopping with activity. I found the city picturesque, if a bit claustrophobic.

"Why do you think the streets are closed in like they are?"

He slid his gaze to me, uncertain. "What do you mean?"

"The streets are tight. They're all one way. There's no room for parking ... although that doesn't stop some people. In most major metropolitan cities, the roads are wider."

"I'm not sure." He stopped to look at the area more closely. "I think this is where the old slave trades took place."

The hair on the back of my neck bristled. "Seriously? That's ... not cool." A black couple happened to be walking past us at the exact moment I decided to stick my foot in my mouth. "I mean ... slavery is never cool. It's wrong. So, so wrong."

Jack pressed his lips together as the couple shot me odd looks. He offered them a conciliatory smile. Without words, he apologized for me being a ninny. The man nodded as he smiled. Apparently my Foot-In-Mouth Disease was fun for the entire family.

Once they were safely out of hearing, he squeezed my hand. "Is it any wonder I can't get enough of you?"

I felt sheepish. "I'm sorry about that. I don't know what made me say it. It just seemed like the thing to say."

"You said it because you're you. It's fine." He leaned in and gave me a kiss, his smile lingering until a serious expression took over. "We need to talk about Harley."

I should've seen this coming. "I know you don't like her."

"It's not about liking her. She's not exactly someone I would choose to spend my time with, but I don't dislike her. She seems exceedingly honest and blunt, which are normally traits I like. The thing is ... ."

"She's a demon," I finished.

"She's a demon," he confirmed. "I can't help but be frightened about what she's capable of."

I pressed the tip of my tongue against the back of my teeth and debated how to answer. Ultimately, I laid it all out. The truth. "People could say the same about me."

"No." He immediately started shaking his head. "You're not dangerous."

"You don't think that. But other people ... ." I swallowed the growing lump in my throat. "How do you think someone would react if they didn't know me and somehow figured out what I was? Heck, I don't even know what I am. I have all these questions and there's nobody to give me answers."

He pulled me close, gently brushing my hair away from my face. "You were adopted. You told me the story not long after we met. I didn't put it together until right now, but ... you think you were abandoned because of what you can do."

"It makes sense."

"No. Whoever left you ... I have to think there was another reason. Your magic came from somewhere. These people — the mother who gave birth to you at the very least — had to realize how powerful you were. I'm guessing they left you to protect you."

"Based on what evidence?"

"Based on ... this." He tapped the spot above his heart. "You were taken care of as a child, Charlie. You told me there was no mistreatment in your files. You found adoptive parents who loved you. Did they know?"

I nodded. "I manifested at a young age. I didn't know enough to keep it quiet back then. When they realized what I could do they started ... training me, I guess, for lack of a better word ... and my father ran me through constant drills to make sure I knew what to do if someone approached me."

"What kind of drills?"

"Mostly Stranger Danger stuff. They didn't want someone approaching me, claiming to be a member of my birth family and trying to steal me."

"That was smart on their part." He smoothed my hair and pulled me close. "You've dealt with a lot. I'm just now starting to realize how much. If you want to try to find your family, I'll help."

"And how will we do that? I'm not saying I want to go that route, but where would we even start?"

"There are places, including DNA databases. We could load up a sample and see if there are any matches."

It was an option that had never been presented to me before. "What if people are looking for me? Or people who have DNA like mine. Won't that lead them straight to me?"

"Not if we make up a fake profile. It's going to require thought and we need to come up with a solid plan. But it's doable."

I nodded as I absorbed the thought. "Can I think about it? I don't want to give you an answer right now."

"That's the smart way to go." He gave me a soft kiss and then released me, linking our fingers and inclining his head down the street. "It's still early. We should look around a bit, let our dinner settle, before heading back."

"You just don't want to see Laura. You know she'll be awake when we get back."

"I never want to see her. It's not as if we have to hang around with her. We can go up to our room or hang out on the patio."

"And look at the ghosts."

He hesitated. "If you want. I can't see them, but you can. I don't know if it makes you feel better or worse to see them anchored out there, but I'm open for whatever you want."

The offer had my mischievous side coming out. "Anything?"

"You are the teacher," he teased.

"I am indeed."

UNFORTUNATELY FOR US, THE LIVING room was packed with people when we got back to the villa. There seemed to be a serious discussion going on.

"I don't see why you have to be such a pain," Laura snapped. "My friend is perfect for this position. I've already told you. He's a real self-starter and will throw himself into the work without complaining."

"And he's friends with you?" Millie challenged. "How did you manage to grow this friendship if you have nothing common?"

If eyes could start fires, Millie would've set a raging inferno in five seconds flat. Laura blasted her with one of the ugliest glares I'd ever seen. "Don't call my work ethic into question. You might not like me, but I'm a good worker. I've always been a good worker."

Chris, who was toiling over a map at the coffee table, pinched the bridge of his nose. "Will you stop arguing? I can't take another second of this."

"What's going on?" Jack asked as he prodded me inside, his expression leery. "It sounds like World War III is about to hit and this is ground zero."

"Oh, look who decided to join us," Laura drawled. "I'm surprised you two bothered to come back. I figured you would be out partying all night again ... like you were last night ... and the night before."

"I don't have to justify my actions to you," Jack shot back. "If Chris has a problem, he'll say something."

"Chris doesn't have a problem with it," our boss announced, speaking of himself in the third person. "The only thing I have a problem with is this constant noise. She hasn't stopped since the two of you left."

On a whim, I decided to take a different tack. "What seems to be the problem, Laura?" I sat on the couch directly next to her and plastered my best "I'm willing to listen, so talk" smile on my face. "You seem disgruntled with life lately. What's up with that?"

Laura's eyes were glittery slits of hate when they landed on me. "Don't make fun of me. I'm trying to talk about a real issue. We need another person on this team. I need someone I can work with who doesn't make me want to slit throats."

"You could always do us all a favor and slit your own throat," Millie suggested.

"Millie." Chris's tone was firm as he briefly focused on his beloved aunt. "Don't add to this insanity."

"I don't know if I can stop," Millie replied blandly. "I'll have to think about it and get back to you. In the meantime, Charlie needs to move over here by me. I'm afraid whatever Laura has is catchy and I want to contain it to one person if I can."

I remained where I was for a moment, practically daring Laura to explain why she was so peeved with life these days. When she didn't open her mouth — a true rarity for her — I switched seats and settled next to Millie.

"Where did you guys go for dinner?" she asked.

"A raw oyster bar."

"Oh. Did you like the oysters?"

I shook my head. "They're a little runny for my taste. We ate all of them, though."

Millie grinned at Jack. "Trying to get your romance on, huh?"

"I don't need oysters for that," he said, moving to kneel next to Chris for a better look at the map. "What do we have going on here?"

"I'm marking the locations where each body was found," Chris responded, his gaze intent as he put an X on the map.

"Why?"

"I'm hoping there's a pattern. When it comes to profiling, the bodies are usually spread in such a manner that it's easy to find a center."

"And that center is where the killer lives," I surmised.

"Or works," Chris agreed. "It's not an exact science, but we're not getting anywhere. Hannah keeps running into roadblocks at the coroner's office. No one there can agree how to classify the deaths."

"What does that mean?" Jack asked Hannah.

"It means that there could be real trouble if some bigwig decides to classify these deaths as natural," Hannah replied. She looked troubled, which was hard to take because she was genuinely a lovely person. "If that happens, there will be no reason for us to stay. Law enforcement will stop cooperating because there will be nothing to investigate."

"I thought you needed a medical reason to declare a death," I interjected. "If it's an unnatural cause, that's still a medical reason. If it's natural causes, there must be something identifiable in the reports."

She nodded her silvery-blond head in agreement. "They're using the compound that was detected as a loophole. They say even though they can't identify it they can deem it the cause of death because it's present in every body."

That was bad news. "And where will they say these women came into contact with the compound?"

"At their little, 'We're going to be television stars' meetings. They did all know each other, by the way. I don't know if the police have confirmed that with you, but I heard them talking in the hallway today. The victims all had regular meetings to brainstorm."

I glanced at Jack. "Are you going to try to confirm that?"

"It's too late to call tonight, but it's on my list for tomorrow. I don't know what good it will do us, but maybe if we can find a location where they met regularly ... ."

"My understanding is that they moved from coffee shop to coffee shop and occasionally even met in parks," Hannah volunteered. "I don't know that there is a central location."

"Which is why this map is important," Chris supplied, leaning back to study his handiwork. "Okay. That's all eight of them. Does anyone see anything important?"

"You know who's good at reading maps?" Laura queried.

"I'm assuming your friend," Chris replied. "I already told you, Laura, I haven't made a decision on our new team member. This has got to be our focus right now. The information you sent on your friend has been forwarded to Human Resources. They'll vet him and we'll go from there."

Laura perked up. "If they don't find anything wrong with him, does that mean he's officially part of the team?"

"No." Chris was firm. "I'll want to meet him, see if he has any personality defects, and even then there might be a better candidate."

Laura's neck stiffened. "Personality defects?"

"He would have to have a few to hang around with you," Millie noted.

"That did it." Laura made a move to stand, but Jack stuck out his foot at an angle and hit the back of her knees, causing her to flop back down on the couch.

"Don't even think about it," Jack warned. "If you go after her I might just let the fight happen. Not only will you get beaten by an older woman, there will be grounds to fire you for assault."

"Oh, whatever." Laura folded her arms over her chest and stared at a blank spot on the wall. "I really hate all of you right now."

"I'm sure that will be something to cry into our pillows about tonight when we all go to bed ... not alone," Hannah offered. She was rarely snarky. I couldn't help being impressed.

I decided to hold on to my accolades until we were alone and I could praise her for putting Laura in her place. "What are we looking for on this map?" I asked, hoping to change the subject.

"A pattern," Chris replied. "Does anyone see anything?"

"Maybe try numbering the deaths," Bernard suggested. He was so quiet sometimes I often forgot he was present. Of course, Millie talked enough for the both of them. "Chronologically, I mean. Maybe there's a pattern in the order they happened."

"Good idea." Chris obligingly checked the files and plotted each death site with an X followed by a number. When he stopped, we all stared at the finished product again.

Laura, of course, was the first to break the silence. "There's nothing there," she groused. "It's a whole big map of nothing. That was a waste of time."

"You could always go to your room and waste time there by yourself," Jack said. "I don't think you would hear any complaints from the rest of us."

She pretended she didn't hear him. "There's no center to that map. There's no central location for the killer. There are points, but then they drop a bit and then go back up."

Jack furrowed his brow as he studied the map. "She's right."

"Of course I'm right."

"Even a broken clock is right twice a day," Millie drawled. "It's still garbage."

Chris lightly smacked his aunt's knee as a form of admonishment. "Do you see something, Jack?"

"I do. Is there a ruler around here?"

"I have one in my bag. Hold on." Chris retrieved a ruler and Jack took the marker from him and started drawing lines between the points. When he finished, we were looking at a rather crude pentagram, one that had more than five points thanks to overlap on several sides and an opening where the final point should be.

"What does that mean?" Laura asked blankly. She was finally interested in the map now that a symbol had appeared. "Isn't that, like, a witch symbol?"

"A pagan symbol," I corrected. "Witches use the pentagram, but so do a lot of other religions."

"And demonic figures," Chris added. "There's clearly a point missing. Can you get a general location?"

I knew what they were trying to ascertain. It was obvious that our killer wasn't yet finished with Charleston. He had at least one more stop.

"I can give us a general location," Jack cautioned. "It's obviously not going to be exact because the lines on this aren't perfect."

"That's probably because he needs a victim who fits his type," I offered. "He can't just go to a point and pick the first person he sees. He has a compulsion to kill women who look alike."

"That right there is a point," Jack noted. "Let's see what we've got." He used a pencil for the final point, probably so we could move the line if we came up empty. "That's it. It looks like a neighborhood that's full of condos and apartments."

"Should we head over there?" Millie asked.

"I think it's better if I contact the police," Chris replied. "As much as I would like to be the first one to see this creature, we have to follow procedure. There's a life in the balance here. We can't put some innocent woman at risk."

TWENTY-ONE

Not long after Chris placed the call to his local police contact, everyone retired for bed. Well, everyone but Laura. She sat on the couch and gave us the evil eye as we tried to have a discussion, which meant we had to disappear upstairs to have a private moment.

"I don't think we should simply ignore this," I said in a low voice. "This is like a gift. If our guy moves tonight and someone dies in that neighborhood, we'll never forgive ourselves."

He didn't immediately answer, instead slipping a strand of hair behind my ear as he debated. Finally, he nodded. "We need to slip out. We can't tell the others."

"I'm fine with that. It will be like a sexy date." I squeezed his hand in a reassuring manner. "I'll protect you."

His expression wavered. "If you say anything like that again, you're staying here."

We both knew that wasn't true. We were a team. However shaky he seemed at the prospect of heading out and hunting a demon, he knew he needed me. Heck, we needed each other.

"You need to change your clothes," he said, looking me up and down. "Go for muted colors but not all black. We're talking grays and dark blue. If we get stopped by the police it's going to be hard to explain why we're dressed as robbers."

"Oh. Good point. I knew I kept you around for a reason."

"You better be keeping me around for multiple reasons." He gave me a playful swat on the behind before moving to his bag. "I'm changing my shirt. With Laura still downstairs, we need to be very quiet sneaking out of this place."

"Why do I feel like that admonishment to be quiet is aimed at me?"

He simply stared at me.

"Fine." I found a dark blue shirt and wore it over black shorts. The only sneakers I'd brought were white, but Jack said there was nothing we could do about it. We went down the back stairs and escaped through the door that led to the beach. We had to hike around the villa to get to the front parking spots.

"Is she still up?" I asked when Jack stopped to look in a window.

He responded by clamping his hand over my mouth and dragging me from the glass pane, shaking his head but remaining silent until we were in the rental. "You know that whispers are like yells when you're on top of glass like that, right?"

Honestly, I didn't know that. "You're so smart. I learn something new every single day."

He shot me a glare and then shook his head. "You are so much work."

"I'm worth it, though, right?"

He stuck the key in the ignition and slid me a look. For a moment, I thought he was going to deny it, but then his expression softened. "You are ... but you're a pain."

I beamed at him. "I think we're the perfect adventuresome couple. Who else can say they go on regular adventures to fight monsters after dark?"

He sobered. "Yeah, you need to do what I say when we get there. I don't want you getting hurt. I can't take it."

"I'll do what you say." *As long as you're not in danger,* I silently added. If the incubus moved on Jack I would do what was necessary to protect him ... and I wouldn't apologize after the fact.

. . .

JACK HAD TO PROGRAM A SPECIFIC address into the GPS so he picked an intersection at the center of the area we were heading. When we got close, I picked up on an entirely different vibe than the one we'd been dealing with earlier.

"This isn't as pretty as the downtown area." I wrinkled my nose and glanced around. "Not even a little bit."

He smirked as he parked on a side street, killed the lights, and looked up and down the roadway for signs of movement. "Tourists don't come to this area. It's still much cleaner and prettier than a lot of other cities I've been in. It doesn't feel unsafe ... except for the fact that we're looking for a demon."

"I'm not saying it's dirty or anything. It's just ... different."

"That can be said of any city." He turned back and fixed me with a pragmatic look. "Okay. Here are the rules."

Ugh. I hated rules. "Can't we just sort of wing it? I'm good at winging it."

"So I've noticed ... and no. Once we get out of this vehicle I need you to be quiet. I know that's difficult, but you can't speak unless you actually see something, and then I want you to whisper."

"I think I can handle that," I said dryly. "In fact ... ." I almost came out of my skin when the back door opened and Millie hopped in behind us. She looked agitated, and maybe a little amused.

"What the hell are you doing here?" Jack snapped, agitation on full display. "Are you trying to kill me?"

"No, Mr. Dramatic," Millie replied. "I've been waiting outside for the two of you for ten minutes. Okay, maybe that's an exaggeration. I followed you here because I knew you would come and now you're just sitting in the rental car like great lumps of nothing."

I pressed my lips together as fury filled Jack's eyes. This was not going to go over well.

"You followed us?" he practically exploded. "Why would you possibly do that?"

"Because I know that Charlie can't stop herself from chasing an adventure ... especially when she thinks she might be able to save someone," Millie said. "I knew the moment Chris said he was calling the police first that you guys were going to head here. I'm not an idiot."

"Yes, you're the smartest woman in the world," Jack drawled. "You followed us to an intersection and wandered around in the dark by yourself even though there might be a demon on the loose. How have you not been named to head Homeland Security?"

I felt a headache coming on, so I rested my elbow on the passenger door and rubbed my forehead. As far as I could see, we were the only ones on the street. The rest of the neighborhood was quiet.

"You're just upset that you're not as stealthy as you think you are," Millie shot back. "By the way, you might want to warn your partner in crime that she shouldn't speak so close to windows because it creates an echo chamber. I think Laura might've heard you guys, but it was so dark she couldn't see out the window."

Jack shot me a look. "I told you."

We'd barely started and already the arguing had gotten out of control. "Can we please not fight?" I meant it. I wasn't in the mood. "We're here to protect a potential victim, not win an argument. We need to focus on the important things and not this ... well ... whatever this is."

Jack grunted but nodded. "Fair enough," he said. "We'll focus on our potential victim. But later I'm totally going to win the argument."

"Only in your dreams," Millie scoffed.

I honestly didn't care which one of them won the argument. I just wanted them to stop talking. And they said I was the loud one. "Let's head out," I suggested. "There's no talking unless we actually see something, Millie. We need to be quiet."

The older woman frowned in response. "Why do I get that admonishment and not you?"

I risked a glance at Jack and found him smiling.

"This is my crack investigative team," he said. "I must've ticked somebody off somewhere."

"I happen to think you're lucky to have us," I countered.

"I *am* lucky to have you."

"Oh, and you totally should've noticed Millie was following us," I added as I opened the door. "That's on you."

He turned sheepish. He couldn't deny the charge.

WE MADE AN INTRIGUING TRIO. Jack apparently didn't think we were stealthy enough.

"I feel like I'm going on a covert mission with my grandmother," he muttered.

"Shh." I lifted my finger to my lips and gave him a pointed look. And he was worried about me being loud.

"Grandmother?" Millie was understandably insulted. "At best I could be your older sister."

Jack shot her a dubious look and then continued moving. He linked his fingers with mine — it would've been easier for us to fade into the background if Jack and I had been allowed to make the trek alone – but that wasn't the scenario we were dealing with. If it was just the two of us we could pass for a couple out for a moonlit stroll. With Millie in tow, it looked as if we needed a chaperone.

Jack's gaze was keen as he glanced around the area. He was obviously trying to get a feel for the buildings. He stood in the same spot and studied them for a long moment and then pointed toward a small park sandwiched between two buildings on the other side of the road.

He lightly tugged on my hand, casting a look over his shoulder to make sure Millie followed. When we reached the heart of the park, we found a swing set, one of those barbecue grills you need to add charcoal to and a picnic table. That's it. It wasn't much of a park, but Jack apparently believed it would serve our needs.

"What are we doing here?" Millie asked, wrinkling her nose in confusion.

"Watching," Jack replied simply. He inclined his head toward the swing. "Hop on and I'll give you a push."

The notion sounded absurd, and yet there was something so sweet about the offer I couldn't turn it down. I happily sat in the swing while Millie rolled her eyes and settled at the table.

"How long do you expect us to sit here?" Millie asked.

I shot her a look and shushed her, something she proceeded to ignore.

"It's okay," Jack offered. "We look like a couple of people just hanging out and talking. Just don't talk too loudly."

Millie made a strange sound. "Why did you look at me when you said that? I'm not loud in the least. You should tell Charlie to be quiet."

"Charlie is being the good one right now," Jack countered. "She's not the one giving me grief. She's being an angel."

Instead of being offended, Millie snorted. "Oh, you've got it bad. It's a little sad how bad you've got it."

Jack ignored her and began pushing me on the swing. I decided to focus on the buildings. "The architecture looks old here," I noted. "These buildings must be about a hundred years old."

Jack nodded as he lifted his eyes. "That sounds about right. They're cool-looking, ornate. A lot of the buildings they erect today are sleek, without character. I like a building with character."

"Me, too."

"I kind of miss my mansion," Millie announced, taking me by surprise. She'd once told me that she didn't care about the trappings of wealth, which was one of the reasons she and Myron were destined to fall apart. It made me like her more, if that was even possible.

"I thought you were happy to give up the mansion," I said. "You said the house was too big and drafty in the winter."

"Yeah, but it had a wine cellar, an indoor pool, a sauna and a butler. I've never been one for hiring a lot of help, but I do miss that butler. He used to run errands for me because I was too lazy to do them myself."

Picturing Millie with a butler made me smile. "You could have your own butler, right? You got enough in the divorce."

"I did, but I really don't miss that life. There are times — like now, for instance — when I wish I had a butler so I could send him on surveillance missions with the two of you. But I'm much happier now."

I could see that. "I don't ever think I'll be rich — and I'm fine with that — but being poor sucks."

Jack held on to the back of the swing long enough to kiss my ear before letting me go again. "You're not poor any longer. You just got a raise and you're getting a bonus," he reminded me.

"I know. I'll be able to eat something other than pizza."

I couldn't see his face, but I heard his groan of disgust. "You didn't have to eat the pizza before. All you had to do was let me buy all the food. How hard is that?"

I didn't answer, so Millie did for me.

"It's harder than you think," she said, turning her body to face us. "Charlie has been taking care of herself for a very long time."

"So have I. I understand pride," Jack noted. "I don't want her going hungry, though."

"I very much doubt she was risking going hungry. It was more that she was subsisting on Ramen noodles to survive."

Jack let loose an involuntary shudder, obviously unhappy at the prospect. "Well, now she can eat. I'm going to force her to vary her diet and fatten her up."

"I'm not getting fat," I interjected quickly.

"It was a joke," he shot back. "I didn't mean fat — not that there's anything wrong with that — as much as ... um ... rounder. You're very thin."

"That's because I run."

"You don't need to run."

"I do if someone is chasing me."

This time when Jack caught the swing and held it he peered around to stare into my eyes. "Do you think about running a lot?"

"Not from you. Don't worry about that. It's a foregone conclusion that someone is going to come for me eventually. I'm not naive enough to think otherwise."

He held his breath and then let it out on a prolonged sigh. "You're not going to be running alone. You're going to have me. Don't ... just don't think about that."

"You'll have me, too," Millie said. "We'll all run together. It will be a fantastic road trip. In fact ... ."

The sound of footsteps on the pavement caused her to trail off. Someone was closing in. Jack stopped pushing and held the swing close again, his eyes trained on the road. At first I thought whoever it was had headed in another direction. Then, right under the lamppost, a figure appeared.

I held my breath and watched as a man stopped in the middle of the road and stared. He was young, in his early to mid-twenties and ... .

"Holy crap!" I jumped out of the swing when I recognized him.

Jack was immediately at my side. "That's your buddy from the bar, right?"

I nodded. "Liam."

"Wait ... you know him?" Millie was obviously confused.

As if momentarily mired in quicksand, Liam remained rooted to his spot. He recognized us. That was obvious. I thought he might actually say something — it was possible he lived in the area after all — but instead he turned on his heel and booked down the street.

"Well, that's not normal," Millie said.

"Stay here," Jack ordered as he gave chase.

"Like hell." I was right on his heels. There was no way I was going to be left behind this time.

WE LOST HIM. TOGETHER. We thought we would be able to catch him until he cut through the gate of a cemetery and disappeared inside.

Jack held up a hand for me to slow my pace — and I did — but once we were inside there was no sign of him. The cemetery was old, one of those ornate ones with the beautiful mausoleums and tombstones. There were cement statues all around, too.

Liam could've been hiding behind any one of them.

I tried using my magic to track him, but the trail was confusing — overlapping lines that caused me to scratch my head and curse under my breath. Jack finally drew me back toward the gate.

"We can't stay here all night," he explained. "If someone sees us they could call the cops."

"So? We're not breaking any laws."

"The hours were posted on the gate. We're definitely past them."

"Oh." I hadn't even seen them. "I guess that means we're going."

"We'll come back and take a look around tomorrow."

"He'll be gone tomorrow."

"Yes, but now we have a face and another name. It's more than we had before we came out here."

We did have that ... though it didn't feel like nearly enough. "We should probably find Millie. I bet she's still in the park."

He grabbed my hand and moved me in front of him, his eyes busy as he searched the shadows. "Did you sense anything different about him?"

I shook my head. "No. I didn't sense anything tonight. We were too far away. The other day, he just seemed like a normal guy."

"Maybe he's more than that."

TWENTY-TWO

When we got back to the park, Millie was annoyed.

"I could've died," she announced, hands on hips.

"You didn't," Jack pointed out. "You should be happy about that."

"Ha, ha, ha." Her expression was dark. "The incubus could've come for me while you were gone."

"You're not exactly the incubus's type," Jack pointed out.

Her eyes narrowed, dangerous energy pooling off her. "Are you insinuating I'm old?"

"No." Jack's expression never changed. "I think you're in your prime. Most women would be thrilled to look like you."

"At my age?"

"At any age."

I had to hand it to him. He was smooth ... much smoother than I'd ever given him credit for. It made me think about things I wasn't exactly keen to think about.

"Well ... that's true," Millie sniffed, looking at her fingernails. "What were we talking about again?"

Jack's lips quirked, but he managed to contain his smirk. "About the fact that you're not the incubus's type. You don't have long, dark hair. I think Charlie should've stayed with you so you could protect each other, but I don't always get a vote in her actions."

"And that's not going to change," I offered.

He barreled forward as if I hadn't spoken. "I'm sorry we left you behind. I wanted to talk to him."

"Where do you even know him from?" Millie turned serious. "I've never seen him before."

"We met him our first day in town. He was at a bar Savannah Billings frequented. He hit on Charlie."

I stiffened. "He didn't hit on me," I argued. "I mean ... he flirted a little bit, but he didn't hit on me. I swear it."

"I didn't say you flirted back," Jack reassured me. "He was most definitely flirting with you. He bought you a drink and seemed extremely disappointed when I showed up."

"Only because the men outnumbered the women and he saw a fresh face and thought he might be able to move in before anyone else did."

"Yeah, I think it was more than that, but it's not worth an argument." He moved his hands to my shoulders and started rubbing. "He disappeared into a cemetery a few blocks away. We couldn't find him."

"A cemetery is a creepy choice for a place to hide," Millie noted. "Do you think he ran in there on purpose or was it just a convenient escape route?"

"That I don't know. Do you remember what he told you about himself, Charlie? Did he say he was local?"

I racked my memory. "Actually, I think he did. He mentioned a place called Drum Island. All I remember thinking at the time was that a chicken drumstick sounded really good. I was anxious for dinner."

Jack gave me a light hug from behind. "You're always hungry. That's one of my favorite things about you. As for Drum Island, it's real. It was created by the dredging in the harbor. It's all marshland."

"He said his parents lived there but he couldn't afford the house once they were gone and he moved into the city to be closer to work. I can't remember if he told me where he worked."

Jack worked his jaw in such a manner that I was instantly alert.

"What?"

"People don't live on Drum Island," he replied. "I think kids boat out there to party occasionally, but nobody lives there."

I didn't know what to say. "Should I have known that?" I asked finally.

"Not unless you decided to study up on Charleston geography during the trip down."

"He lied to me, though. If I'd have known that wasn't a thing we could've caught him right then."

Amusement flitted over Jack's features. "Really? You would've assumed a guy who lied about his parents having a nice house on an island was a demon? That seems quite a stretch."

He had a point, but still ... . I was feeling obstinate. "It would've proved he's not a local like he pretended," I insisted. "A local would've known to pick an inhabited island."

He hesitated. "I guess that's true, but that's still a leap, especially when you're talking about a demon."

"I agree with Jack," Millie offered. "Not that you asked or anything. By the way, seeing as you two have decided to play the 'You're the only person in the world who matters' game, I'm going to head out. We're done here, right? There aren't any more adventures to be had, are there?"

"We're done," Jack confirmed. "We'll walk you back to your vehicle."

Goodbyes were non-existent and Millie offered only a half wave before tearing out. She was obviously over the evening's hijinks.

"Well, that sucks," I lamented. "I thought we might actually cover some ground tonight."

He slid his eyes to me, his expression unreadable. "Who says we're done?"

"You just told Millie the adventures were over."

"Because Millie would stick out where we're going. As much as I love her — and I do — I've had my fill for the evening. The next adventure is going to be just you and me."

"Where are we going?"

"The one place we've seen Liam before."

Why didn't I think of that?

BLESSED WAS HOPPING, the music pounding in the background and people spread out all over the beach. The atmosphere felt sweaty and closed in ... which was fairly impressive because we were outside.

"I thought this place was much cooler during the day," I complained, wrinkling my nose.

Jack, who wasn't much for busy places, slid his arm around my waist and anchored me to his side. "Make me a promise."

I didn't even have to ask what he was fishing for. "I won't leave your side this time."

"Thank you."

"I'm not an idiot," I reminded him. "These circumstances are vastly different from the first time we were here. It's dark now ... and there are people everywhere. They're crawling around like ants."

"That's a lovely picture." He kept his hand firm on my hip. "We'll take one of those outside tables, on the far side over there. I think people aren't at them because they can't hear the music as well, but that's a bonus for us."

"Definitely."

I stuck close to Jack as he ordered our drinks and was grateful when we moved away from the drums that had been echoing in my rib cage. "I don't like the noise," I admitted as I sat down. I'd always been overly sensitive to extremely loud noises. I had no idea why, but I'd refrained from going to concerts once I realized how adverse I was to banging music.

"I don't either." He sat across from me and patted my hand. "I wouldn't put either of us through this, but I think we need to see if we can find any of Liam's friends. If he has a chance to talk to them before we question them ... ."

He didn't have to finish the sentence. I understood the ramifications. "They might alter what they say."

He bobbed his head and took a drink from his beer. "Do you recognize anyone?"

I tapped my bottom lip and scanned the crowd, my eyes ultimately falling on a familiar blonde. "The woman who hit on you that day is here."

He followed my gaze. It was dark, but I swear his cheeks flushed. "She didn't hit on me," he countered.

"Oh, please." I didn't bother to hide my eye roll. "Who do you think you're fooling? I saw her. She couldn't lean over far enough so you could see down her shirt ... not that I would call that a shirt."

He leaned back in his chair, delight flitting through his eyes. "Are you jealous?"

It was an interesting question. I'd been taught to consider it insulting, but I didn't think it was. Sure, "jealous" was one of those words middle-school girls (and women acting like pre-teens) threw around daily. It was rarely true, but there were instances where it was.

"I think jealousy is a reasonable thing that can't always be controlled," I hedged. "I don't say that as a way to encourage you to act like an alpha dog on steroids whenever I talk to a man. I'm still annoyed about how you acted the other day."

"Even though that guy might be our killer?"

I didn't like that he might have a point. "It doesn't matter. I wasn't doing anything and he wasn't really doing anything either. Well, unless he was trying to soften me up in an attempt to get me alone because he's a sex demon who steals the essence of others. Wait ... this conversation is getting away from me."

Jack's laugh was rich and low and served to put me at ease. The music was no longer overpowering. The strong breeze ruffled my hair and I could smell the saltwater. It was a lovely location ... and I felt relaxed despite the number of people buzzing around us.

"I agree that jealousy is natural," he said when he recovered. "There's a level of jealousy that isn't healthy. I think we've both seen that with Laura. A little jealousy — the kind where we tease each other and can laugh about it — isn't so bad."

"I'm not going to let you use it as an excuse," I warned. "Just because you might've been right in this particular instance doesn't mean it will always be that way. That said, your little girlfriend looks to be a regular here. She might be worth talking to."

Jack looked resigned. "For the record, you're my only girlfriend. She's not even my type."

"What is your type?"

"You."

"Do you want to expound on that?"

"Are you fishing for compliments?"

"How is that fishing for compliments?"

"Because you want me to say you're so magical, so beautiful, that you became the only example of my type to ever exist."

"Um ... I most certainly didn't say I want that."

"But it's true." He cast me a fond smile. "Somehow, you managed to do something I never thought possible. I wouldn't trade you for anything, but I'm still baffled." He raised his finger in the air to get the blonde's attention. "Try not to rip her face off. I promise that I'll be thinking of you the whole time."

CELESTE LYNN was as oily as she looked. She told Jack she was twenty-three — she'd largely ignored me since joining us — but a quick poke through her head told me she'd shaved ten years off that number. I had to be honest, she looked good in her tiny top.

I still didn't like her.

"Are you in town for business or pleasure?" Celeste asked with a grating giggle. Every time she let it loose it was as if my insides were being scraped by a blunt spoon.

"A little of both," Jack replied, offering me a wink that Celeste clearly ignored. She'd managed to box me out of the conversation, to the point I looked like the third wheel on my own date. I wasn't happy with the turn of events, but she had information we needed.

That didn't mean I couldn't lob a few mean thoughts in her direction.

"Will you be hanging around for a while?" Celeste asked, twirling a strand of what was obviously dyed hair around her finger.

"It depends on how things go," Jack answered. "I'm actually looking for someone. I thought you might be able to help me."

"You're looking for someone? I'm right here. Look no further." She laughed at her own joke, which was enough to make me strain something rolling my eyes. She didn't as much as look at me, so I wasn't worried about her noticing.

"I'm looking for a man."

I pressed my lips together to keep from laughing as the smile slipped from Celeste's face.

"Oh. Well ... oh." Disappointment was evident, but she gave his arm a small squeeze. "That's okay. I should've seen that coming. You're too good looking to like women. I don't have luck like that."

It took Jack a moment to understand what she was saying, and when he did his reaction was hysterical. "I didn't mean that. I like women. One woman. That woman." He pointed at me. "I'm looking for a man for my job. He frequents this establishment quite often."

"Her?" Celeste had obviously tuned the rest out as she focused her full attention on me ... and she didn't look happy. "Why her? I mean ... I thought she was your sister."

If the situation wasn't so sad it would've been hilarious.

"She's my girlfriend." Jack was firm. "We have to travel all over the place for work. I won't be here more than a few more days so ... you're better off without me. Trust me."

"Definitely," I agreed, earning a stern glare from Jack. "He's not all he's cracked up to be," I added. "He can be a little overbearing."

"Thank you, Charlie." He forced a smile on his face when he turned back to Celeste. "There's a guy who hangs out here. His name is Liam. I'm pretty sure he's a regular. Do you know him?"

Celeste pursed her plump red lips and nodded after a moment. "I know the guy you're talking about. Well-built. Twenty-five. Always drooling over any woman who will pay attention to him ... as long as she has dark hair."

"That sounds like him," Jack confirmed. "I was wondering if you've ever seen him here with a woman."

"Tons of them. This is a hookup joint. Look around." Now that she knew Jack was off the menu her attitude was less than pleasant. "I would say he scored a good fifty percent of the time he was here. He's got a certain appeal some women like. Not me, of course, but other people."

"If I showed you a photograph do you think you would be able to tell me if he ever left with a specific woman?" Jack asked. It was a long shot.

"I guess, but I didn't really pay attention to his dates. I don't really care about them because ... well ... they're not my dates. I only have enough time to worry about me."

"It's a terrible burden, isn't it?" I drawled "To be so beautiful and have to carry the torch for all women."

Celeste either didn't register or ignored the sarcasm. "It's the worst," she agreed. "People don't understand how hard it is for me."

Jack shot me a warning look and then held out his phone. "Just give it a look, okay?"

I looked over Celeste's shoulder so I could see what he was showing her. Savannah Billings. That was a good choice. She was the most recent woman to die.

"You know, now that you mention it, she does kind of look familiar," Celeste hedged. "The thing is, now that I think about it, all the women he left with looked the same. He had a specific type. It was a boring type if you ask me, but he obviously liked boring women."

"Can you describe the type?" Jack asked.

"Sure." Celeste swiveled on her chair until she was facing me. "They all looked exactly like her. Seriously, if he was here right now he would be all over her."

Speaking of that ... . "Was he here earlier this evening?" I asked.

"I don't think so. I don't really know. It's not like we hang out. We have nothing in common. I want to marry a rich man and have lots of babies. You know, be a homemaker with a yacht and a Ferrari." She adopted a far-off expression.

"That sounds like a lovely life." Jack drained the rest of his beer and stood, holding out his hand for me. "Thank you a great deal for your time, Celeste. You've been a big help."

"Is that it?" She jutted out her lower lip. "I thought we would spend some time alone together. You know ... talk and stuff." She did the hair twirl again. That was obviously her go-to move.

"I'm going to go home with my girlfriend," Jack countered. "I appreciate all you told us. Thank you." His hand was firm at the small of my back as he prodded me toward the exit. "Let's get out of here."

"Oh, come on," I teased. "Don't you want to buy her a Ferrari and make her a homemaker?"

"I would rather deafen myself with Q-tips and die alone."

"That's rather extreme."

"That's how I feel." He didn't stop until we were on the street in front of the bar, away from the noise and sweating bodies. When he looked at me something smoldered in his gaze. "I wasn't joking. I have exactly one type. You. Not women who act like you. Not women who look like you. Just you. That woman in there is ... horrible."

I couldn't help agreeing with him. "We didn't get much," I pointed out. "I mean ... she sort of confirmed it, but that doesn't necessarily mean anything."

"No, but it's something."

We headed toward the car. He made to come to my side to open the door, but I was too tired.

"Let's just go home and go to bed," I suggested. "I'm exhausted."

He headed to the driver's side, his gaze intent on his keys. In that instant, I felt a pair of eyes on the back of my neck.

When I lifted my head and whipped it in that direction, I found nothing but darkness beckoning. No one was there ... and yet someone was. I felt it.

A chill swept through me.

"Get in the car, Charlie," Jack ordered. "I want to go to bed."

"Yeah. Sure." Just as soon as it threatened to overtake me, the feeling was gone. Someone had definitely been there, but the space was empty now.

So ... who was it? And why was he watching me?

TWENTY-THREE

I slid into sleep within seconds of climbing between the sheets. When I woke, it wasn't Jack's face I found staring at me.

"What the ... ?" I clutched the sheet tighter to my chest and fixed Harley with an incredulous stare. "Do you knock?"

She snorted in amusement and eased herself to a reclining position on my side of the bed. "I didn't think that was wise given the fact that people are up and bustling about downstairs. I figured you wouldn't want to explain that."

On my other side, Jack stirred ... and went rigid when he realized we weren't alone. "You've got to be kidding me." He viciously swore under his breath as he fixed Harley with a hateful look. "This has to be a nightmare. There's no other way to explain it."

She chuckled. "Oh, don't pretend you didn't have dreams about this."

"I guarantee you've never been in anything but my nightmares."

"Okay, maybe not me specifically, but there's no guy in the world who hasn't dreamt about having two women in bed with him at the same time."

"Me." He thumped his chest. "I'm the guy. I'm more than happy with my one woman."

"Oh, isn't he the cutest?" Harley winked at me and stretched out her legs. "So ... I haven't been to bed yet. And, if you're wondering, I do sleep. I can get by with less than a normal person, but looking this good isn't easy. Beauty sleep is a must. Still, I knew how important confirmation was to you, so I went on a trip last night. Well, actually I went on three trips."

I was dressed in an oversized T-shirt and a pair of Jack's boxer shorts, so I let the sheet slide down and propped myself up on the pillow to look her straight in the eye. "And?"

"There are ghosts anchored in the water in each city," Harley confirmed, sobering. "Do you want to know how many?"

"I want you out of the bed," Jack replied. "This is weird."

"You're fine." Harley offered up a dismissive wave. "You need to unclench occasionally. If you're not careful you're going to die with that stick up your butt and it's going to make for an uncomfortable funeral."

Jack's only response was a low growl. I patted his hand in an effort to soothe but kept my eyes on Harley. "How many ghosts did you find?"

"Seventy."

If she hadn't been crowding the edge of the bed I would've fallen out of it. "Seventy?" That couldn't possibly be right. "That's ... no way."

"I'm afraid so. I was a little surprised myself." All traces of mirth were missing from her features. "There're a lot of dead people in those cities and all the souls left behind are being ... tortured."

Jack, apparently forgetting his annoyance with Harley, shifted so he was sharing my pillow. The expression on his face was hard to read. "How are the souls being tortured?"

"Would you want to be anchored outside of the city where you were killed for a millennium?"

"Not particularly, but other than being trapped, what are we talking about?"

"I don't know. I've never seen anything like it." Harley plucked at the sheet and tilted her head, considering. "The way the souls are being harvested reminds me of what a wraith would do. Are you familiar with wraiths?"

Slowly, Jack shook his head and glanced at me. "Are you?"

"I've heard of them, but ... I've never seen one," I replied. "Everything I've read about them suggests I don't want to see one. They're monsters."

"Apparently there are a lot of monsters out there I wasn't aware of." He rested his hand on top of mine. "How does a wraith kill?"

"Wraiths are former humans who sacrificed parts of their own souls to stave off death," Harley explained. "Most of the time we're talking about people who weren't very good in life and were terrified of what was to come once they crossed into the great beyond. They essentially didn't want to go to Hell, so they created a hell on earth."

Jack frowned. "Are you telling me Hell is real?"

Her smile was enigmatic. "I forget you were a nonbeliever before Charlie came into your life. I'll try to keep that in mind. You're dealing with a steep learning curve — I get that — but you need to at least try to keep up.

"In a nutshell, it's all real ... at least to a certain extent," she continued. "Heaven, Hell, Olam Haba, Hades, Paradise, Moksha, Nirvana, Samsara. Where you end up depends on what you believe in life. There's a good and bad place for all practitioners of those religions.

"When an individual dies, a reaper comes for the soul. The soul is absorbed and then sent through the gate, where the souls are sorted and sent on to their final resting places. Wraiths interrupt the mechanics of that system. They kill humans by sucking their souls ... and essentially devouring them."

Jack wrinkled his nose. "Are you saying wraiths eat humans?"

"Not their bodies, but they do eat the most important thing. Think about it this way: You and Charlie are together in this life. You'll do your best to keep each other alive and hopefully grow old together. Once one of you dies, you'll move on to a different place ... and, in theory, the other will eventually join the first. There you'll have until the end of time together."

My cheeks colored at her example. "I think you're getting a bit ahead of yourself there."

Jack barreled forward as if I hadn't spoken. "So there really is something beyond this life?"

Harley's lips curved. "Did you doubt that?"

"I don't know. I've been wondering about a lot of things lately. Before this — before Charlie — I would've considered myself an atheist. Now, ..." He trailed off, uncertain. "It's a lot to absorb."

"It is and you'll be fine." Harley was back to her perky self. "When you don't have that stick up your behind, you're a fantastic man. You need to keep that in mind going forward. When in doubt, remove stick. It's a pretty simple philosophy."

Jack's scowl was back. "Are you done here?"

"Not even close." She turned her eyes back to me. "I know you figured there would be souls anchored in the water, but the sheer amount of dead people we're talking about here has probably shaken you. I'm sorry for that. I wish I had better news."

"Are you sure about the number?" I asked.

She nodded. "I counted in each location. I guess it's possible that there could be more bodies even farther out, but somehow I doubt it. Whoever did this wanted the women to be close enough to see the lives they lost. Also, if he ever stopped by for a visit he might want to review his handiwork."

"Like a serial killer," Jack noted. "There are some who like to revisit the bodies because ... well, they're sick. There's also something instinctive in the act. They're drawn there as part of the ritual."

Harley bobbed her head. "I think it could be that way for our guy. I still don't know what kind of creature you're dealing with. I'm sorry. I think to save the ghosts you've got to eradicate whatever this ... thing ... is."

Jack rubbed the back of his neck. "I have to go back to the searches. Somewhere in that mountain of information we've started to amass is our guy. He has to be someone who works on a ship ... or at least travels a lot. Maybe our guy Liam is the one we're looking for. There has to be a way to track him down."

"See. You're proactive when there's no stick." Harley winked at him. "I like this Jack."

"Oh, stuff it."

She made a tsking sound. "And the stick is back. He's a master at hiding that thing, isn't he?"

I didn't want to laugh. It seemed disloyal to Jack. I couldn't stop myself, though. "I kind of like the stick."

"You would."

HARLEY DECIDED TO HANG AROUND while Jack conducted his searches, which made things tense.

"Do you have to breathe directly on me?" Jack complained as he sat at the desk and worked on his computer. He insisted on tossing on a shirt when he got out of bed — even though he normally wouldn't have bothered — and the wolf whistle Harley graced him with had been enough to set his teeth on edge before he even got started. Things had only gotten worse since then.

"I do if I don't want to die," Harley shot back. "Do you want me to die, Jack? Is that what you're saying?"

"Shh." I shot them both glares and then checked the door. We were at the far end of the hallway, so I surreptitiously stuck out my head, looked in the direction Millie and Bernard were located, and then pulled back and shut the door. "If you guys aren't careful someone will check on us ... and one guess who that someone is."

"Laura?" Harley made a face as she stepped away from Jack and flopped on the bed, rolling to her back and staring at the ceiling. "She's a real pill, huh?"

"That's not the word I would use for her," Jack replied.

"That's because you're a crab." Harley gave him an amused look and then shook her head when he made a face regarding her current location. "Oh, don't give me grief. I'm not doing anything to soil your little love nest with Charlie. Don't get all worked up."

I blew out a sigh as I sank into one of the chairs in the corner of the room. When Jack and I had first stepped into the room, I marveled at how big it was. Now it felt small because three big personalities were eating up all the space. "You guys are giving me a headache."

Jack slid his eyes to me for a moment and watched as I pinched the bridge of my nose. He leaned over and dug into his smaller bag and came back with a container of aspirin before wordlessly tossing it to me.

"Thanks." I brightened. "This should actually help."

Harley snickered. "He's like a Boy Scout. He's always prepared."

"I happen to like that he's a Boy Scout," I argued as I popped the aspirin in my mouth and grabbed a bottle of water from the mini-fridge in the dresser. "I've always had a thing about Boy Scouts."

He graced me with an indulgent look before pinning Harley with one laced with warning. "Don't give her a hard time. Can't you see she has a headache?"

Harley's smile only widened. "Good grief you guys are cute. How have your co-workers not killed you?"

"It could be coming with Laura," I noted. "She absolutely hates us. Well, she hates me. She wouldn't be all that upset if there was a freak accident and somehow I stepped in front of a bus and she had to console Jack over my death with her breasts."

He lifted his head. "You've spent a little too much time thinking about this, baby."

"I'm not the one thinking about it. Most of her fantasies are right on the surface. They're hard to miss."

He stilled. "Are you sure that's a fantasy and not something she intends to really act on?"

I had to laugh. "Jack, most people have random thoughts like that and they mean absolutely nothing. I don't like getting into people's heads because it's an invasion of privacy, but sometimes I can't help myself with Laura.

"At first I used to think she'd had a lot of sex with you and that's what some of those things she pictured were about," I continued. "This is before we hooked up. Then, after seeing you naked, I realized that she was making it all up in her head because she always misses the little details. Like that cute birthmark you have on your butt that looks like a pair of lips."

"Oh, that sounds adorable," Harley drawled. "I would love to see it."

Jack's cheeks flushed and he turned back to the computer. "You're not supposed to tell anyone about the birthmark. You don't hear me telling people about the way you snort like a pig in your sleep."

I was pretty sure I should be offended. "I don't snort like a pig."

"It's a very cute pig but still a pig, Charlie ... but you snort. I find it adorable. Others might be less inclined to think the same. Laura would use it as a weapon to bash you over the head."

He wasn't wrong there. "What I'm saying is that she spends a lot of time in her head, and because of that, I can't always avoid what she's thinking. She hates me. She wants Jack so badly she can practically taste it. She would legitimately like to do harm to Millie, but is afraid of her at the same time. She finds Hannah annoying because everyone thinks she's the prettiest female in the group and Laura is used to that title being granted to her. Oh, and she respects Chris but thinks he might be crazy."

"I think there are times we all believe that," Jack said as he clicked on a file and brought it up. "As for Hannah, she's definitely pretty, but you're prettier."

I didn't bother to hide my eye roll. "Oh, don't give me that. I like a good ego massage as much as the next person but let's get out of La-La Land, huh?"

"I'm serious. She's definitely pretty. I would never say otherwise. It's a remote beauty, though, and she comes across as having a bland personality. I mean ... she might be a firecracker in private, shy on the outside and a raging beast on the inside or something, but she's not my cup of tea.

"You, on the other hand, are physically beautiful and you have an engaging personality that makes me laugh out loud," he continued. "When you combine that, you're simply breathtaking."

I sat there a moment, unsure what to say. Then Harley responded for me.

"Aw." She made an exaggerated face. "And that right there is why you're worth the effort despite the stick problem. Give me a hug." She moved to climb off the bed, but he swiftly turned back to his computer.

"I have something," he announced, directing the conversation back to something important.

"What?" I was thankful to have something to focus on.

"I've been able to rule out Brock Wilson. He was out of town on two different occasions when women died. In one instance, he was in North Carolina for a conference. In the other, he was at a funeral two hours away and stayed the night. I have the hotel receipts and there's an online footprint suggesting he's telling the truth."

"I think we both figured he wasn't our guy after the weird way he reacted when I accidentally knocked him down yesterday," I said. "Still, it's good to have confirmation."

"There was nothing accidental about the way you took him down," Jack pointed out. "You tackled him and then magicked up your elbow and slammed it into his back. He's probably going to be walking funny for two weeks."

I couldn't work up much sympathy about that. "He lies to women to get them to have sex. He had it coming."

"Fair enough." Jack turned back to the computer. "The one I'm having trouble tracking is Liam. You provided me with a last name but ... as far as I can tell, he doesn't exist."

I drew my eyebrows together. "How can that be? We've both seen him. He obviously exists."

"Not on paper, which seems to indicate that he's either using a fake name or he has no digital footprint, which doesn't seem possible. Everyone has a digital footprint today."

"So he was lying from the start," I surmised. "There can be only one reason for that."

"While I don't want to jump to conclusions, I agree that it's suspect. Between him showing up at the point on the pentagram and taking off into the cemetery and the fact that he's not really who he says he is, it's looking more and more likely that he's our man."

"Which means we need to find him," I said. "Do you have any ideas on that?"

"None that are foolproof. I need to give it some thought. First, I need to shower and we need to get breakfast. I'm starving."

"Yeah. Me, too." I absently started to the bathroom and pulled up short when I realized Jack was glowering at Harley, who showed no signs of moving. "Oh, don't get in a fight. That will give me something worse than a headache before I've even had my coffee."

Jack remained focused on the blonde. "Don't you think it's time for you to go?"

Harley didn't back down despite the glare. "I don't know. Are you going to ask nicely?"

"This is my room. I don't have to ask nicely."

"I disagree."

Oh, geez. I felt as if I was fourteen and trapped babysitting the Gunderson twins all over again. "Knock it off," I warned, aiming a finger at Harley. "Stop toying with him. You're just doing it to get a rise out of him now and it's not necessary."

Harley's chuckle was warm. "Oh, you do like to ruin my fun." She hopped to her feet. "I'll tap some sources and see if I can get a line on this Liam guy ... or at least see if anyone has any ideas about what's going on. I'll be in touch."

"Knock next time," Jack ordered.

"What fun would that be?"

TWENTY-FOUR

Once Harley was gone, Jack relaxed ... though only marginally. Her presence obviously bothered him, but I didn't know what to say to make him feel better. Instead, I simply stood in front of the sliding glass doors and stared at the ghosts — even the ones I couldn't see — and contemplated our options.

"How are we going to find Liam?"

"I don't know yet." He looked up from the end of the bed where he sat tying his shoes. "I don't want you working yourself into a knot over this. We will figure it out."

"He knows we're on to him." I turned to him. "What's to stop him from running? If you were in his position, would you stay? I would get out of here as soon as possible. I would run as fast as I could and not look back."

"I would, too, but I'm not sure our guy can manage that."

"Why? If it is an incubus he's been alive for a very long time. He's not stupid."

"No, but he is compulsive," Jack argued. "Look at the map again, Charlie. He needs to kill. He can't stop himself. He also has to follow a pattern. He can't seem to deviate from it. That's going to benefit us."

"Yeah, well ... ." I trailed off and decided to change course. "Have you talked to Chris at all? Is he aware of the Liam situation?"

"I went to bed with you last night. I didn't see him."

"Yeah, but you were on your computer typing when I was in the bathroom before passing out."

He turned sheepish. "I didn't realize you were aware of that."

"I'm smarter than I look." I playfully tapped the side of my head as he moved toward me, drew me into his arms.

"You're definitely smart." He swayed as he rested his lips against my forehead. "I think he's going to go back to the same neighborhood. He won't be able to stop himself because ... well ... he just can't. He's compulsive.

"I bet if we take the time to map the other locations we'll find pentagrams there, too," he continued. "I think it's part of a ritual. We'll have to take him alive to question him regarding the intricacies."

"We'll debate between catching and killing him once we find him," I said.

He kissed my forehead and then released me. "Once this is over, we're going to come up with some ground rules for Harley. I don't like that she can just pop into our bedroom whenever she feels like it. That's ... uncomfortable."

"She's kind of funny."

"Oh, yeah? How would you feel if the tables were turned and it was a man who kept popping into our bedroom without knocking?"

I made a face. "Not that great," I conceded after a beat. "I didn't really think about it before, but ... um ... I'll try to talk to her next time I see her."

"That would be great." He prodded me toward the door. "Let's get some breakfast and we'll come up with a plan. By the way, I did message Chris before going to bed. I'm sure he's aware we had a late night."

"Millie will be angry when we get down there," I warned. "When she finds out we went to a bar without her ... well ... you might want to put on a cup."

Jack let loose a heavy sigh. "My life was less colorful before you were a part of it."

"Does it make you sad looking back because things for you were bleak and you didn't even realize it?"

I was teasing him but his response was serious. "Yeah. It really does."

THE ENTIRE GROUP WAS IN THE kitchen — McDonald's bags everywhere — and there seemed to be a lot of activity for so early in the morning.

"What's going on?" Jack asked, glancing around. "What happened?"

"I got breakfast for everyone because we need to talk over our plan of action," Chris replied, an Egg McMuffin and hash brown resting in front of him on the table. "I thought it best if we were alone for this conversation."

"Because it's going to be about demons?" I asked, grabbing one of the nearby bags and looking inside.

"Pretty much." Chris's smile was bright. Very little ever got him down and he wasn't about to break that streak here. "So, get breakfast and then sit at the table. We have a lot to talk about. I want to hear about your adventure last night."

"So do I," Millie said dryly from her spot next to Chris. There was an edge to her voice. "I want to hear all about the adventure the two of you went on after sending me home early."

"You should get used to that," Laura offered as she shuffled into the room. "Jack and Charlie are in their own little world these days. They don't let anyone join in on the adventures with them. They're exclusionary."

"Or maybe we just have standards where you're concerned," Jack shot back, accepting the breakfast sandwich I handed him. "My usual?"

I smiled and nodded, the expression faltering when I caught a hint of movement behind Laura. Then, to my utter surprise, a strange man walked into the room behind her.

He was young, probably twenty-seven-ish — which made him younger than Laura but older than me — with dark brown hair and broad shoulders. He was criminally attractive as though he could be a male model ... or maybe even a professional actor ... and his cheekbones were cut and high.

"Hello." His eyes fell on me first and his smile was quick and easy. "Nice morning, isn't it?"

I was caught off guard and looked to Jack for help.

"Who are you?" Jack asked, instantly on alert. "Did Laura pick you up at the bar last night?"

If looks could kill, Jack would be dead. I was almost surprised when death rays didn't spark out of her eyes and smash into Jack's face. "Your wit astounds me," she seethed.

Despite the argument, which was turning into a regular thing, the man's smile never wavered. He looked happy to be here. I was starting to wonder if he was deranged because his expression never changed.

"This is Casey Stephens," Laura volunteered. "He's the friend I was telling you about. Chris allowed him to help on this case — for free — to see how he meshes with the rest of the group. When I called and told him, he couldn't wait to get down here. He'll be with us for the duration now ... and probably long after that." The smile she shot him was adoring, but it sparked more questions than answers.

"I don't understand," I said. "You flew overnight to join us on a case even though you're not getting paid?"

Casey nodded without hesitation. "Absolutely. I know this is a great opportunity — maybe the best I'll ever have — and I want to make a good impression. This is exactly the sort of outfit I've always wanted to work with."

I didn't know what to say. Thankfully, Jack didn't have that problem.

"And you live in Boston?" Jack asked, dropping his breakfast on the table before returning to the bags. He searched through the sandwiches until he found what he was looking for and then grabbed two hash browns. I didn't realize they were for me until he pulled out a chair and inclined his head toward the table. "Sit, Charlie. You need some food."

"I live in Boston now," Casey replied. If he thought Jack's tone was odd, he didn't show it. He seemed perfectly happy to answer the questions the team peppered him with. "I grew up in the Midwest."

"Where in the Midwest?" I asked as I settled next to Jack. Surprisingly, I was hungry. I wouldn't have expected it given the shenanigans of last evening and the surprises of this morning, but apparently nothing could diminish my appetite.

"We moved around," Casey replied. "My father was military intelligence. We moved to various bases when I was a kid and almost all of them were in the Midwest because that's what my father preferred. He got to pick his locations, which was nice, but I wouldn't have minded visiting Hawaii or Georgia for the weather."

"That sounds like a lot," I noted. "Um ... It's nice to meet you."

"It's nice to meet you, too. I didn't get your name."

I felt like a first-class jerk. "Charlie Rhodes." I extended my hand and shook his. Jack introduced himself and did the same. "I hope things work out for you the way you want them to," I offered. "This is a fun group."

"Yes, we're tons of fun," Millie drawled. "Like last night, for example. Charlie, Jack and I went to stake out an intersection to see if we could catch an incubus, and when our suspect took off I assumed we were coming back here. Instead, they went out and had a grand old time at a bar. Without me. Can you believe that?"

Yup. I knew this was coming. "We're sorry, Millie."

"We're not sorry," Jack countered, firm. "We needed to fly under the radar. We looked like a normal couple out for a night of entertainment while looking for Liam at the first place we interacted with him. If we'd taken you along it would've been like we ... ." He trailed off when Millie pointed a warning finger at him.

"Like we had our older sister with us," I offered lamely.

"Right, like we had our older sister with us," Jack echoed, although his expression was dubious. "We didn't want potential informants to think we were those sort of people."

Millie rolled her eyes and folded her arms across her chest. "I know exactly what the two of you were up to and I don't appreciate it ... at all. You guys totally abandoned me. Twice. Yeah, they did it twice." She seemingly warmed to her story. "The minute they saw Liam, they took off after him and left me to fend for myself. What would've happened if the incubus had returned?"

Laura snorted. "The incubus is after young brunettes," she pointed out. "You're neither. Your hair is gray and you're definitely not young. But I don't understand why Charlie went after him. If something had happened to Jack during the chase she likely would've been his next victim."

Jack stirred beside me. "I didn't consider that."

I didn't want him mired in that frame of mind. "I was perfectly fine. Nothing will happen to Jack." I would make certain of that, even if I had to unload every ounce of magic I had at my disposal. There was nothing I wouldn't do to protect him.

"No, but it probably wasn't smart for you to follow me," Jack offered. "You would've been walking directly into a trap if I went down."

"Let it go." I briefly rested my hand on his wrist. "It's done. Besides, we're a team. I'm not going to let you race off after a potential demon by yourself simply because you have testicles and I don't."

Jack nearly choked on his breakfast sandwich. "W-what?"

"She's saying you're being an alpha jerkface," Laura offered. "You think you should be able to chase the demon by yourself because you're a man. That's a double standard and not fair to us women who can hold our own in a fight ... not that I want to take Charlie's side in any of this or anything."

"Yes, perish the thought," Millie drawled.

Casey, apparently oblivious to the current of unease running through the room, seemed perfectly happy to select a breakfast sandwich and sit between Laura and me. "I love McDonald's breakfast sandwiches," he enthused. "Is there anything better than a McGriddle?"

"Not that I'm aware of," Jack said dryly.

"I want to know if you found anything at the bar," Chris countered. "Your notes weren't very specific."

"I'm sorry. We were tired when we got back. We didn't get much at the bar. But one of the women we saw there — she was there the first day, which is why we decided to question her — said that Liam's a regular and he leaves with a different dark-haired woman every night."

"Did she recognize any of the victims?" Hannah queried. "That would be even better."

"She thought she might've recognized them," Jack replied. "She couldn't be sure. She said they all looked alike." Slowly, his eyes tracked to me. "And then she said that Charlie was his exact type."

I wanted to choke him for pointing that out. "Let's not go there again," I argued, my temper getting the better of me. "I don't want to sit around and stress over this. I won't let him get his hands on me, so this isn't an issue. You need to let it go."

"While I agree we can't dwell on it, I think it's best if we make sure Charlie is covered at all times," Chris noted.

Jack's lips curved and smugness reverberated from him. "I was thinking the same thing. Thank you for backing me up."

"No problem." Chris returned the smile. "With that in mind, I think I'm going to send Laura and Casey with you today. Casey needs to learn the lay of the land and he can serve as an extra protective force. With four of you together, Liam is unlikely to approach Charlie."

Oh, no. That was the absolute worst idea. Ever. In the history of ideas, that was the idea that sank the Titanic, ignited the Hindenberg and mixed the grape Kool-Aid at Jonestown. We couldn't spend our day with them.

"I think that's probably a waste of their talents," I argued. "Maybe they should go with Millie and Bernard instead."

"Oh, no." Millie started shaking her finger. "That's not going to happen. I took that viper with me yesterday and she made my life a living hell. I've done my penance for this group. It's somebody else's turn. Hannah took her to the morgue the first day, so I believe you're up."

Panic licked my skin as I turned to Jack for help. He looked legitimately caught. "Do something," I hissed under my breath.

"Before you start arguing about how you don't want Laura with you — a sentiment I totally understand — you might want to consider this the best thing to keep Charlie safe," Chris offered pragmatically.

There are times I think Chris is out of touch with reality. There are also times when he comes across as a master manipulator. This was one of those times.

Jack was resigned as he nodded in acquiescence. "I think Laura and Casey coming with us sounds like a fine idea."

Ugh. If yesterday was my lucky day, today was going to be the exact opposite. I should've seen this coming. Things couldn't keep rolling right along for me in the best way possible forever.

"That's great." Chris's smile never wavered. "Let's talk about what we're going to do today. It seems to me that we all need to shift our focus to Liam. It shouldn't be difficult to track him down. He introduced himself to Charlie that first day."

"He did," Jack agreed. "He also lied. He told her that he lived on Drum Island, which is impossible. She didn't know enough to question him at the time. I tried searching for him and came up empty. He doesn't exist on paper ... which means it's a fake identity. It might not be as easy to track him as we would like."

"Have you tried calling the police?" Chris asked. "You met that detective who was helpful. It might not be a bad idea to tap him again."

"That's the plan," Jack agreed. "We're going to meet him at the market again and then go from there. I'm hoping he'll be able to point us toward Liam's apartment. Even better, I'm hoping he'll allow us to go with him when he searches it."

"What are the odds of that?" Laura challenged. "I mean ... why would he possibly want to help us? What's the benefit for him?"

"I think at least part of him believes that something paranormal is happening here," Jack replied. "He didn't come right out and say it, but he made us aware that he was familiar with our mission. He didn't seem weird about it. I'm hopeful he'll allow us to play the game — at least to a certain extent — right alongside him. He also seemed to like Charlie, so I'm hoping that helps us. He found her entertaining."

"Yes, she's a real laugh a minute," Laura drawled. "We should all be like Charlie."

Jack ignored her. "We'll finish our breakfast and head out. What are you guys going to do?"

"Hannah and I are heading back down to the bar. Uncle Myron has called in a favor and the owner has agreed to let us review the security footage. We might be able to put Liam with several of the victims, which will help the police."

"And Bernard and I are going back to the docks," Millie volunteered. "I don't have a photo of Liam but I have a good description. We're hoping someone will recognize it and maybe link him to a ship. I still think there's a good chance our guy works on a tanker or something."

"I think that's a good possibility, too," Jack agreed. "It sounds like we all have our assignments. It's time to work them."

TWENTY-FIVE

Rick met us in the same outdoor cafe. He already had coffee and a muffin in front of him. Jack instructed Laura and Casey to get drinks for us — something that obviously chafed Laura — but she didn't put up a fight in public.

"I see your group is larger today," Rick said as he inclined his head in the direction of their retreating backs.

"The case is starting to heat up," Jack supplied.

"And how is it that you think you've uncovered the identity of our killer?"

"It's kind of a long story." Jack laid it all out, including showing Rick a photo of the map Chris had outlined. "Chris called the higher-ups in your department to share the information. I'm assuming you saw it."

"I did," Rick confirmed. "It's an interesting idea, but I seem to be the only one who believes that. Others in my department believe the overlapping kills show that it can't possibly be a pentagram."

"Unless it's more than one pentagram on top of one another," I noted, my mind busy as I thought about the sheer number of ghosts Harley found anchored in the water in the other cities. "Maybe he does more than one pentagram and if we tear it apart again we'll see that pattern."

"What makes you think that?" Rick asked.

I couldn't very well tell him about Harley, so I wasn't sure what to say. Thankfully, Jack smoothly slid in and answered for me.

"We've done a little digging and found clusters of similar victims in other cities," he explained. "We're talking Boston, Atlantic City and Virginia Beach."

"All coastal cities." Rick stroked his chin, thoughtful. "I didn't think about doing that. It was smart. How many victims are we talking about?"

"I don't have firm numbers," Jack replied. "All combined, I think we could be looking at a total of seventy victims ... not including the eight you have here."

"Seventy?" Rick was flabbergasted. "But ... that would make him one of the most prolific serial killers in history."

"We don't know that it's a man," I pointed out. "You know why our group was called in and the things we tend to investigate. We could be dealing with something entirely different from your garden-variety serial killer."

"This demon thing you were talking about," his expression was hard to read but I didn't see outright disbelief reflected in his eyes. "How do you think we'll catch this man — or beast, if you prefer — if he has magic at his disposal? That is what you're insinuating, right?"

I opened my mouth to answer, but Laura beat me to it.

"I think we're dealing with a serial killer who has somehow perfected a poison that doesn't show up on most of the tox screens," she offered. She came across as well-informed and diligent when she wanted, and this was one of those instances. "I think he knocks the women out, rapes them, and then waits for the poison to do its work. I don't think we're talking about anything more magical than that."

Her tone grated. "Oh, really?" I didn't want to argue in front of Rick, but I couldn't stop myself. "What about the open windows? Why would those women invite him in if he wasn't paranormal? Also, some of those windows were on the second floor. How did he get up there?"

"Maybe he used a ladder or climbed a tree," Laura shot back, irritation flashing in the depths of her eyes. "As for the windows, people sleep with open windows all the time. It's not unheard of."

"It is in Charleston this time of year," I fired back. "It's hot and muggy. Most people have their AC going twenty-four hours a day."

Laura looked to Rick for confirmation. "People sleep with their windows open at night here, don't they?"

I'd originally gotten the information from him, so I knew how Rick was going to respond.

"Actually, no one I know sleeps with open windows," Rick replied. He almost looked amused by the conversation ... and my righteous indignation at Laura's suggestion. He didn't mention that I'd believed the same thing days before. I appreciated that. "It's simply not done."

"Oh." Laura shifted on her chair. "I guess I hadn't considered that."

I was about to admit I was in the same position as her originally, but Jack stopped me.

"I guess you're just not as smart as Charlie," he said, earning a glare for his efforts before he turned back to Rick. "We need information on this Liam we've uncovered. He has a place in Charleston ... somewhere. I'm guessing it's close to Folly Beach."

"Why would you think that?"

Jack hesitated. He'd essentially talked himself into a corner and we both knew it.

"It's a feeling we have, and it's an idea I suggested," I offered hurriedly. If he was going to step in and save me from myself, I could do the same on the rare occasions when he stuck his foot in his mouth. "It makes sense with our water hunch. We think he likes the water ... or that he works on the water."

"I don't really know what to tell you," Rick said. "But I do like your idea that we're dealing with a transient worker. It makes the most sense.

"Human serial killers usually start by mutilating small animals," he continued. "Some even start nuisance fires before building up to kills like this. We've had none of that here. Plus, with the sexual component, it seems to me there would've been a spate of young women with dark hair and blue eyes complaining about a creepy guy trying to sexually assault them. We don't have that either.

"If there are similar murders in other cities, it makes sense that our killer is on a ship. I'm going to send some guys down to the docks to ask questions. Maybe we'll find our guy that way. The thing is, if he's on a ship, he doesn't likely have an apartment here. Why would he rent something that he would have to lease for at least a month when he could be called back to the ship at any time?"

"That's something I didn't think about," Jack admitted, leaning back in his chair and sipping his coffee. "Well ... that could be why I couldn't find anything rented in his name. I assumed it was because he gave Charlie a fake name — and I'm still not convinced that's his real name because I can find no paper trail on him — but what if he's staying in temporary digs?"

"What does that leave?" Casey asked, speaking for the first time. To his credit, he seemed to be taking it all in and trying to learn on the job. He was much more dignified than I was when I started. He seemed fine so far, despite his ties to Laura. That could mean he would turn into the devil eventually, but I was still waiting to see horns protrude from the top of his head. "Should we be looking at hotels?"

"Hotels are a possibility," Rick hedged. "The thing is, they're expensive in this area. Even the bad hotels aren't exactly something that's easily affordable to a guy who spends all his time working on a ship. There's another option."

"And what's that?" Jack asked.

"They're kind of like youth hostels but for the men who work on the ships. They're community living spaces. They're basically big houses, old houses, with multiple rooms, kitchen and laundry facilities, and cheap prices. There are a lot of them over by the docks. There's also one on Folly Beach. It's about half a mile from your hotel."

I straightened as I ran the notion through my head. Something inside dinged and my intuition immediately glommed on to the idea.

"I like that idea a great deal. We should definitely check out the one in Folly Beach. By any chance, does it look out at the water?"

Rick nodded. "It does. It's a former warehouse. There's no manufacturing base out at Folly Beach any longer, so the building was refurbished. It can house about twenty, I think. I'm betting our guy is staying in one of those locations."

"It's a place to start," Jack agreed. "We'll head out to the Folly Beach site while you send guys to the other locations. If we find anything, we'll let you know."

"That sounds like a plan."

THE WOMAN RUNNING THE Folly Beach Temporary Hotel (that was its actual name and it almost made me laugh out loud) was open to questions. She was bubbly, all smiles when we entered, and her gaze immediately went to Jack and Casey.

While I still found Jack the superior specimen, I could see why women might go weak at the knees for Casey. He was attractive, amiable and charming. It was an interesting combination ... and one that had me questioning why Laura was still panting around after Jack if she had this guy available to her.

"The guy you're looking for is staying here." Her name was Susie and it seemed to fit. She had dark blond hair and a smattering of freckles over her nose. She was short, barely five feet, and she had one of those ski-slope noses that made her look pert. "He didn't come back last night. He's a late owl and usually rolls in around two or so, but not last night. We lock the doors at two and nobody is allowed in after that, so he wouldn't have been able to enter."

"Even if he rented a room?" I asked, confused. "That's a little ... stringent."

"Nothing good happens after two o'clock," Susie replied primly. "That's what the owner says anyway. He sets the rules."

"Well ... ." I glanced at Jack and found he was equally amused. "Can we look through his room?"

"Sure." Susie shrugged. She didn't seem bothered by the thought that she was allowing us to invade Liam's personal space. She was more than happy to let us in the room and didn't seem bothered when we started poking into his things. "I don't really care. But if you find any money, you can't steal it."

"We won't take any money," Jack promised, waiting until she disappeared to point at various places in the room. "There's not much here. It won't take long to go through things. We need to split up and check everything. There has to be a clue here."

"Good idea," Laura said. "I'll take the bedroom with you."

Jack looked as if he was going to argue, but I was too worried about the fact that Liam was apparently on the run to care if Laura wanted to make a fool of herself. "Fine," he said when I immediately moved into the living room with Casey. "Don't do anything annoying."

"I think you have me confused with your girlfriend."

"That will never happen."

I tried to tune out the sound of their muted sniping and focused on the living room. It was barebones: a coffee table, ratty couch and an entertainment stand. "There's not much here to go on."

"No, but we should still look." Casey immediately went to the couch and started removing cushions. "I know I just met you, but can I ask you a question?"

I was expecting this. He couldn't possibly think Laura's behavior was normal. "Yes, she's always like this. No, I don't know why."

He let loose a low chuckle. "Not that. I know that Laura is ... well ... Laura. She can't seem to help herself. I think it stems from a place of insecurity. Some people turn inward when they feel inadequate. She turns outward and attacks anyone in her general vicinity. You probably shouldn't take it to heart. She simply can't help herself."

That was an interesting observation, and it was one I'd come to believe myself. I was hardly a psychology student, but I took a few classes in college to round out my requirements. Laura was a textbook case. "How long have you known her?"

"About two months."

"Are you dating?"

"We ... spend time together socially."

Well, that was a very diplomatic answer. Reading between the lines, it meant they were getting busy but leaving emotions out of it. From his point of view, maybe that was the smart move. Laura's brain had to be a minefield. But if that was true, I felt a bit sad for Laura. No wonder she was panting after Jack.

"You said you had a question and it didn't turn out to be about Laura," I said, changing the subject. "What's your question?"

"It's about you."

"Go ahead."

"Laura doesn't seem to like you at all," he offered. "I expected you to be evil, but you're enthusiastic and fairly nice. Laura is definitely jealous of you, but I think that goes back to her feeling inadequate. What I want to know is how you put up with her? If I were in your position, I would get her fired."

Hmm. That smelled like a trap. Could Laura sense that Chris was trying to amass enough information to have her removed from her position? Did she realize he was almost there? Did she bring this guy in to get confirmation? If so, it was smart to send him after me first. I have an absolutely huge mouth and don't know when to shut it.

"I don't really think that way," I replied after a moment. I decided to opt for the truth. "I feel more sorry for Laura than vindictive."

"Jack doesn't feel that way."

"In Jack's mind she's attacked us – both of us – so many times she's a legitimate threat. If she would just back off ... well, they wouldn't be friends but he wouldn't be so agitated all the time. She purposely pushes him. It's as if she thinks she's going to be able to turn him to her way of thinking, but if she believes that she doesn't know him at all."

"You read people well, too," Casey said as he went back to his search. "You seem to fit in well with the group. It's obvious Laura is the odd one out."

"Does that bother you?"

"No. I plan to make a name for myself separate from her. I am curious about you, though. She mentioned you were an orphan, abandoned by your parents and then adopted. You grew up in the Midwest and then put yourself through school. Do you know anything about your real parents?"

"The Rhodes were my real parents." My gaze fell on something familiar on the small table by the door and I immediately started walking toward it. "The people who abandoned me aren't real to me. I don't really care about them. They didn't want me, so I don't see why I should care about them."

"You're not even a little curious? If I found out I was adopted all I would think about was the real family I was separated from. I would be obsessed with it."

"Well ... I don't think that. I don't think of the people who left me as my real anything. They're just the people who decided they didn't want me." I picked up the book on the table and frowned when I flipped it over. I definitely recognized it. "Jack!" I called out his name. The space was so small he was back in two seconds.

"What's wrong?" He was instantly alert.

"Look at this." I held up the Bible.

He narrowed his eyes when he saw it. "That's the same Bible Savannah Billings had in her apartment. Does it have the same stamp inside?"

I opened it to check and found a business card inside. "It does have the same stamp. It's definitely from the same church."

"What's that?" Jack asked, moving closer when he saw the card. "Is that from the church, too?"

I studied the card and shook my head. "No. It's from something called the Down & Dirty. It's a bar by the docks and it apparently prides itself on having places in the dirt to pass out if you drink too much."

Jack pursed his lips. "Another bar. Maybe it's another hunting ground."

"Maybe," I agreed. "It's probably not open yet. We need to check out the church first."

"I'm right there with you. It's too much of a coincidence to ignore."

TWENTY-SIX

The church was cool and quiet when we entered a second time. The stillness was shattered by Laura, who let out a huge exclamation of dismay when she saw the ornate crucifix on the wall. It really was ostentatious ... and a little bloody for my taste.

"Well ... that's just all kinds of wrong," she complained. "Good God, who chose that ugly thing?"

The only person in the vestibule was Gretchen and she didn't look happy to see us. "Back again I see," she noted, her gaze bouncing between us. "And this time you brought sinners with you."

The statement would've been hilarious if I didn't think she meant it to her very core. "Just one sinner. She desperately wants to repent."

Confusion etched itself in Laura's features. "Are you referring to me? Am I supposed to be the sinner? You're the one practically living in sin with Jack. I mean ... the way you two carry on."

"Shut it," Jack ordered, his tone no-nonsense. When he turned back to Gretchen he had a pleasant expression on his face, but it didn't make it all the way to his eyes. He was clearly starting to feel the strain of having Laura along on this excursion. I had to wonder what happened in Liam's bedroom when my back was turned. Ah, well, it didn't really matter. I trusted Jack implicitly, just as I trusted Laura wanted to cause trouble however she could.

"Hey, Gretchen," Jack offered. "I was wondering if Reverend Rodriguez might have a few moments for us. It's important."

I noticed he didn't ask to see the older reverend. Alexander was just a bit too curmudgeonly for even him to handle.

"He's very busy," Gretchen replied. "I'm not sure he has time for you."

"We're investigating multiple murders," Jack reminded her. "Perhaps that's more important than whatever he's doing. I think he would want to help. I would appreciate it if you would at least ask him if he can spare a few minutes."

Gretchen's face was a mask of unidentifiable emotions. She heaved out a dramatic sigh and nodded. "I'll check with him. You're to wait here." She started toward the back offices and then stilled before turning back. "Don't touch anything. And, remember, God is watching." She gestured toward the crucifix on the wall before disappearing.

"Well, she's great," Laura said when she was gone. "I don't know why every church doesn't have one of her. I mean ... she's a real people pleaser, a party person for the new millennium."

"Shut up, Laura," Jack snapped. "We need a favor from these people. Deriding them won't get it."

"Oh, like you weren't thinking it," she shot back.

We spent the next three minutes in absolute silence. When Gretchen returned, she didn't look happy. "He asked that I bring you back." It was clear what she thought of that request, but she was, if anything, subservient to the two reverends ... perhaps one more than the other.

Samuel had tea ready when we joined him. He looked apologetic. "I'm sorry you had to wait. I don't think Gretchen understands how important your work is."

"It's fine," Jack replied, sitting in one of the free chairs, which left me to share the couch with Laura and Casey. He clearly didn't want to risk Laura playing games in a house of worship. "We don't want to take up much of your time, but we have a situation. He proceeded to lay things out in a concise manner, but he left out certain things that he probably felt the reverend didn't need to know about. He ended with a description of Liam. "Does that individual sound familiar?"

"I don't know." Samuel looked perplexed. "That could be any number of people. Do you have a photograph?"

"I'm sorry but we don't. At the time we first interacted with him it didn't feel necessary and the second time ... well ... he wasn't exactly open to the suggestion of posing for photographs."

"No, I imagine not." Samuel leaned back in his chair. "I don't want to infringe on your privacy — I know how important that is for individuals in your line of work — but after you left, I did a little research on the Legacy Foundation. What I found was ... intriguing."

I sensed trouble. For a man of religious persuasion, chasing ghosts and hobgoblins might seem like blasphemy. I assumed Jack recognized the potential trouble, but it wasn't as if I could warn him of what might come next. He was the leader of our little group. He would have to tread carefully on his own.

"You did research or Gretchen did?" Jack queried, perhaps to buy himself time.

Samuel's chuckle was low and throaty. "It's true that she initiated the research. She was ... perplexed ... following your first visit. I can't say I blame her. Your friend's interaction with Alexander set off a few warning bells." He inclined his head toward me.

"What did you do?" Laura's tone was accusatory when she slid her eyes to me. "This is why you shouldn't be allowed to question people. You're bad at it."

"On the contrary, Charlie was forthcoming and honest, two things I greatly appreciate," Samuel countered. "It's obvious you're looking for something outside the realm of the normal. Savannah was a regular parishioner, and we're interested in making sure she gets justice.

"The thing is, what I've learned about your group is ... difficult to wrap my head around," he continued. "I think, simply to put all our minds at ease, it would be nice if we could be honest with one another."

"No more lies," Gretchen yelled from the hallway, causing me to swivel in that direction. Sure enough, the door remained open. Apparently she was loitering in the darkness. There was nothing wrong with her hearing, but her personality and observation skills left much to be desired.

"Gretchen, either come in and join us or go back to your duties," Samuel ordered. "I don't appreciate being eavesdropped on. We've had this discussion before."

There was nothing sheepish about Gretchen's expression when she entered the room. She didn't look as if she felt guilty in the least about getting caught. I had to admire her moxie. "I wasn't eavesdropping," she countered. "I was cleaning and happened to overhear part of your conversation."

"There's nothing to clean in that hallway," Samuel argued.

"I was washing the floor."

"With what?" I asked, ignoring the dark look she shot in my direction. "I don't see a mop or anything. What were you cleaning with?"

"The power of prayer."

Oh, well .... "I'll have to look into that since I can't afford a maid," I offered lamely. When I risked a glance at Jack I found him shaking his head.

"Charlie is enthusiastic," Jack offered. "She wants to believe in everything. She has a curious mind. If she offended you, I'm sorry. She doesn't have a mean bone in her body."

"You misunderstand." The look Samuel shot me was apologetic. "I have no problem with Charlie's enthusiasm. It's more that I'm ... intrigued. She mentioned a demon. My fellow reverend assumed she was talking about demons as a metaphor for aberrant human behavior. I think she was talking about something specific."

Jack hesitated, his gaze shooting to me. He looked caught. Because I didn't want this falling on his shoulders, however strong, I decided to take control.

"I'm talking about an incubus," I announced, causing Laura to groan and Casey to sit up straighter. "Do you know what that is?"

If Samuel was surprised by my answer, he didn't show it. His expression remained flat. "Only in very academic terms. I know it's a demon that seduces women and feeds on their souls."

"That's pretty much it in a nutshell," I agreed.

"That's blasphemous," Gretchen announced, her eyes flashing. "You can't talk about creatures from another world in the house of God."

"Actually, that's not true in the least," Samuel countered. "She's talking about demons, which have strong ties to God. Remember, the angels fell for a reason." He pinned Gretchen with a pointed look. "According to the Bible, what happens to angels when they fall?"

Gretchen was taken aback. "They ... become demons."

"Exactly." Samuel nodded once. "If it is a demon, we must be involved. God is involved. He banished the demons in the first place, didn't he?"

Well, that was a unique way of looking at it. "So ... you believe me?" I had trouble wrapping my head around the notion that he wasn't at least going to put up token resistance.

"I don't know that I believe incubi are real," Samuel cautioned. "I'm simply not as prone to denying the possibility outright. I find the possibility intriguing. May I ask what has caused you to come to this conclusion?"

"Multiple things," Jack answered for me. He proceeded to lay out our case in a precise manner, no embellishments. He didn't catch my gaze while he was talking, which made me wonder if he was angry about me blurting out the big secret. It would hardly be the first time my mouth got ahead of my brain. I would have to wait until later for the fallout. He wouldn't chastise me in front of an audience, especially when that audience included Laura. He didn't want to give her any ammunition.

"I tend to straddle a line when it comes to believing these things," Jack continued, earning a snort from Laura.

"Since when?" she challenged. "You're always the one who doesn't believe, even until the bitter end. And you're almost always right."

Jack ignored her. "I don't think we're dealing with a human monster in this particular case." He obviously couldn't mention the ghosts. Nobody but Jack and I — and, well, Harley — knew about them. "I think this thing has to be a monster. Charlie believes with her whole heart. This time, so do I. I'm not asking you to believe if it's too much of a leap. We just need to find this man. Even if he's not a demon, he knows something."

"I don't know what to tell you," Samuel replied after a moment's contemplation. "Your description could apply to multiple members of my congregation, but nobody goes by that name here. I'm reticent to point you in the direction of potentially innocent individuals. I'm sorry."

Jack shook his head. "I understand." He motioned for me to stand with him. "We apologize for taking up your time. We'll show ourselves out."

"I'm sorry I couldn't be more help." He shadowed us to the hallway. "If you manage to get your hands on a photograph, please return. I'll make sure Gretchen knows to show you back to my office immediately."

"We'll do that," Jack promised.

I was the first to enter the hallway and I almost came out of my skin when I realized Alexander was standing directly on the other side of the door. His expression was dark, as if something terrible had happened and he was about to deliver some bad news. His eyes were directly on me as we filed out.

"Good afternoon, reverend," I offered. I felt awkward, as if I should say something, even if it was all kinds of lame. "How are you today?"

"Fighting sinners, as always," he replied. "I received word that you were here for another interview. I see you're already finished. That means you're leaving?"

The way he phrased it made me think Gretchen wasn't the only one with an eavesdropping problem. She probably wasn't even in the hallway alone. He was most likely with her because she couldn't wait to tattle on us. She took the fall when Samuel called out because Alexander had to be protected and she served as his shield.

"We're leaving," I reassured him. The man made me feel distinctly uncomfortable. There was something off about him ... and not just because religion always made me itchy. I grew up with genuine fear that I would be struck dead if I entered a church because I was somehow an abomination. That fear had dissipated some with age, but remnants remained. Alexander's countenance was doing little to ease my fear. "We'll try not to come back unless we absolutely have to."

"That's probably for the best," he agreed. "You might want to pray in front of our savior on your way out. It couldn't possibly hurt."

He wasn't wrong, but that felt hypocritical so I simply smiled and nodded. "I'll consider it. Have a nice day."

"Goodbye."

WE RETURNED TO THE VILLA BECAUSE we needed to strategize. Plus, I think part of Jack believed that we might be able to dump Laura and Casey if they became distracted by something else. He returned to Chris's map and fetched a different colored marker so he could start working on my multiple pentagrams idea.

"I should've grabbed another map so I could start fresh," he complained. "This one is going to be a mess."

That was such a Jack thing to worry about. I couldn't help but smile. "I think we'll muddle through. We don't need to waste the paper of another map."

He snorted. "Only you would worry about that."

Hmm. Apparently we both had our "things" we worried about. We were opposites in some respects, but somehow we fit together. Sure, the fit wasn't always comfortable, but it was exactly what both of us needed.

"I'll help." I settled on the floor next to him and grabbed a ruler. "What did you think about what happened at the church?"

Laura and Casey were on the back patio, drinking iced tea and chatting. If I had to guess, the conversation revolved around Jack and me — especially how much she hated me — but I didn't care enough to check on them.

"I think Samuel wanted to help but didn't feel as if he could because he's the sort of man who wouldn't forgive himself if he pointed us in the direction of the wrong man. I can't really blame him. We don't have a photograph of Liam, so ... it is what it is."

"Not that part. I agree about Samuel. He's the open sort and wants to help, even if he doesn't believe."

"I'm not so sure he doesn't believe. In case you didn't notice, he was very interested in what we were saying ... and he looked to you for answers. The only reason I took control is because I didn't want you going overboard. If he's terrified of what we're telling him, he might not want to get involved."

"I'm not offended, Jack. I thought I'd probably gone too far when I said it. I believed there was a chance you were angry with me."

"I'm very rarely angry with you."

I arched a dubious eyebrow. "Define 'very rarely'?"

"There are times you do things that frustrate me," he clarified. "Believe it or not, I have trouble being angry with you because you're just so cute." He poked my side. "But when you put yourself in danger I reserve the right to be angry. The other stuff, that's just details, baby."

I couldn't stop myself from laughing. "You're more easygoing than I first thought. I guess that's because you have a tough exterior. Once you get past that, you're kind of a Twinkie with a gooey center."

"That's always what I want people to think of me." He was quiet for a moment as he watched me work, and then stirred. "If you weren't talking about Samuel's reaction to the demon bomb, what were you referencing at the church?"

"Alexander. He was obviously listening to us on the other side of the door. He's all kinds of creepy."

"I think he's just set in his ways."

"I think it's more than that, but it doesn't matter. Okay, this is what I've come up with. The first pentagram has all but one point. The other one is missing two."

Jack studied the map. "You were right. It's two pentagrams. He's working on two pentagrams. That is ... so smart." He smacked a loud kiss against my cheek. "I always knew you were a genius. We need to map the other two points. We might be able to track Liam at one of those points, but we'll have to split up to do it."

"And make sure Rick is aware," I added as I started adding dashes to find the points. It was at the fifth point of the second pentagram that I stopped. "Look at this, Jack."

He stared at the map as I pointed. "What am I looking at?"

"It's a bar downtown. The Down & Dirty."

He stiffened beside me and raised his chin. "That was the card you found in the Bible."

"Yeah."

"Do you think that's the next place he wants to hit?"

"I guess it depends on if there's someone specific he wants there ... or maybe an apartment across the road."

"It's definitely worth a look." He planted a hard kiss on my mouth and then scrambled to stand. "That's three points we need to monitor tonight. We'll take the Down & Dirty. We'll have the others split up and take the other locations. "I wasn't joking when I said you were a genius, Charlie. You are amazing."

I went warm all over. "I am pretty good, huh?"

"The best."

TWENTY-SEVEN

Jack looked up the Down & Dirty and found that it had a unique reputation.

"That's a strip club." I was looking over his shoulder and was horrified by the photos I saw on his computer screen. "I can't go to a strip club."

"It's a strip club for couples," he corrected. "That makes it a ... different ... experience."

He was obviously shining me on. "I'm not going to a strip club." I was adamant. "I just ... wait. If it's for couples, do they expect me to get up there and strip? I'm not doing that. If other people are stripping, I'll go."

He chuckled. "That was a quick turnaround. And, no, you're not stripping. I think we can both agree on that. I believe some of the women get into the act, but I've never been to one of these establishments. I've only heard about them."

I eyed him suspiciously. "No offense, Jack, but you know a lot about these establishments you claim to have never been to."

"I know people."

That seemed a lame excuse, but we hardly had time for an argument. "So we have to go as a couple. We won't have to worry about the others. If something happens, that's probably best."

His eyes were thoughtful as he slid them to me. "We need to talk about that. What do you plan to do if we find him?"

The question caught me off guard. "What do you mean?"

"I'm guessing he's going to need to be taken out, Charlie. It's not as if he can be rehabilitated. Besides, police officers will have no idea what to do with him."

"He definitely has to be taken out," I agreed, rolling my neck as I thought. Part of my mind was on what I was going to wear to the strip club. The other part was trying to unsnarl the busy strands of my brain when it came to potential battle. "I think the only way to free the ghosts is to kill him. I mean ... I'm by no means an expert, but that's what makes sense to me."

Jack hesitated a moment before barreling forward. "Should we call Harley? She might be helpful. She was with the zombies."

That was true. Unfortunately, a relationship with Harley came with strings. "Do you want to owe her more than dinner? We can't ask for her help. She appeared out of nowhere and volunteered it in New Orleans."

Jack cocked his head, contemplating, and then shook it. "No. I don't want to owe her more than I already do. Dinner will be painful enough."

Actually, I was looking forward to dinner. I thought it had the potential to be amusing ... and then some. "I think we have to do it ourselves."

"Right." He moved to the gun case he kept in the closet and removed it. He was always prepared but didn't feel the need to always be armed, which was something I admired about him. He kept the case locked so nobody could get at his weapon, and when he removed the revolver my heart gave a little lurch. "Can he be shot?"

He was asking questions I couldn't answer. "I'm sure he can be. Whether the bullets will do him any harm is up for debate. I don't know what to tell you."

"Yeah, well ... ." He heaved out a sigh. "I'll be careful. I very much doubt a strip club will let me in armed, so I'll keep it in the rental."

"And I'm always armed," I reminded him.

"You are," he agreed. "The thing is, I don't want this always falling on you. This is bound to be a busy place and if someone sees ... ."

He didn't have to finish. It was his worst fear. I don't know what terrified him in the dark corners of his mind before I came into his life, but I understood I had taken the reins of that particular stage-coach at this point. He was convinced if someone found out what I could do they would take me. It was a fear I always lived with but vowed not to let take me over. He was going to have to unclench a bit.

"I appreciate that, Jack, but in this particular case I don't see that we have many options. He can't live. Women are dying. We need to try to lure him away from the bar."

"And how do you suggest we do that?"

"Me. I'm his type. If he sees me alone, he'll give chase."

Jack growled. "You're not using yourself as bait."

"What other choice do we have?"

"We'll think of something."

"Jack." Exasperation took me over.

"We'll think of something," he repeated. "I'm not okay putting you in danger. I believe you're strong and capable. I would never say otherwise. But you can't get me to be okay with you purposely putting yourself in danger. I won't let that happen."

It was a step too far, but he would have to get used to it before the end of the night. For now, though, I would cede to his need for order. "We'll figure something out," I agreed. "I need to decide what to wear. What does one wear to a strip club?"

His smile was back. "I'll leave that up to you. I suggest dressing so you don't stand out, though. The last thing we want to do is draw attention to ourselves."

That made sense ... but sounded like zero fun.

. . .

JACK WAS STILL SHAKING HIS HEAD about my choice of outfits when we parked around the corner from the bar.

"I don't understand how you managed to find leather pants," he complained.

"They're vinyl," I corrected. "I found them at one of the shops by the hotel. They have shark teeth on the butt and urge you to take a bite out of Folly Beach. I thought they would be perfect for a strip club."

Jack's expression told me I might've guessed wrong on that front. "I don't think you wearing leather — er, vinyl — pants will help us fly under the radar. Everybody will be looking at your butt."

"Are you going to be looking at my butt?"

"I always look at your butt. I just make sure you're not looking at my butt at the time because I figure if our pervert tendencies overlap the world will end."

I choked on a laugh. I was beyond amused. "That is ... funny. It's also likely true."

"It's definitely true," he agreed. "Just ... stick close to me once we're inside, okay? It's important that we're not separated."

"I have no intention of being separated from you."

"That means you have to lay off the liquids because I can't go into the restroom with you."

"That's never going to be a thing no matter how comfortable we get with one another. You've been warned."

"So noted."

Jack kept close once we were on the sidewalk. He'd agonized when it came to deciding where we should park. Ultimately he chose a spot that was a decent way from the bar simply because he thought there was a chance Liam would recognize the rental. It was a trade-off. He wouldn't be close to his weapon, but we'd be unobtrusive. I knew he was nervous about it, but there was nothing more we could do.

"I hate to admit it — and I might deny it later if I have to get into a fight to protect your honor — but the shark teeth on your butt are ridiculously hot," he admitted as he stood behind me on the sidewalk. "I mean ... so freaking hot. It should be outlawed."

I cast a look over my shoulder and grinned. "Oh, you're so sweet. I … ." I frowned when a shadow emerged from the darkness behind us. "Get out of the way!" I shoved Jack as hard as I could and stepped in front of him, coming face to face with Liam. "Don't touch him." There was venom in my tone. "I'll rip you apart if you touch him."

Liam merely sighed. "I have no intention of hurting him. In fact, it's quite the opposite. I'm here to help you."

That sounded unlikely. "How are you going to help us?"

Jack was back in the thick of things within seconds. "What the hell, Charlie?" he complained, incredulous. "That is not working as a team. We talked about this."

"We'll have to argue about that later," I shot back. "For now, we have a different problem."

Jack recovered quickly. "Oh, right." He pinned Liam with a dark look. "We're here to end your life, demon. How do you want it to go?"

My mouth dropped open as I slid him a sidelong look. "And people think I say stupid things."

Instead of reacting with anger or threats, Liam merely shook his head. "I'm not a demon. We need to talk."

"About you not being a demon?" I asked.

He nodded. "I'm definitely not a demon, We're looking for the same thing. I … can we please sit down and talk? I promise I won't do whatever it is you think I'm going to do if you promise to not kill me. I really do think we can help each other."

Jack didn't look convinced. "Fine." He gestured toward a small outdoor patio for a restaurant that was closed. The picnic tables in front of it remained in place. "We can talk over there. If you move on Charlie, … ." The threat was more inventive because he didn't finish it.

"I don't want to move on Charlie. I promise."

"Then let's talk."

ONCE WE WERE SITUATED AT ONE of the tables — Jack and me on one side and Liam on the other — conversation ground to a halt. It appeared none of us knew how to proceed. Finally, Jack took control.

"If you're not a demon, what are you?" he boldly asked.

"A man," Liam replied. "I'm just a man."

"You're obviously more than that," I pressed. "You know things. You're here. You don't really exist."

"I exist. I'm just not who I said I was. Although ... I didn't really lie all that much to you when we first crossed paths. Most of it was true."

"You can't live on Drum Island," I shot back.

He chuckled hollowly. "No, and I didn't realize that when I told the lie. That was pointed out to me by a local the same day I met you two. I need you to know that I didn't zero in on you because I wanted to hurt you, Charlie. I wanted to protect you. I realized right away that you would be an enticing target for the incubus."

"How do you know what it is?" Jack asked, his hands resting on the table. It was clear he was ready to spring into action should Liam make a move. That was starting to seem unlikely. I wasn't always the best judge of character — I wanted to see the best in people — but something about Liam's demeanor told me he was telling the truth.

"I conducted a lot of research on the topic," he replied. "You see ... my sister Elizabeth was one of the first victims in Boston. That was more than a year ago. Even though the medical examiner told me she likely died of natural causes — even though they couldn't narrow the reason down — I knew that wasn't right.

"Liz was ... healthy," he explained, his voice plaintive. "She took care of herself, went to the doctor regularly, and if there was something wrong she would've known. She wasn't the sort of person who just dies in her sleep."

"I hate to break it to you, but people die in their sleep all the time," Jack pointed out. "Still, I'm sorry for your loss. You had to have more than an assumption when you embarked on this journey, though. That couldn't have been enough."

"We were twins," Liam explained. "Liam and Liz. That's my real first name. My last name is Peterson."

Jack removed his phone from his pocket and started typing. After a few moments he nodded. "Here she is. Elizabeth Peterson. She was your sister?"

"She was," Liam confirmed, nodding. "She was also my best friend. We were unbelievably tight. I was rocked by her death. I wouldn't believe what the medical examiner told me and I was determined to find a different answer.

"I started following the obituary reports and noticed a trend consisting of young women who looked a lot like my sister dying in their sleep," he continued. "I started tracking and realized what I was dealing with after a lot of research. Even then I wasn't sure I could trust my instincts. Not until I found him on the streets of Boston one night. I was chasing one of his pentagrams and lucked out."

I slid a glance to Jack. "We were right about the pentagrams."

"*You* were right," he corrected, his gaze never leaving Liam's face. "You're saying that you've seen this creature. Do you know who it is?"

"That's the thing. He can change his looks. I didn't realize that at first. I found this guy named Travis Jones. He was a real man. The incubus killed him and took over his identity. I fought him and thought I won — Travis's body was even discovered by the police a few days later even though I ran that night because I didn't want to be arrested — and I thought it was over."

Sympathy washed over me. "When did you realize he'd simply changed cities?"

"It wasn't that easy for me," Liam replied. "When the police discovered his body, he'd been dead for months. That's what the media reports said. I thought there must've been a mistake. I mean … how was that even possible? I thought maybe the demon reanimated a corpse or something ... and then I heard what was happening in Atlantic City.

"I set up a Google alert to track unexplained deaths of women and then hand sorted them. A lot started coming in from Atlantic City. That's when I knew that I hadn't really killed him despite the knife I'd plunged into his chest. He'd simply moved on and changed his identity.

"I loved my sister. I mean ... she was important to me. I made a promise to catch her killer. So I picked up stakes and followed. I got close again in Atlantic City, when he was going by the name Jerry

Trawley. Then again in Virginia Beach when he was Mark Tremblay. I've been in Charleston for two weeks. I'm always behind because I have to wait for the death reports before I can move.

"Once I'm in a city, I follow the pentagram points," he explained. "I figure that's what you were doing last night. But when I first saw you, I thought maybe Jack was the incubus. You're the creature's type, Charlie. That's why I attached myself to you that day at the bar. That's why I followed you the day you kayaked out on the water … although I panicked when I thought you saw me and took off. I was trying to protect you from the start."

"Well … thank you." Things started slipping into place. "You ran because you thought Jack was the incubus and you believed he would follow you because he recognized you."

"We hate each other," Liam confirmed. "We want to kill each other. When you started chasing me I was confused. I listened to you in the cemetery. You didn't speak like him, Jack, and you genuinely seemed to care about her. I was just about to reveal myself when you left. I needed to think about what you were talking about, so I followed far enough behind to get your license plate number. I paid to have it run and it tracked back to a rental place. A woman there told me the name of the company that rented it. Then I ran the Legacy Foundation and realized what you did for a living. That's when I decided to trust you. I figured you would come to this spot once you searched my room at the hostel."

"Sorry about that," Jack said ruefully. It was obvious he was coming around to the idea of trusting Liam. "We assumed you were the guilty party, especially when I couldn't find a real record of you anywhere."

"I don't blame you." Liam rubbed his chin and shifted his eyes to the darkened street. "He's going to come here tonight, hunting. He's going to kill another woman if we don't stop him. I need your help to finish this, and that's not easy for me to admit."

"We'll help you," Jack promised. "We'll work together. Do you know what identity he's going by here?"

"I don't. I haven't gotten that far yet. I've been spending my nights trying to protect women at the bars because I don't know what else to do."

"That's a noble pursuit," Jack reassured him. "We need to be even more proactive."

"What do you suggest?"

"We add bait to the mix," I replied simply.

Jack shifted next to me and when I risked a glance at his face I found his eyes pressed shut.

"What bait?" Liam was clearly confused. "What are you talking about."

"You said it yourself," I replied briskly. "I'm his type. I say we use that, draw him into a trap, and then end him for good. If a knife to the chest doesn't work, we'll have to try something else. We'll all work together. We'll get it done."

"Charlie … ." Jack's voice sounded strangled. "I don't like this."

"Do you have another idea?"

"No, but … ."

"We have to do this." I was firm. "We can't let another woman die. We have to free those souls."

He held my gaze for what felt like forever and then nodded. "Fine. You're going to be so careful that you'll win an award for being a strategic thinker tonight. I will not lose you."

"You won't," I promised him. "I already have a plan."

"Am I going to like this plan?"

"Probably not, but it's totally awesome."

"Of course it is."

TWENTY-EIGHT

Jack took control of the plan. If I was to be used as bait, he wanted to think through every scenario. He finally agreed that we had no other choice and it was our best shot, but he was hardly happy about it.

"You know what to do, right?" He ran his hands over my shoulders and stared into my eyes as we prepared to separate.

"I do. It'll be fine, Jack. I swear it."

He didn't look convinced, but nodded. "Don't take any unnecessary chances. I won't lecture you about the necessary ones because I know there's no stopping you when you put your mind to something."

"In this particular case, there's not. It'll be okay. This is better than going into the strip club."

That nudged a small, reluctant smile out of him. "You just didn't want to dance."

"Pretty much." I rolled up to the balls of my feet and pressed a kiss to the corner of his mouth. "Don't move unless I give you the signal. Also, maybe try to distract Liam. If I have to use magic … ."

He solemnly nodded. "I won't let him hurt you. I know he's been through a lot, but so have you. He'll have to deal with how we handle things. That's all there is to it."

"Just keep an eye on him," I instructed. "If it comes to it, maybe leave me to handle this and take him someplace else."

Jack immediately started shaking his head. "That's not going to happen, Charlie. You're not facing this alone. Don't even ... ." His face flushed with anger. "Just don't. You agreed that we would do this together. You can't back out now."

"I'm not backing out," I reassured him. "I'm just trying to ensure we get the best possible outcome."

"We will. One thing I've learned since this entire thing started is that we're better together, stronger. This will prove that."

I had no doubt he was right.

I WALKED THE SIDEWALK IN FRONT OF the Down & Dirty, holding my phone to my ear and pretending to have a conversation. "I don't want to go in by myself, Jack." He wasn't on the other end of the call, of course. I was putting on a show. "I'll just wait for you here." I waited a moment, as if listening to his end of the conversation. "No. I won't go inside without you. I told you I was uncomfortable with this. I'm just going to walk around the block." Another beat of silence. "I'll be fine. You're only thirty minutes behind me. I think I can keep out of trouble until you get here." I said some hasty goodbyes and then shoved the phone in my pocket, muttering to myself as if frustrated.

If this plan was to work, we had to assume the incubus was already here and watching the area. I'd just given him a brief opening. I was his type. I was alone. It wouldn't get any better than this.

Jack and Liam were secluded in Liam's truck, parked across the road. They could see me but were still a fair distance away. Jack didn't like that in the least, but I had to remind him that we were dealing with a demon, and he would be detected if he tried to stick too close. He was reluctant but didn't argue further.

I pretended to be bored, scuffing my feet against the sidewalk. A loud noise in front of the bar drew my attention. A raucous couple yukking it up as they drunkenly leaned on each other. They were a bit loud for my taste, so I rounded the corner. Jack and Liam could still see me, but I was a bit farther away.

My phone buzzed in my pocket and when I pulled it out I read a message from Jack.

Don't go very far.

I could practically feel the worry emanating from him even though he was two-hundred feet away. He was anxious to the point of making himself sick. This wasn't how he wanted to handle things and yet he knew this was our best chance, so he shuttered his emotions and worked with me instead of against. I wouldn't forget this. It felt like an important chapter in our story.

I typed back a reassuring message and returned the phone to my pocket, pulling up short when a shadow crossed my path. I assumed it was someone heading toward the bar, There was an apology on my lips when I raised my eyes. All thoughts of saying "I'm sorry" died when I recognized the face in front of me.

"Seriously?" I was at a loss. "It's you?"

Reverend Alexander was dressed in street clothes, jeans and a simple shirt. He had a small bag clutched in one hand, one that looked like the sort a doctor would carry for house calls. He looked just as surprised to see me as I was to see him.

"What are you doing here?" he blurted out.

"I asked you first." I held my ground. He wasn't nearly as scary in the real world as he was in his church. Well, unless he was the demon. Then he was even scarier.

"I don't have time for games, young lady," Alexander snapped. "What are you doing here?" His gaze drifted toward the bar, which was rocking thanks to the ridiculous music. "You're not a performer, are you?"

Well, now I was officially offended. "Don't be absurd. I'm here ... looking for a guy." Wait. That might've come out wrong.

Alexander furrowed his brow. "I thought you were with the young man you who was with you when you visited the church. I got a particular vibe off you."

Oh, that was a load of crap. "You mean your nutty minion Gretchen told you we were together. Why do you even care?"

"I'm trying to figure out why you're here."

Something occurred to me. "Wait ... why are you here? Are you here for the show? This is a bar for couples. Ugh. Please tell me Gretchen isn't your partner. I'll have nightmares for years."

The look he shot me was withering. "I'm not here for the show."

"Then why are you here?"

"You tell me first."

"No, you tell me." I folded my arms over my chest and pinned him with my best "You will do what I say whether you like it or not" glare. When my phone dinged in my pocket, I growled and retrieved it. I didn't even have to look to know it was from Jack.

Is Alexander the incubus?

That was an interesting question. I didn't have an answer. I hesitated and worked my jaw before asking the obvious question. "Okay, this is going to sound weird but I don't really have a choice in the matter. I'm sorry if this upsets you ... or makes you think I'm crazy ... or gives you more fodder to talk about with your crazy girlfriend. I have to ask. Are you an incubus?"

Instead of reacting with outrage or hysterical guffaws, Alexander narrowed his eyes. "Not last time I checked. Are you hunting an incubus?"

"Maybe." I had a wild notion and decided to go with it. "Are you hunting an incubus?"

"Maybe." He mimicked my tone to perfection. "Why are you here?" This time there was no accusation to the question, just honest curiosity.

"I'm looking for the creature killing women. This is one of the points on his pentagram map. I believe he's going to show up here tonight. When I saw you, well, I naturally assumed you were our guy."

He made a face. "You shouldn't assume things. It makes you look like a dolt, and you have enough marks in that column to overcome."

I glared. "Don't insult me. I don't need to put up with your crap.

You're just as much of a dolt as me, but you don't have the excuse of youth. You're old and still act like an idiot. What's up with that?"

"I think this conversation is done," Alexander snapped. "Be on your way. I have work to do here." He looked determined as he tried to push past me ... and then frowned when his gaze landed on something. I turned to see what it was and sighed when I realized it was Liam and Jack. "You're not alone," he murmured.

"Do you really think Jack would allow me to come to this place without backup? Come on. I know you're out of touch, but you need to buy a clue. That's like buying a vowel on *Wheel of Fortune* if you're confused."

"I'm familiar with *Wheel of Fortune*." Alexander worked his jaw. "You're here for the same reason I am."

"The incubus? Maybe. But why are you here searching for the incubus? How do you even know?"

Footsteps on the sidewalk interrupted Alexander. When I turned to greet what I was sure was another drunken strip club couple I was doubly shocked to find Samuel joining the party. "Oh, he roped you into this, too, huh? You poor thing. Unless ... um ... are you the other half of his couple?"

Alexander didn't yell at me for asking the question. Instead his gaze went dark as he focused on the younger reverend. There was something in his countenance that I couldn't identify, but it felt a lot like loathing.

"What's going on?" Samuel asked. He momentarily looked shocked when he first registered us, but recovered quickly. I was surprised by the reaction. "What are you doing here?"

"That seems to be the question of the evening," I replied. "Aren't you two here together?" I couldn't for the life of me fathom how they would show up at the same strip club if they didn't arrive as a pair.

"We're not together," Alexander gritted out, his eyes full of fire. "We haven't been together for weeks."

I was sincerely having trouble putting things together. "Is this like a lover's spat?"

Before either could respond, I heard a door slam and risked a glance toward the truck where Liam and Jack were waiting. They were both out of the vehicle and heading in my direction. Liam looked as if he was going to start mowing bodies down to get to us.

"I won't let you get away again," he howled.

My eyes first went to Alexander because he seemed the obvious choice for the threat. If anyone was a demon in human form, it had to be him. To my utter surprise, though, he didn't react to Liam at all. No, that honor went to Samuel.

"No way." The words escaped from my mouth in a whoosh and my eyes went wide. "No freaking way!"

Samuel wasn't waiting around to hear accusations lobbed at him. He took off in the direction he came from. Because I was closest, I didn't have a choice. I gave chase. Unfortunately for Jack and Liam, a group of rowdy patrons from the bar decided to get involved, too, and they joined in, even though they had no idea who they were chasing or why.

"Let's get him," one of the men yelled.

I had to stop looking over my shoulder and focus on what was in front of me when Jack got tied up with the growing group. He would have to take care of himself. I couldn't let the incubus get away. This might be our only chance to stop him.

Samuel was fast, but I was determined. I put my head down and gave it my all as I followed him into the night. He zigged down an alley and then zagged up a one-way street in an attempt to lose me. He went around another three corners and never diminished his pace. Neither did I. By the time he came upon a dead end behind what looked to be an old grocery store we were completely separated from the rest of the group.

"End of the line," I gasped, lowering my hands to the front of my thighs and fighting to catch my breath. "There's nowhere left to run."

"I was going to say the same to you." This time when Samuel turned, his eyes glowed an odd blue. They definitely weren't human ... and he wasn't gasping for breath at all.

Uh-oh.

I sucked in oxygen and fought to maintain control of my reaction.

He was a demon, I reminded myself. Somehow he'd talked himself into those other women's bedrooms. That meant he had mind power. I had to keep him out of my head. Even now I could feel him poking and prodding as he looked for a way in.

"You're probably going to want to stop doing that," I said, slamming shut the door to my mind and putting a bit of extra magic behind it as I slapped him back.

His eyes went wide. "What are you?" He didn't sound upset that I was something other than human. In fact, he sounded intrigued.

"I was about to ask you the same question. We've been working under the assumption that you're an incubus."

"I am one of the oldest creatures imaginable," he fired back. "I am more than one thing. So are you. You're ... different." He lifted his nose to the air and scented. "You're amazing. I caught your scent at the church but couldn't allow myself to dwell on it. What are you?"

He seemed enraptured. I hoped I could work that to my advantage. "I'm an Aquarius," I replied without hesitation. "And you're ... wearing another man's body." That's when the full brunt of what I was dealing with hit me. "The real Samuel Rodriguez is dead, isn't he?"

"Long dead," the incubus confirmed, seemingly amused by the sorrow that momentarily coursed through me. "I wouldn't be too upset if I were you. He was a real ass. That's how I managed to overtake him in the first place. The bitterness growing in his heart regarding Alexander's refusal to hand over the church made him easy pickings. He wasn't my first clergyman, but I always get a little thrill when I can overtake one."

"That's part of it?" I mused. I was buying time until I could figure out what to do. I was genuinely at a loss. "You need the people you inhabit to have a black heart."

"No, just a fractured soul," he replied. "Samuel had one. He was having an affair with that insipid Gretchen. I ended that right away, which made her a little mad. Crazy mad, not angry mad ... although she's a little of both now that I think about it.

"I probably should've given more thought to my actions because she's the reason I'm in this situation to begin with," he lamented. "I've been in this city for almost two months. I sign on with ships when I need to move. It's not as easy to get a driver's license as it used to be since September 11th. Basically I stick on the ship until I find a place I like and then depart. I remain in a city until I'm bored with it – or run out by that idiot Liam, which seems to be the norm these days – and then get on with another ship. It's a cycle I enjoy because I get bored if I stay in one place too long.

"I found Samuel on my third day. He was easy to overpower. I found out about Gretchen the day after because she was a bit needy. When I ended the affair, she started whispering in Alexander's ear. She told him there was something wrong with me ... and then he caught me in a lie because I didn't do enough research before taking over this persona. He's been suspicious of me ever since. I guess that's why he's here."

"There *is* something wrong with you," I pointed out. "You're a sick, sick man. Of course, you're not even a man."

"Neither are you."

"A man? You're right."

"You're not human. At least not entirely. You're something else."

"Sweet talking me will get you nowhere."

"I think it's going to get me exactly where I want." He took a menacing step toward me, but I held my ground. "You're different but still the same, Charlie. You look like the others, like Savannah and her friends – who made it far too easy by clustering together in that little group. But you're more. You're a challenge, unlike them. They lined up and wanted to be slaughtered. I think part of them wanted it.

"You, however, are completely different and yet look the same. You won't make it easy. You'll fight ... and I do love a good fight. I haven't had one in decades. I need you for my work."

"Your work?" My stomach turned at the thought. "Is that what you call it? You seduce women and steal their essences to live."

"It's not my fault. I was created this way. I cannot change. Every creature in the world has the compulsion to survive. I'm no different. I'm not truly bad. I'm just a survivor."

"Oh, really?" I was done playing games. "Then what about the trapped souls you've left between Boston and here? You've anchored them to the water, forced them to look at a world they're no longer a part of, and made it so they can't interact with each other or their surroundings. That's evil on a level that's hard to even grasp."

He couldn't hide his surprise. "How ... ?" He trailed off. "You really are a magical being, aren't you?"

"I'm more than one thing," I replied, clenching my fists at my sides. I was going to have to move without Jack. It was probably better this way. "I can't let you leave. I've come to the conclusion that the only way to free those souls is to kill you."

He tossed back his head and barked out a laugh that was eerie enough to chill me to the bone. "I've been around for centuries, little girl. Do you really think you have the strength to stop me? Let me save you the trouble of over-taxing that simple brain of yours. You don't have the power. I am forever ... and you are no more."

As if to prove it, he lifted his hands and let loose a wisp of magic. I couldn't really see it, but I could feel it. There was a lullaby woven into it, a soft song meant to soothe any impulses I might have to fight. That's how he got the women to open their windows. He parked outside, used his magic and convinced them it was a good idea to let him in.

Well, no more. I wouldn't allow it to happen again.

"Close your eyes," he instructed in a voice as soft as cotton. "Listen to the beat of my heart. Let your heart join it."

That sounded like the most ridiculous thing I'd ever heard, but I played along. I needed to draw him in.

"Do you hear that?" he asked. He was closer now. I had to use my senses to keep track of him. He thought I was under his thrall ... but he was wrong. "That sound is forever beckoning. It's quiet ... and peaceful ... and sounds like the ocean. That's the happiest place in the world, you know."

For a moment I could almost see myself in his version of utopia. The lulling waves, the saltwater scent. It was majestic. And then I pictured Jack sitting on my couch as we argued over pizza toppings ... and the way he snored when he slept ... and the way his stubble tickled me when we cuddled in the morning. The ocean might be his happy place, but Jack was mine.

When I felt him finally move into my space I used my magic to tap into his head. He was so far gone into what he was doing he didn't even feel me. Instead, he focused on what he was doing and ignored the signs that he was failing.

"It's almost time, Charlie," he whispered.

"There's no almost about it," I replied, my eyes popping open as I extended my hands and pressed them into his chest. "It's definitely time."

I poured all the magic I could muster into him at the same moment he realized I'd fooled him. He gasped, tried to twist away, but the magic was already entrenched inside him.

"What are you doing?" He writhed, lashed out with hands that somehow resembled claws. I expected the attack and held him back. "Stop that. It ... burns!"

"It's supposed to burn," I replied dully. The amount of magic I was expending was tremendous, but I knew better than to stop. "I'm cleansing the demon out of you. It's not a picnic in the park."

"Stop!" He was getting desperate now as he fought against me. "I'm not done yet. I can't leave them unfinished. The pentagrams, they need to be finished. I ... stop!" Now his cry was anguished. That only caused me to add to the magic.

"The world is better off without you," I murmured as his cry trailed off and he began to sag. "No one will mourn you. Most won't even know you ever existed. The world will go on without you ... and we'll be just fine."

I poured the last of my magic into him and then sank to the ground. I was exhausted, empty, and all I wanted to do was sleep. I dully heard voices approaching. One of them belonged to Jack. I felt him before I even heard him ... and then his arms were around me.

"Charlie?" His worried eyes swam into view as I smiled at him.

"He's gone. I burned him away."

"Baby." He stroked his fingers down my cheek as he held me close. "What do I do? Do I need to take you to the hospital? Are you okay?"

"I'm okay," I promised him, my words slurring. "I just need sleep. Take me to bed. I'm ... okay."

The last thing I heard was him crying out as he swung me up into his arms. Then blissful sleep washed over me. Even then I could feel it. The demon might've emptied it out of me, but Jack was replenishing all of it.

We'd figured it out ... and we were okay.

TWENTY-NINE

Jack sat vigil until I woke the next morning. The relief on his face was palpable, and it reminded me of another time he had done the same thing. That was before we admitted our feelings to each other, but I was pretty sure the roots of what we were growing were already there. Just like then, I'd never been so happy to see anyone in my entire life.

"What happened ... after?" My voice was raspy as he fetched a bottle of water from the nightstand. I couldn't remember anything from the previous night after Jack arrived.

"Rick came. I had to call him because ... well, because it was the right thing to do."

Fear washed over me as I propped myself on the bed to accept the water. "Is he coming to talk to me?"

"No, baby, he's not." Jack shifted from the chair he'd situated so he could watch me the entire night and slid in next to me, being gentle as he brought me to his side. His lips were warm against my forehead and his proximity allowed me to let loose a pent-up shudder.

"Don't you be afraid," he whispered. "He's not coming for you. There's nothing to be afraid of. I promise."

I pulled myself together. I was still shaky, weak, but I was markedly better than I had been following the incident. "What happened?"

Jack was calm as he filled in the gaps for me. "Liam and Alexander were with me when I got to you. They heard what you said but assumed you were confused because you'd been hurt. Er, well, I thought that's what Alexander assumed. He said the right things, but ... well ... it became clear pretty quickly that he was covering for you."

"Why would he do that?"

"He understood that you didn't kill Samuel as much as you killed the creature that took his face. He's known for some time that Samuel was gone, almost from the start. He grieves for the young man he knew, but is thankful for what you did."

"And Liam?"

"Liam doesn't believe you ended the incubus." He was obviously choosing his words carefully to keep me calm. "He says that he thought he killed the incubus but it somehow managed to escape, jump bodies so to speak, and he's going to keep watching. He thanked us for our help and hoped you would feel better soon, but he plans to move down the coast to keep looking."

"That's a waste of time, Jack."

"I know, but ... there's nothing I can do to change his mind."

"I could try telling him the truth."

"I would prefer you didn't. He's too excitable. And, while I don't like the idea of him chasing a creature that no longer exists, I think he needs to come to that conclusion himself. He's not ready to give up the fight because it's all he's had since the death of his sister. When no more murders pop up, he'll be forced to deal with what's really bothering him ... that he's alone. We can't fix that for him."

It was a fairly profound deduction. "I still feel bad."

"Hey." He tapped my chin to get me to look into his eyes. "You're the hero of this story, Charlie. You saved the day last night. You took on that creature by yourself — and I'm still kind of angry about that, by the way, but you get a pass because you scared the dickens out of me. You freed all those souls."

I stirred. "How do you know that? Did you see them leave?"

He shook his head. "No. Harley stopped by to check on you. She was ready to influence the fight but didn't get to us in time. She said she had a job. She was angry — hopping up and down mad — and I think her boss has been getting an earful. She checked for me, though, and she didn't even try to make a deal. She volunteered before I could ask because I knew you would want to know."

"She checked all the places?"

"She did. They're all gone."

"They've been released."

"All but the one who belonged to Harley. She said she managed to reap her soul and that her business in Charleston was concluded. She said she would be in Boston to see us in a few weeks, when I make good on her dinner."

I pressed my lips together to keep from laughing at his mournful expression. "I'm sorry. You only made the deal to protect me."

"I would make a lot more deals like that — and probably worse — to protect you." He lowered his mouth to mine and gave me a kiss so sweet it was almost aching. "You scared me." He rested his forehead against mine. "You have to stop doing that."

"I told you I would be okay. I was just drained."

"I know but ... you were so pale ... and quiet ... and you wouldn't open your eyes. I had to sneak you in here and put you to bed so the others wouldn't ask too many questions."

Uh-oh. That begged another question. "What do they know?"

"The official story that we told the police is that Samuel was a normal man who went on a killing spree," Jack replied calmly. "Rick helped fill in the blanks. I think he knew something big went down, but he was so thankful it was over he didn't question anything when it was time to fill out the report. Alexander lying was a benefit, too. Who is going to challenge an eighty-year-old reverend who was close with the dead guy?"

"But that doesn't make things right for the real Samuel. He wasn't a murderer."

"No, but Alexander said he would be okay with how things went down. He was once a good man who wanted to do right by the world.

Somehow he got twisted throughout the years. If he was a good person, the incubus wouldn't have been able to invade him the way it did."

"Still ... ."

"We can't always have everything we want, Charlie." Jack was firm. "I'm sorry. I know you don't want to hear it, but it's the truth. We can't sew this up neatly and put a bow on it. We're lucky that Alexander is helping us at all."

"What did he say?"

"Not to come back to his church."

Jack's response, and especially the way he delivered it, would've been funny under different circumstances. "Seriously?"

"Pretty much. He was there because he'd overheard Samuel taunting Gretchen. She's apparently off her rocker and Alexander promises to get her help. He decided to take on Samuel himself. That bag he was carrying had a crucifix, holy water from a neighboring church, salt because he saw it on a television show and a Bible. He was going to take him down with his faith."

"I don't think that would have worked."

"You can't tell him that. But it doesn't matter. What matters is that the incubus is gone."

"What about Samuel's real body? It's out there somewhere."

"It is, and I don't know how that's going to be dealt with. There's nothing we can do about it but wait."

That wasn't my strong suit, but I was too tired to press the issue. Instead, I snuggled closer to Jack. "And our group? They know which version of the story?"

"That Samuel was evil and tried to hurt you. That during a struggle he keeled over and didn't get back up. There were no marks on his body. I'm guessing, when they conduct his autopsy, they'll find the same compound that was in the women. I think he creates it when he ... has sex with them."

That was a disturbing thought so I made a face and focused on something else. "So ... they think I fainted during a fight with a serial killer."

"They think you were brave during a fight with a serial killer and then, yes, fainted. I'm sorry. It's the only thing I could come up with."

"Ah, well. I guess it could be worse. I'm sure Laura will be laughing about it for weeks."

"Who cares what she thinks?" He tightened his arms around me. "I know the truth. You're a hero and ... I'm really proud of you."

I swallowed the lump that formed in my throat. "Thank you."

"I'm also really angry because you allowed yourself to get separated and took on a monster by yourself. We'll argue about that later, though."

"That sounds like a good plan."

"I thought you would like it."

We rested like that for a good twenty minutes before I stirred. "You know what?"

"Hmm?"

"I make enough money to buy you dinner when we get back to town. What do you say to a fun night of fish and chips, and a walk on the beach?"

"That's the best offer I've had all day."

WITHIN THREE HOURS, CHRIS MADE the call. We were heading back to headquarters. Our work in Charleston was done. As usual, Chris was disappointed. Hannah was already consoling him, and I figured his bad mood wouldn't last.

I spent time on the balcony searching for signs of the ghosts, but they were indeed gone. That was a relief. I could leave with less weight on my shoulders, although the idea of the real Samuel going down as a murderer was an ache I couldn't quite shake. Jack was right, though. We couldn't have everything.

By the time we made our way downstairs with our luggage, only Casey remained. I thought he would've hitched a ride with Laura's group when they left for the airport.

"Are you riding with us?" Jack asked as he carried our bags, making sure to keep one eye on me should I threaten to topple over again.

"I am," Casey replied. "The other vehicles were kind of full. Laura manages to take up two seats because of her mouth."

"Yeah. Get used to that." Jack flicked his eyes to me. "I'll take the bags out. Can you do a swing around the living room and kitchen to make sure we don't leave anything behind? I'll be back to help you to the car in a few minutes."

"I can walk to the car myself."

"Except you won't. I get to take care of you all day today ... and tomorrow ... and through the weekend. That's all there is to it. I don't want to hear any argument."

I offered up an exaggerated eye roll but didn't fight him. There was no point.

Once he was gone, I flashed a small smile for Casey's benefit and started the search. He followed me, which I found weird. The more time I spent with him — which admittedly wasn't much at this point — the odder I found him.

"I don't see anything, do you?" I asked to break the uncomfortable silence.

"No." Casey leaned against the wall and folded his arms over his chest. The gaze he shot me was piercing. "So ... you used your magic to take out the incubus. You should probably learn to regulate your energy output. You don't have to put that much effort into a spell. Still, it was pretty impressive ... at least I gather that because I couldn't get too close."

I had no idea what to say. "W-what?"

His smirk was smug. "Did you really think I didn't know? The others might believe that story Jack told, but it was so full of holes it should've been on a Reuben sandwich. I mean ... come on. I guess it was the best he could do on the fly, though."

I fervently wished for Jack to return as my cheeks burned. "I don't know what you're talking about."

"And we don't have much time, so lies are really unnecessary. Jack will be back any second. I wanted to ride to the airport alone with you, but dislodging that guy from your side is pretty much impossible."

Suspicion grabbed my heart and squeezed. "Who are you?"

"Do you really not know?"

"I have no idea."

"I'm your brother."

I thought I was going to pass out again. I had to extend my hand to brace myself against the counter. I saw black spots whirling in my peripheral vision. This made no sense.

"You're not my brother." The words were strangled as they escaped my mouth. "You're ... something else. Did Laura put you up to this? That would be just like her."

Even as I said the words, I knew they couldn't possibly be right. Laura had no idea who I was or what I could do. If she had, she would have blurted it out to the others a long time ago.

"Laura is not really a part of this. Well, other than getting me the job. She did prove useful on that front. This isn't about her. It's about you and me. The reason I know what you can do is because you're my sister. I wasn't lying."

He had to be lying. There was no other explanation. "I don't know what game you're playing ... ."

"I'm not playing a game. Far from it. I'm here to talk to you. You're the only reason I joined this idiotic outfit. Now, I don't expect you to believe me. You would have to be stupid to believe some random guy you just met. While you're naive, you're not stupid. I'll submit to a DNA test. The faster we can get that done, the faster we can move on to Phase Two."

I had no idea what Phase One was, let alone Phase Two. I didn't really want to know. "I don't think ... ."

"It doesn't matter what you think." He was no-nonsense. "This is happening. It's real. We have a lot to talk about. We can't move forward until you have your confirmation. That's simply the way it is."

Jack picked that moment to return. He was momentarily oblivious. "Everyone ready?" When I didn't immediately answer, he shifted his gaze to me ... and then was on me in two long strides. "What's wrong?" His hand was on my forehead. "Are you relapsing? Do you need to go to the hospital? You know what? You're going whether you like it or not. That's all there is to it."

The look Casey shot me was full of warning. He was silently admonishing me to keep my mouth shut. I'd done that before, though, and I had no intention of doing it again.

"He says he's my brother." I blurted out the words, earning a scowl from Casey. "He says he's my brother and knows ... everything."

Jack immediately pushed himself between us, standing as a buffer between Casey and me. Fury radiated off him in waves. "I knew there had to be something wrong with you. No one can put up with Laura. Who are you? What's your game?"

The sigh Casey let loose was long and drawn out. "I'm Charlie's brother ... though I used to call her something else. That's for another time. Before you start, Jack, you should know that I've already volunteered to take a DNA test. I don't expect her to swallow this information on faith alone."

"How awesome of you," Jack drawled. "Why are you here? What do you want from her?"

"That's to be discussed once the DNA test is finalized. She's not going to believe until she has proof. She's always had a hard head."

I felt sick to my stomach and bent over at the waist. "Jack ... ."

He immediately moved his hand to my back. "It's okay. I won't let him hurt you ... or take you. We'll get rid of him."

"Oh, don't be so hasty," Casey chided. "How are you going to explain wanting to oust me? If you try, I'll tell Chris what she can do. You'll leave me no other choice. Is that what you want?"

"You're blackmailing us?" I was incredulous. "So much for family bonding."

"There's a lot you don't know, Charlie," Casey countered. "I'm being as expedient as I can. There is a specific outcome here that needs to be achieved. Make no mistake about it, we will come to a meeting of the minds."

"And what happens if we don't agree to your terms?" Jack challenged.

"You'll find out that she can be taken after all." Casey was firm.

"Don't fight me on this, Jack. You'll lose." With those words, he strolled toward the door. "We should get moving. They're waiting for us at the airport."

Jack pulled me into his arms the second he disappeared. "It's okay." He kissed my forehead and hugged me tight. "It's going to be okay. We'll figure this out."

I wanted to laugh, but it would've been hollow. How were we supposed to figure this out?

"It's going to be okay," he repeated, hugging me as tightly as he could. "If this guy wants a war, he's got one. I'll fight him."

I believed that. The question was: Would Jack be capable of stopping him?

Made in the USA
Monee, IL
02 January 2021

56048355R00163